ROYAL FAKE FIANCÉ

VIVIAN WOOD

AUTHOR'S COPYRIGHT

ROYAL FAKE FIANCÈ

Thank you so much to Antje, Rachael, Jenn, and Belinda. Thanks to my beta reader Patricia. And most of all, thanks to Shawn Mendes, who will forever be who I picture when I envision Lars in my mind.

1

——————

LARS

Standing on the highest balcony at the school, I shiver. My eyes trace the jaw dropping beauty of the Swiss Alps. The scene is set dramatically with two nearly vertical cliff faces. Each is snow-capped and soars impossibly high, chilling the dark stone foundations of the school I'm standing on. A waterfall crashes down nearby, providing a perfect frame for the backdrop of more snowy, white peaks.

I sniffle as the wind picks up, bringing with it the season's first fat flakes of snow. The balcony I'm on is barely three feet deep and a dozen feet long, easily accessible through a thick wooden door. It's one of a dozen small balconies clinging to the castle's upper floors; in medieval times, this was probably meant for archers to be able to pop out and fire rapidly.

We've been studying castles and the feudal system during history and the castle itself has been rather illustrious.

Too bad that I hate it here.

Bracing myself against the cold, I will myself to stop crying.

Princes don't cry.

It's just that this boarding school is very far away from home. I was sent here last month after being kicked out of yet another prep school back in Copenhagen. And it hasn't been an easy adjustment.

St. Matthew's is housed in an old castle, drafty in the winter and dark all the time. Back home, I slept in adjoining rooms with my older brother Stellan; here I feel alone nearly all the time.

Not to mention the fact that the kids that attend St. Matthew's are the dictionary definition of a clique. So far, I only seem to be able to piss off the boys and make the girls turn up their noses.

It really hasn't been a very good start to the second half of my seventh grade year.

I stare out at the mountains in the distance, I wish I were like their dark, rocky surfaces. Hard, impenetrable, cold. I'm very much not those things. Instead, I'm slipping away from my pre-algebra class to sneak outside for privacy and bawl like a little baby. If anybody in school found out that I did this regularly, I would be humiliated.

As I grapple with my runaway emotions, the heavy wood door creaks open. One of my classmates sticks her head of bright copper curls out, checking to see if anyone is here.

God, please don't let her come out here. Please don't let her see me like this. I wipe my face, waiting for a second.

Then she steps out, looking away toward the majestic waterfall. I suck in a breath and slip away from her, pressing against the building facade. Thank god the building turns ever so slightly and hides my presence.

I watch as the girl steps out, letting the door close behind her and leaning on the dark stone balcony railing. She's slender and willowy, her skin as fair as cream. She has light colored eyes and an upturned button nose. Her crown of curls spirals down her shoulders, falling almost to her waist. She's only wearing her uniform: a white button up shirt, a heavy black sweater with the school logo stitched into it, a pleated gray plaid skirt, and thick black tights. I'm wearing my heaviest coat and I'm still freezing. She has to be crazy.

Tilting my head, I try to put a name with her face. Unfortunately I haven't really learned everyone yet, especially not the people who aren't popular. My eyes slide over her again, head to toe.

I'm a little surprised at not recognizing this girl, because she is really pretty.

No, pretty isn't right.

As she raises her eyes to the sky, her lips moving silently, she makes my heart skip a beat. She's beautiful.

I'm not expecting her to start weeping, though. She murmurs something that I can't quite hear, dropping her head low. Her face contorts. Her eyes shimmer with tears.

I straighten my head, looking away. She's clearly expecting privacy. I try to give it to her, although there isn't much room on the balcony to move.

I inch away from her, shivering. There is a small pebble on the floor, something that I thoughtlessly kick out of my way. She suddenly looks up, her eyes wide.

When she speaks, her breath condenses in the air. "Is someone there?"

Her accent is foreign, perhaps British. Her voice is smooth and light, melodic to my ears.

I freeze. Before I can decide whether or not to call out, she takes a step closer, coming around the sharp point in the facade. Her eyes go wide with alarm.

"What are you doing here?"

She wraps her arms around herself, her words sounding like an accusation.

I straighten my spine, my head cocking. "I could ask you the same question. I was just out here, minding my own business. You are intruding into my space, technically."

Her eyes narrow as she takes me in. I'm dark haired and scrawny, probably only emphasized by the fact that I'm wearing a huge coat.

"Who are you?" she asks.

My neck heats. "My name is Lars."

I see the moment that she realizes who I am; something clicks and there is a second of acknowledgement in her clear blue eyes.

"Ah. You're the prince."

My expression sours. "Yes. Go ahead, make your jokes."

Her eyebrows rise. "I'm sorry?"

I turn away, looking out toward the mountains. "You heard me. That's what I've heard from everyone in this school so far. So go ahead, question my lineage. Talk about how my parents planned well when they decided to have me. My brother is the heir, I'm just the spare."

I spit on the ground, bracing for whatever she is about to say. My angry breath leaves me mouth in distinct huffs. I'm certain that she's about to tear into me, tell me I barely qualify to be a prince.

"It's my second week here."

My eyebrows rise; I look over at her, thrown off by her words. "What?"

She shivers, wiping her nose on her sleeve. "I'm new here. If the other children tease you, they certainly don't share it with me." Her mouth twists. "Haven't you heard? I'm a scholarship student. A charity case. In the pecking order, you definitely come above me."

My mouth opens. I'm not quite sure what to make of this little spitfire. She huffs a laugh, turning away.

"Great, now you too. Everybody at this school looks down on me because I am not a titled heir with a huge fortune. Even the teachers look at me with pity."

She says it with such anger and conviction, her hands balling into fists.

I pull a face. "I wasn't thinking that."

She frowns. "You weren't?"

I shake my head. "I wasn't. I was just wondering two things."

She looks uncertain. "What?"

I exhale, feeling a little shaky. "First, I was wondering if you were ever going to tell me your name."

Two spots of bright pink appear in the apples of her cheeks. "I'm Pippa. Pippa Welch."

I step forward, holding out my hand. She looks at me for a second, as if she's trying to decide whether I'm serious or not. Then she takes a couple of steps, taking my hand. I shiver as electricity washes over my skin.

From this close, I can make out the freckles that span the bridge of her nose.

I give her the tiniest smile. "It's nice to meet you, Pippa."

She sniffs, taking her hand back and shivering again. "What was the other thing that you were wondering?"

My smile broadens. "I was wondering if you wanted to head inside." I pause, scrunching up one side of my face. "I have a hot plate and some cocoa in my room. It's contraband, obviously—"

She cuts in. "I'm freezing. So yes, cocoa sounds nice." She turns around, moving toward the door. "Where is your room?"

I blush. It just now occurs to me that I have invited her to my room and… well, she's a girl.

A pretty girl.

"It's in the east wing," I say, following her.

She looks back at me, wrinkling her nose as she pulls the heavy wooden door open. "I've never snuck into a boy's room, much less a prince."

Just now, I have a funny feeling in the pit of my stomach. Pippa's eyes sparkle mischievously. I clear my throat, trying to come up with a proper response to that.

"I won't tell if you won't," I end up saying.

She wrinkles her nose, amused, and tosses her upper curls as she heads inside. And I follow her, feeling my whole world shift on its axis.

It takes me a few hours to realize what the feeling fluttering around my stomach is: stupid, blind, complete love.

God help me.

2

LARS

MODERN TIMES

I sit at the far end of a dimly lit, crowded cocktail bar, drumming my fingers on the counter and looking at my watch. It's getting late, well past midnight.

Pippa was supposed to meet me here at exactly twelve.

The bar is noisy. The patrons are talking and laughing over the sophisticated notes of jazz in the background.

Any minute, I expect to see Pippa: tall, lithe, and redheaded. From this distance, I'll be able to see the two spots in the apples of her cheeks as she rushes toward me, dressed in some sort of a flowy designer gown. Her eyes are this almost electric shade of teal. When she looks at you, her gaze seems to pin you in place.

But only if she's here, of course. I glance at my watch again with a sigh.

We've been best friends for long enough that I expect her usual tardiness. Pippa is exceptionally late though, even by her standards.

I look down at my whiskey and soda in its glass tumbler. I'm up at the crack of dawn every single day to train for the one thing I've wanted since I was seven years old: to be a member of the National Space Institute's next class of astronauts.

I know it's a crazy goal. You have to be the best of the best and the brightest of bright to be accepted to the program. You have to have a ridiculous, impossible to maintain physique and your mind must be sharp enough to cut.

I've got that part down. The only thing that might hold me back, funnily enough, is my title. See, I'm not the heir… but I am supposed to be waiting in the wings in case anything happens to King Stellan.

I'm not much of the wait and see what happens type, but that's neither here nor there.

At any rate, I try not to drink too much while I'm still training.

Draining the last drops of whiskey, I push my glass away. When the bartender comes by, asking if I want another drink, I shake my head. He nods and replaces my drink with a glass of water. I sigh, looking around the bar again.

That's when I notice a couple of girls looking my way. As a member of Denmark's royal family, I'm used to getting those stares. The ones people give you when they can't quite place you at first…

If I were my brother Stellan, the King of Denmark, I would be too famous to even lurk in this dark corner of the bar. But as second in line to the throne, people are much slower to recognize me.

I glance over at the girls again, trying to decide if they recognize me as Prince Lars or the just think I'm some guy in the bar that's attractive. They bow their heads together, giggling softly. I really hope that it is the latter of the two and that the girls are just flirting with me.

That would be optimal, because I'm seriously done with being royal at this moment.

After a moment, both girls approach me. I cast my gaze over them, my stomach starting to sink. Normally if there are girls that think I'm attractive in a bar, they don't come right up to me and tell me about it. No, I'm pretty sure that their approach means that they have figured out who I am.

I raise my hand to the bartender, signaling that I do want another whiskey soda. I'll hurt tomorrow because of it, but so be it.

One of the girls is a pretty ash blonde. She leads the way over to me while her friend slinks behind her, a more timid brunette. The blonde smiles as she tucks her hair behind her ear, gesturing to show that she means no harm.

"Excuse me, you wouldn't happen to be Prince Lars, would you?"

I exhale slowly, looking her up and down. She is very young, probably only eighteen, but her tiny black dress shows off her cleavage and her supermodel legs. I spin in my chair, favoring her and her friend with a smirk. "Who is asking?"

Both of the girls blush an enchanting pink. The blonde speaks for both of them. "I'm Anya and this is Katya."

I toy with the rim of my glass, looking at them. So young, so sweet, so innocent…

It happens in the same manner that it *always* happens.

The rational, thinking half of my brain switches off. And the base, impulsive half of my brain turns on instead. One minute, I'm thinking of Greene's latest article on string theory. The next minute, I'm thinking of the way this pretty blonde's tongue will feel as she uses it to tease my cock.

It happens so quickly, between breaths. There's nothing I can do to stop it, not that I particularly want to.

Biting my lip, I lean forward with an inviting smirk.

"You've found me out," I say. I tilt my head to the side, eyeing both of the girls up and down. "Aren't you two clever?"

Both of them flush an alluring dark pink. The blonde ducks her head. "We were wondering why you are here at the bar all alone. Do you want some company?"

My smirk deepens. I know just how good looking I am. I know that I'm a prince. I hold all the cards here.

"I wouldn't say no to that offer."

The seats on either side of me are unoccupied and the girls slide onto the leather stools, the blonde on my left and the brunette on my right. This isn't the first time that this exact thing has happened. I sit back, raising my hand to signal the bartender.

"Let me get you both a drink," I say.

The blonde smiles widely at me while her brunette friend looks on, still red as a beet. While the bartender makes them a couple of fruity cocktails, I sit back and take in the blonde's cleavage and short, tight skirt.

"Are you two in school somewhere?" I ask.

The blonde is in the middle of sipping her drink so the brunette clears her throat. "We're in our first semester at the Copenhagen Academy of Fashion. Do you know it?"

I dip my head in a nod. "*Ja*. My friend Pippa went there for a year."

The blonde arches a brow. "Your *friend* probably dropped out because it's hard."

I frown at the way she used the word friend to mean… something else. I sip my water, feeling myself check out of the conversation. Looking bored, I shrug. "She left to pursue journalism, if that's what you mean."

The brunette cuts in, giving her friend a sharp glance. "I'm sure that Anya didn't mean anything by that. We are both having the damnedest time with our course loads, that's all."

Anya shoots her friend an irritated glance. "Thanks, Katya. But really, who wants to talk about our boring lives? You're a real, live prince. What is that like?"

I find myself checking my watch, wondering when Pippa will be here. "What part, exactly?"

My eyes are already roving the bar, looking for something more interesting than these two can offer. I know exactly how the rest of this conversation will go, down to the moment when the blonde leans in and whispers that we should leave together. I'm not against it, and certainly I have no problem with women expressing their sexuality.

Quite the opposite, actually.

It would just be nice if one of these women did something surprising for a change. Something more stimulating than batting their eyelashes and subtly toying with their hair.

It's nice. It's just been done so many times before.

"Ummm, what is King Stellan like? Ohh, and Queen Margot! You must love spending time with them."

My gaze wanders to Anya again. I put zero thought into how I'm going to answer that question.

"Stellan is the same asshole he's always been. And Margot is as sweet as sugar for putting up with him."

She laughs, leaning in and putting her hand on my forearm. "That's amazing. Tell me, how is it that you are still single? I mean, you're very handsome and very eligible…"

My gaze slides over to the brunette, who has pulled out her phone and isn't paying attention anymore. I take another sip of my water. "I don't know. I'm only twenty five. That leaves me plenty of time to settle down, I think. Besides, I'm incredibly choosy about the girls I sleep with."

That's just a bald-faced lie, but it slips past my lips unchecked and unheeded. Anya laughs again, gripping my arm.

God, I'm so tired of how meaningless this conversation is. So deeply, deeply exhausted.

I open my mouth to excuse myself, looking out across the bar. And that's the moment when I see Pippa.

She's wearing a billowy beige lace dress with a dramatic slash of cleavage in the front, an enormous black faux-fur coat, and black high heels. Her beautiful copper hair is wound in braids around her head; her blue-green eyes stand out even from this distance; her delicate pink mouth is twisted in an almost-grimace as she heads straight toward me.

For a moment, my stomach flip flops. The two girls I was talking to are all but forgotten as I rise, sure that my height will call Pippa's attention more than my black leather jacket, black cotton t-shirt, or dark jeans ever could.

I would wave, but I'm certain that I would look like a complete fool. So I just stand for a second, a head above the next tallest person here.

It does the trick. She looks my way. Our eyes clash.

She gives me the most sheepish smile, biting her lower lip as she rushes over to me. Warmth splashes through my insides like warm water, filling me to the brim.

Thank god.

"Sorry! I'm so, so late!" Pippa exclaims, elbowing two guys out of her way. Her accent is British, her o's short and her a's choppy.

She stops short, hugging herself nervously as her eyes dance over me. There has always been an unspoken rule between us, ever since we were kids.

No hugging.

No touching.

Trust me, it's been a savior for me, time and time again.

I shrug, pointing to a booth. "Want to go sit down?"

I can see hesitance on her heart shaped face. "What about your, uh… friends?"

I turn my head, only at this moment remembering that the other girls are still at the bar. The blonde is currently looking at Pippa with judgmental, jealous eyes.

"Oh. You girls don't mind if I go talk to my friend, do you?" I paste on my fakest, most charming smirk. "I'll be back in a bit, if you're still here."

It's not really a question. I'm not interested in their input, really.

I lean in, brushing against the blonde and wink as I scoop up my glass of water. Then I make eye contact with the bartender, holding up two fingers and pointing to the booth where I'll be at. He nods and I walk away, swaggering over to the dark little booth where Pippa is making herself at home.

I slide into the other side of the cracked black leather booth, peeling off my jacket. Pippa pushes her coat off, spreading her palms flat against the dark wood of the table. She sighs, craning her neck.

I let my eyes wander down her pale, graceful neck and slip down to her pronounced collarbones. I don't look at her slash of exposed cleavage; that's another unspoken rule.

Don't touch her. Don't even look at her.

And if you do look, don't get caught staring.

"It has been the longest day ever," she declares, running her hand over her face. "When did other people become so bothersome?"

My laugh leaves my chest in a rumble. I tilt my head at her. "I've always thought they were pretty awful."

She wrinkles her nose. "Some of them are."

The bartender brings us two fresh drinks. We come here quite a bit, enough for him to know what we drink. A fizzy cocktail for Pippa, a whiskey soda for me.

"Thanks," I say, lifting the glass at him.

Pippa's lips curve and she raises her glass, clinking it against mine. "Here's to people being the worst."

I smile as I take a sip, the honeyed sweetness of the whiskey balanced by the bubbles and sharp tang of alcohol. Rolling it around in my mouth for a moment, I sit back.

She makes a satisfied sound. "That's a nice cocktail. Speaking of which, I thought you were laying off the liquor for the next few months."

"Thanks, *mor*. I am bending my own rules a little, *ja*. But I will be the one who pays the price when my alarm goes off at five. Besides, I wouldn't even still be here if you weren't so late."

Her cheeks color a little. "I said I was sorry. And anyway, you seemed to have found your own company, as usual."

She arches a brow and gestures to where I left the girls sitting at the bar. The corners of my mouth curl upward. "You left me to fend for myself. What can I say?"

She sighs, shaking her head. "You are a womanizer, through and through."

I shrug, sipping my drink. "I think we can both agree that I'm not the best choice for anyone. Fathers, lock up your daughters!"

I chuckle to myself. Pippa rolls her eyes.

"Yes, yes. You're a big, brooding bad boy. I get it, okay? Trust me, everybody gets that it's your *thing*."

I laugh at her dismissiveness. "*Ja, ja*. I just tell it like it is."

Her lips quirk. "I think you're just afraid to let yourself get comfortable. Every night, a new bed. Every day, you're doing some harebrained, dare-devil stunt for the sake of… I don't know… adrenaline, I guess?"

She shudders.

"Hey, don't act like I haven't grown up in the… what, four-teen years you've known me?" I smirk at her.

"Fifteen years," she says, toying with the rim of her glass. "Okay, example one. You're still a pilot in the Royal Air Force. Example two, I know about you applying for the Danish Space Institute, or whatever. The royal family may think that you've matured, but I am not fooled so easily." Her eyes sparkle as she sips her cocktail.

I lean in, liking the feistiness of her words. "I'll have you know that I only race expensive yachts and go base jumping on weeks when I'm not scheduled to fly in the RAF."

She rolls her eyes. "You are so irresponsible. Perpetually, I fear."

"You wound me." I smirk again, belying my own words.

Her slow smile tells me everything I need to know. She shakes her head. "Hey, speaking of which. Did you get the invitation for St. Matthew's winter celebration?"

I snort. "No. Maybe our alma mater realizes I live here in Denmark and have no interest in flying back to the Swiss Alps in this weather."

"I am wholly certain that they sent it to you and you just didn't read it. It's okay though, because I'm pretty sure that they're just asking alumnus to come back as a fancy way to open our checkbooks."

I nod slowly. "It is always about the money with them. In any case, I'm sure that the royal family just writes them a big fat check every year. The next time that they donate, I should just have them add your name to the roster."

Pippa glances down into her drink, frowning for a split second. I realize I've accidentally tripped over my own tongue. Pippa and I both went to an elite boarding school, but we went under very different circumstances.

Pippa is an orphan who attended the school thanks to a mysterious benefactor.

And me?

I attended because I was such a bad kid at ten years old that I had been kicked out of every notable prep school in Denmark.

I clear my throat, changing the subject to cover my gaffe. "You're coming to the palace tomorrow, *ja?*"

She smiles softly at me. "If you want me to be there, I will."

"I always want you," I say. The words just tumble out of my mouth, unchecked.

When Pippa's cheeks go pink, my neck heats. I look down at my drink, shaking my head. "You know what I meant. Just come, please. Save me from my own family like you do every year."

She smiles. For a moment, I can't tell if her expression is genuine or not. "I will come. Thanks, Froggy."

Her use of my childhood nickname draws a laugh from my lips. "Anything for you, little witch."

She looks up, catching my gaze for just a second. She bites one of her soft, full lips.

Those kissable, perfectly plump lips. So close and yet…

So very, very off limits.

I swallow. Just now, I know a moment of pure want.

God, I could just reach across the table right now, drag Pippa over here, and plunder those sexy fucking lips.

Then she breaks the spell by tipping up her glass, finishing the last drops, and grabbing her voluminous coat. "All right. I should get home. And you should too, though somehow I don't think you will find yourself there anytime soon…"

She tips her head toward the bar. I look over and see the blonde from earlier still waiting there. I squint, looking back to Pippa with a shrug.

"Let me drive you home," I say, yawning. "I'm tired anyway."

Pippa stands up, shaking her head. "No. You stay. Have a good time!" She gives me a quick grin, touching my shoulder as she passes me. "I'll see you tomorrow, Lars."

I move my hand up my chest to touch hers as it lands against my skin. I'm too slow, though. She's gone before I can do anything else, leaving my heart aching just a bit.

Isn't that always the way of things? Pippa slipping away, while I'm still trying to tamp down my more dangerous emotions around her.

Quaffing the rest of my drink, I stand up, turning to watch Pippa's elegant form disappearing through the crowd. Taking my wallet out of my pants pocket, I toss a wad of cash on the table. Then I make eye contact with the simpering blonde from earlier.

I only have to cock a brow and jerk my head toward the exit. She positively beams at me, nodding her head enthusiastically. I grab my leather jacket, putting it on.

There is something wrong though.

I know it even as I head for the door.

The blonde's smile doesn't light me up inside the way Pippa's does.

No one else even comes close.

As I push the heavy door open and try to put that thought out of my mind as I escort the blonde out to my waiting chauffeured car.

3

____

PIPPA

G OD, HOW BEAUTIFUL THE WORLD IS RIGHT NOW. I BLINK UP into the winter sky, thankful that it's actually clear and sunny. It's still cold as all get out though. Huge snow drifts are everywhere I look. As I hurry down the cobbled streets of Copenhagen, a hushed sort of wonderland is all around me.

Most of the cars are still snowed in from last night. Lights twinkle nearly everywhere I look. This is the fanciest part of town, full of lavish window displays and signs proclaiming _Jul_ cheer. Every window I pass has cute gingerbread men or simple red and white paper hearts pressed against the glass. All the shops and businesses are closed for _Julaften_, the Danish version of Christmas Eve.

When I turn the corner, I see Amalienborg palace rising just at the end of the street. The snow has been all but vanquished here, shoveled away by unseen hands. There are four massive beige brick buildings all huddled in a circle, all saluting a rather large statue of a man on a horse. With their white-trimmed windows, dark roofs covered by snow drifts, and guards dressed in scarlet, the palaces definitely proudly exude *money*.

I check my slender silver wristwatch as I scurry up to the palace, stopping at the newly-installed guard station. It's made entirely of plastic sheeting and PVC piping, looking like a strong enough gust of wind might blow it away entirely.

I try not to voice my frustrations out loud; the palace has been implementing more stringent rules lately because of *elevated threat levels,* whatever that means.

Two scarlet-clad guards are standing between me and the palace door. I can't help but start to feel nervous as I clear my throat, reaching into my bag and fishing out my identification.

The new checkpoint has nothing to do with you, I remind myself calmly.

"*Haj,*" I greet the guards. "*Glædelig jul!*" I say brightly. Roughly translated, it means Merry Christmas.

The guard is all business. He holds out his hand, expectant. I can't help but notice my hand is trembling ever so slightly as I offer them my driver's license. "Here you go."

"*Taak.* One moment." One of the guards bows his head, takes my ID, and then disappears into the little tent.

Breathe, I reprimand myself. *You are not of any interest to these guards. No one is going around, digging up fifteen year old secrets. They are just doing their job.*

The guard is taking his time with my ID, though. I can feel a few droplets of sweat start to break out on the back of my neck. I clench and unclench my fists, trying not to seem agitated.

The guard that is waiting outside with me shoots me a polite smile. "It will just be another minute, I'm sure."

I shiver, wrapping my coat more snugly around myself. The guard in the booth emerges at last, my identification card pinches between two fingers. His gaze narrows on my face.

My stomach drops as he stalks over to me.

"I'm sorry, frøken, but the system doesn't recognize your ID. It says your records don't exist. I can't let you into the palace without the proper clearance."

My eyes go wide. I stammer out, "What?"

They can't know. It's *impossible*. My identification card is real. Pippa Welch might not have existed when I took the name at eleven, but definitely exists now.

"Pippa!"

I glance up to find Lars bursting out of the heavy double doors on the other side of the guard booth. With his dark hair, his intense blue eyes, and his ruddy complexion, he looks like he just walked off a damn runway. His black cable knit sweater and casual black jeans fit him like a glove.

And he's about to find out that his best friend in the entire world is a liar.

Oh god, this is the last thing I want.

He can't find out like this.

I open my mouth, trying to explain away the guards. But Lars just storms up to the guards, taking them to task.

"What is the problem here?" he snarls at the guard closest to him. He snatches my ID card out of the man's hand, his eyes flickering with anger.

Lars has a fiery temper, to put it lightly. Usually I would step in and defend the poor guard, but in this case… I just lick my lips nervously and say nothing.

"Your highness, I am just following protocol…" the guard says, turning pink.

"It's Julaften," Lars says, tilting his head. "In the spirit of the holiday, I'm going to restrain myself." He steps closer to the guard, making him step back. "Pippa Welch is here as my guest. She is *always* welcome. If you've got a list of names somewhere, you'd better write hers down. I don't want to have this conversation again."

The guard swallows, nodding. "Yes, your highness."

Lars shakes his head, turning to me. He beckons to me, his voice still curt. "Come on, Pippa."

I walk toward the heavy wood double doors, my heart pounding, my palms still a bit damp. Lifting my chin, I stride through the doors as they are opened for me. I don't even give the guard stand a second glance.

As we walk inside, I feel Lars put his hand on the small of my back. My stride breaks for a moment.

Cool down, I tell myself. *Be a lady, for god's sake.*

I exhale and shed my coat, handing it off to a servant. Lars eyes me as we start climbing the white marble stairs that lead up into the palace proper. I feel his gaze on my slinky gold dress, judging me like I'm a prize heifer.

"Stop staring," I scold him, not even looking over to see if it's true or not. "I'm wearing a perfectly presentable dress, if that's what you are worried about."

I hear the smile in his voice. "I wasn't thinking about that."

"Then why are you looking at me?"

I turn, shooting him a glare. He shrugs, his little smirk maddening. "You look nice, that's all."

Wrinkling up my face at him, I huff. "Well, quit it. I'm not some blonde at the bar. You can't chat me up and take me back to someplace dark for a bit of fun. We're best friends, not fuck buddies."

Lars chuckles. "Fair enough, little witch."

I shoot him an irritated look and pick up the hem of my dress, holding it up as we keep climbing.

We make it up the steep stairs and I stop, my eyes widening. The palace is always something to behold. Gray marble floors, gray marble columns flanking both sides of the hall-way, an incredible arched and carved white marble ceiling.

I've never seen it decorated quite so thoroughly, though.

Towering trees stand between each column. Each one is festively decorated with delicate red paper hearts, crisp white paper snowflakes, and shimmering gold tinsel. There is a cheerful red runner on the floor and garlands of tiny red and white flags strung overhead. At the far end of the hall, I can just make out the shapes of gingerbread men and toy soldiers plastered against the floor to ceiling window.

"Whoa," I say.

Lars rolls his eyes at the decorations, pulling at my hand. "Margot went a little nuts with the decorating. Come on, the sooner we get into the sitting room, the sooner we can leave."

A laugh bubbles to my lips as I let him lead me toward the party. "Where have you got to be? Everyone you know is here."

He gives his head a shake, not interested in explaining. There is only one door open in the grand hallway. Light spills out and as I get closer, I can hear laughter.

A chill runs down my spine. This is far from my first Julaften, but I swear I will never tire of how much this family enjoys being around each other. Lars goes through the doorway just ahead of me. When I step through, it's exactly as I would have hoped it would be. A beautifully decorated sitting room, with a full decorated tree in one corner and a whole buffet of delicious-smelling foods up against one wall. All of Lars's extended family is clustered together around the fireplace, sitting near their partners.

Dark-haired Stellan is standing closest to the fire, beaming down at his pink-haired pixie of a wife Margot. On the couch beside Margot is Lars's lovely blonde sister Annika, and her enormous blond fiancé Erik.

Lars's parents, Mor and Dar, are sitting on a couch on the other side of the fireplace. His brothers Finn and Anders have pulled up chairs just beside them. And there is an empty loveseat facing the fireplace, obviously meant for Lars and me to occupy it.

Margot lays eyes on me and pops up out of her seat, her eyes shining with genuine joy. "Pippa!"

My lips curl upward. Margot is one of my oldest friends. It just so happens that she fell head over heels for Stellan this spring after I introduced them. So I always look forward to seeing her, especially now during the holidays. I throw my hands wide, greeting the room.

"Glædelig jul!" I declare, wishing her a merry Christmas.

Margot runs over to me and I embrace her, setting an arm around her small body. She is dainty and delicate like a child, but I know the rebel heart that beats in her chest. "Merry Christmas," I murmur in her ear.

She pulls back, tears glimmering in her eyes. Margot didn't exactly have an easy childhood. Looking at all the over the top decorations that the palace doesn't usually have this time of year, it's obvious that this Christmas is her way of living out her childhood fantasies.

"Here, here," she says. She ushers me over to the loveseat, pushing on my shoulder. "Sit down. Let me get you a mug of cocoa."

I pull a face but she isn't listening to me.

"Margot's too wrapped up in all the Christmas cheer, it seems." Lars sits down beside me, taking up most of the room on the loveseat. I shoot him a look and he shrugs innocently.

Nika leans forward, looking elegant as always. "Hello, Pippa. Merry Christmas."

I cast a gaze over her. She and Erik are sitting with their hands clasped. I smile because three months ago, that would've been a really big deal.

"You too. How's the charity work?"

She beams, excited. "It's good. Remind me to catch you later and bend your ear about my latest project. It's inspired, if I do say so myself."

Margot has moved over to the buffet that is laid out for our gathering. Stellan shakes his head, calling over to her. "Margot, let Lars make Pippa I drink. You don't have to do everything for everybody, darling."

I notice Lars's parents have been unusually quiet. On any normal day, I expect them to be making everyone pay attention to them and dote on them. That definitely seems like the commonality between his parents. But it seems that I have missed their antics today. His mother drains her glass of champagne while his father just looks extremely tired.

Lars's mother and father stand up, his father yawning a little. She looks at him, putting her arm in his quite tenderly. "I think that we should say good night now. Your father isn't feeling too well. It was nice to see you all, though."

Lars looks a little concerned but he lets it pass unremarked. Instead, he gets up and kisses his mother on the cheek and claps his father on the back. I watch the exchange warily; we've known for a while that Lars's father is terminally ill.

Margot carries my drink over to me as Stellan's parents exit. I take the mug from her thankfully, clutching it as I look around the room. Margot settles in where Lars's mother just was and Stellan joins her, his arm going around her shoulders. I look at that small gesture of intimacy with no small amount of longing.

I want that. I have the familiarity with Lars part down, but I don't see how we will ever get to be as close as Margot and Stellan are. It's the only sort of limitation placed on my friendship with Lars.

We follow the unspoken rule that there is just absolutely no touching for *any* reason.

I clear my throat and swing my gaze over to Annika, only to find her whispering something in Erik's ear.

Ugh. This place is full of people who have fallen deeply and irrevocably in love with each other… And it's really killing my buzz.

Lars must feel the same way, because he pipes up. "Could you guys please save it for the bedroom? Some of us are just trying to live our lives over here, you know?"

As my lips curl up, I notice that my knee brushes Lars's. I shrink myself back from him a few inches, wishing like hell that we were sitting on anything but this loveseat. Lars doesn't even seem to notice. He clears his throat.

"Stellan, now that our parents are gone, do you think that we could add some booze to this party?"

Stellan grins. "I thought you would never asked."

For the next couple of minutes, the room is a flurry of motion. Stellan gets a bottle of champagne and look pops it; champagne flutes are filled and handed out. I raise my eyebrow at Margot, making sure that she sees my expression.

She flushes just a little bit. I know her big secret… she is pregnant. I'm not even sure why Stellan would pour her a glass of champagne, honestly.

She holds up one finger, which I take to mean that I need to wait just a minute.

Anders raises his glass. "What should we toast to? Just Merry Christmas?"

Stellan's smile widens. He puts his free hand on Margot's me. "Actually, we have some news. We're not telling people yet, obviously. But we're expecting."

Margot looks slightly embarrassed, tucking her bright pink hair behind her ear. I beam as I look at her. She looks like she is truly, enviably happy. And she found that happy ending with the king of Denmark, no less. As she takes Stellan's hand, I feel a strange pinch. I want the kind of love that they have.

"Hear, hear!" I say, raising my glass.

Everyone else cheers, congratulating the couple.

Even though I knew about the pregnancy news ahead of time, my eyes still fill with tears of happiness. I beam at Margot. She's basically living my most basic bitch dreams.

Not that I would ever tell anyone, but all I have ever wanted is to end up living in a big house with a white picket fence. Two point five children, scruffy little dog, and a husband that loves me to the ends of the earth.

My life has never resembled a Norman Rockwell painting, but a voice inside tells me that I really should expect it still.

I know, it's stupid. It goes hand in hand with my idiotic longing for Lars.

I try to ignore it as best I can.

Margot wipes her eyes. "Thanks, guys."

Lars interjects. "When are you due?"

I arched my brow at him, wondering how he knows to even ask that question. He meets my gaze and shrugs.

Margot smiles prettily at us. "In the middle of May."

Stellan clears his throat. "We're both very excited. It goes without saying that the news doesn't leave this room. I don't even want my parents to know, much less anyone that would leak the information to the press. Sorry, Pippa."

I blush. He's referring to my job at *Politiken*, the Copenhagen daily newspaper.

I'm quick to assure him that I won't tell anyone. "It's not my news to share. I think you should keep it secret as long as you can, honestly."

He grins down at Margot, squeezing her in a side hug. "I'm going to try."

Lars moves to get more comfortable, squishing me in the process. He's arranged himself so that his thigh presses against mine. I sigh, shooting him a look.

We have established some age-old boundaries with each other, not the least of which is that we expend effort to avoid casually touching each other. He glances at me, his eyebrow arching.

"What?" he asks.

I shake my head, pushing his knee away and starting to get up. Too late though, I realize that Finn and Anders have started to reenact a skit of some sort in the middle of the semicircle of seats.

So I'm forced to sit back. Lars looks at me, his eyes twinkling, and throws his arm around my shoulders. It's too much; he's touching my thigh, my hip, and my shoulders. Everywhere he is touching me vaguely tingles. I think that the sensation of knowing I shouldn't be so close to the guy secretly I'm in love with is too intense to handle.

I immediately start to squirm out of his hold. He grips my shoulder to keep me in place.

"Oh, little witch," he teases me. "I know you hate being touched, but just deal with it for a minute. Come on. You secretly like it, I think."

My cheeks flood with heat and I look down. It's not that I dislike being touched.

Not, it's the opposite.

I crave it.

I want him to do it more.

But Lars and I don't have that kind of intimacy. We can't, not without it turning into something more.

And I won't be one of those nameless, faceless girls that he never sees again.

I couldn't handle that.

Pushing myself up and out of his grasp, I stand up, straightening my dress. I shoot him a purposeful look as I walk around the circle, crouching down next to Margot.

She's delighted to see me and starts chattering away.

But I still feel his eyes on me.

Watching.

Waiting.

For what, I don't know.

4

———

LARS

THERE IS NOTHING SO EXHILARATING AS FLYING THIS FUCKING jet. My eyes are as wide as can be, scanning the horizon. My mind is almost blank as I pilot the jet, making a thousand tiny alterations to my speed and altitude and direction. My heart pounds.

There is something zen about having so much to focus on at once. It's very much like running a marathon in the way that every single resource you have is pulled into doing it; mentally, physically, you have to give it your all.

Or else…

Well, I would fall from the sky.

I look out my window, glancing at the ground. Up here, the world is carved into little blocks of dull gray, dark brown, and black. I can see the block of runway that I'm heading for; from the distance, it just looks like a long Tetris block of heather gray. If I really stare hard enough, I could probably make out the bright yellow runway markings.

"Tower, looking for permission to land," I say into my headset.

There's a second of silence. My heartbeat pounds in my ears.

A crackle informs me that my request has been heard. "This is tower one. Permission granted."

"Coming in now," I say into my headset.

I point myself down and find that same state of electric zenness as I hurtle toward the ground. The world rushes by, but I barely notice. It's all just muscle memory at this point.

As I smoothly taxi my little jet down the RDAF runway, I feel the surge of adrenaline rushing through my system. As I glide into the parking bay, I look around. I push the brake to stop the jet and unbuckle my helmet. I push the button to stop the engine and open the cockpit.

A rush of cool air prickles across my scalp, raising the hairs on the back of my neck. I undo my seat belt and use the jets outside steps to get down to the ground, jumping down the last step. When I hit the ground, I look up to find Erik standing there, waiting for me. Erik and I are old friends, going back to the first days of his unofficial adoption into the palace.

I flash him a grin. We are closer probably even than he and Stellan are, but don't tell either of them that.

He is also an officer in the Royal Air Force, although he has since retired. Arching a brow, I stride toward him. He looks me up and down, smirking a little at my jumpsuit.

"So just an average morning for you then?"

I grin at him. "Yup. Hey, I'm just finishing here. Do you want to go grab a drink?"

He looks at his watch, squinting. "It's not five yet."

I clapped him on his shoulder. "It's five somewhere. Come on."

He follows me for a second. "Actually, I have something to drop off to a friend. Go ahead and change and I'll meet you in the canteen."

I shake my head, continuing through the space and into the men's locker rooms. I shower and change with my usual efficiency, putting on a pair of dark jeans and a dark gray sweater. By the time I head out to the canteen, one of the only places for people to gather and socialize on the base, Erik is sitting at a table already.

He is dressed in a white button down shirts and dark blue trousers, looking for all the world like he belongs on the cover of GQ or something. If I didn't know better, I would think he had gotten quite lost on the way here.

I sit down at the little gray aluminum table, just as Erik is pouring amber beer out of a pitcher into two pint glasses. The Royal Air Force canteen is not exactly known for having a great beer selection on tap. In fact, they only have the shittiest beer and the most bargain-basement labels of hard alcohol.

Given the choice, I think Erik made the right decision.

I raise my pint glass toward him. He clinks his glass against the rim of mine and we both take a long sip. It's cheap and it tastes like water. But hey, a drink's a drink, I guess.

Erik looks at me, quirking his lips. "So… I hear you are training to be an astronaut."

I look up at him, a frown on my face. "Who told you that?"

He shrugs. "A friendly face here on the base. He told me in confidence, if it makes you feel any better."

I pull a face. "It doesn't really. No one is supposed to know that I'm even training for it. It's all very hush-hush."

"My source says that it's a bit of a long shot. Add in the fact that you, as a member of the royal family, are considered one of the country's important resources… It puts you pretty solidly in the 'will not happen' category."

I roll my eyes. "I've heard that. But I've also asked command if my being second in line to the throne puts me out of the running entirely. And no one has said yet that I won't get the mission just because of who I am. That's pretty much against the code of the Royal Air Force. So I'm just going to keep running for it as long as I can."

Erik sips his beer, watching me over the rim of his pint glass. When he is done, he licks a bit of foam from his lips and continues asking questions. "If you're pretty sure that you're not going to get it, why do you keep going? What motivates that kind of thinking?"

I shrug a shoulder. "It's a chance to go to space, man. If I did that… If I actually made it to space, I would be…" I trail after second and then shake my head. "I don't want to go down in history as the second in line to the throne. I want my name to mean something to somebody. I want to be remembered."

His brows shoot up in surprise. "Really?"

I nod, feeling a bit sheepish. But he purses his lips again, seeming pensive.

"That's a hell of a way to start a legacy. Most people just get married and have kids."

I chuckled dryly, shaking my head. "Not me, man. I can't even meet a girl that I like, much less one that I want to marry."

Erik huffs out a laugh. "I think that Pippa would disagree about that."

I rock back in my chair. "Besides Pippa, I mean. She doesn't count, obviously."

"No? What's wrong with Pippa?"

I fixed him with a stare. "We've already been over this 100 times. She's my best friend, not a potential mate. Girls are so flighty. They're really only after my title. Pippa isn't like that. But that's just because we been friends for well over fifteen years. I don't want to rock the boat and risk losing my oldest, closest friend." I set my beer down with a smirk. "Besides, Pippa is so busy with her life that I don't even know where I would fit in."

I say the last line as a joke, but the rest of it I really mean. I spent hours agonizing over how to tell Pippa how I feel, only to realize that this imagined love may only run one way. I would rather risk never finding someone to love me then to risk what I have with Pippa.

It's just not worth it.

Erik leans his elbows on the table. "But what if she loves you just like you love her?"

I roll my eyes, tipping up my pint glass to drain the contents in a few swallows when I'm done, I grab the pitcher and refill my glass. "I don't want to talk about her anymore. Let's change the subject. How about we poke around in your private business with Nika?"

That earns me a scowl. I slide the beer pitcher over to him and he accepts it with a frown. "That's not very funny."

I huff a laugh. "And yet, it's more entertaining than talking about why Pippa and I aren't an item. I think at this point, I have to admit to myself that I don't think I'm cut out for love. Being in love, believing in love, the whole thing is just very…" I wrinkle my face up.

Erik takes a few moments to fill his glass and take a sip. He looks up at me after he's done, his keen eyes pinning me in place. "It's funny you say that, because not that long ago, I was saying that too. And then… there was Annika. Your sister hit me like a hurricane and I had no choice but to fall in love with her." He smiles into his beer. "She's very lovable."

I give him a smarmy smile. "You two would have never gotten together if it hadn't been for Stellan and my grandmother sticking their big fat noses in where they didn't along. It created a tension, a sense of taboo, where there wasn't one before. I blame that entirely on you and Nika."

Erik fans his hand out. "Maybe. I think there is more to love than the sense of forbidden longing though."

I purse my lips. "Maybe that is why I haven't ever been in love. I don't even think I'm capable of it."

He frowns. "I'm sure that's not true."

"It really is. And that's okay. Someone has to stand out among all the rest."

He rolls his eyes. "I wouldn't word it like that."

"Look, I know that I'm not the safest of choices. But I will still be a handsome retired Royal Air Force pilot and a prince when I am seventy years old. Hell, I might have even been to space! I have difficulty believing that I will never be able to walk into a bar and get any girl that catches my eye. That's not something that most people can say."

He laughs a little at that. "I think that's your age talking. When you are fifty years old, you will be watching Pippa and whatever guy she settles down with. And you'll feel sorry that you ever thought that you would always be able to get all the pussy you want."

I roll my eyes. "For the longest time, Pippa and I have been facing questions about our friendship. The fact that we've managed to keep close but separate is honestly a miracle."

He gives me a look and shakes his head. "I guess it is whatever makes you happy."

My lips curve upward. "Exactly. Pippa isn't your average girl. She is exceptional in every way. And that includes the fact that I'm not interested in her in that way."

He arches a brow. "So you don't think Pippa is hot?"

I shoot him a little smile. "All my friends are hot."

He shakes his head again. "You're crazy." He stands up, quaffing the rest of his drink. "I think I need some fries to go with this beer. You want anything?"

"Hah. The RDAF has some of the worst food on the planet. So I'll stick to their watery beer for now."

He nods a little as he heads to the canteen counter. I watch him go, sighing. He's told me a hundred times before that he doesn't understand my relationship with Pippa.

She's right there. You're both attractive. You like each other enough. Just go for it.

Each and every time he brings it up, I rebuff him. It's a tale as old as time, to be perfectly frank. And not to mention that it's boring as fuck, feeling like I have to explain to Erik and everyone else.

Why won't people just mind their own business?

Taking a sip of my beer, I mull it over again in my head.

Pippa is wonderful. She's sweet. She's smart. She's playful. She knows my history.

Hell, she's been there for a lot of it.

Plus there is the fact that she's absolutely fucking smoking hot.

But there is an edge to her. There is a point at which she grows uncomfortable with closeness, pushes everyone away, including me. I have the vague sense that there is just more to her that I can't quite touch. She is a lake whose depths are yet-unknown to anyone. And as you delve deeper, the water gets cold as ice.

I don't know for sure, but I get the feeling that at the bottom is a solid, frozen wall.

So yes, I may have a thing for her.

But there is definitely no way that I'm about to take it further. Even if I could, I'm not sure I would want to.

A bird in the hand is worth two in the bush. I have Pippa's friendship. Asking for more than that seems… greedy, some- how. It's better to have the closest friendship than to have no Pippa at all.

I stare down at my empty glass, trying to reassure myself.

5

PIPPA

Sylvie Martin. That was the name that I was born with.

Sitting on my couch in my tiny apartment, I open my laptop and type the name in. Swallowing quickly, I hit return.

A million results are returned in my search box. I guess Sylvie Martin is a pretty common name. But I keep scrolling down, looking for old mentions of myself. Clicking next on every page of links that don't have anything to do with me, I finally find a link to an old newspaper article on the sixth page.

The old newspaper article is in French, though it's only the work of a minute to translate it with Google. It reads, *Ansel Martin sentenced to thirty life sentences this week. The terrorist that bombed French Parliament is survived by his daughters Sylvie and Stella. The two girls have gone to live with a close family friend, although authorities will not release that guardian's name. It is believed that they will be placed in witness protection and start new lives under new names...*

I swallow, closing the page. I want more than anything to know exactly what happened to my little sister Stella. She disappeared from my life around the same time that I went to a Swiss boarding school and changed my name to Pippa Welch.

That's my biggest regret: I have no real idea what happened to Stella. By the time that I reached out to the family friend who got me accepted to St. Matthew's boarding school, the family friend and my little sister had disappeared without a trace.

In retrospect, I should've asked a lot more questions. But at the time, it seemed like I just had to get away from my old life. I let Stella go as part of the deal.

Biting my lip, I figure a little digital snooping won't hurt anyone. I type *in what happened to Ansel Martin's daughters?* and *Paris* into the search bar and get a million fresh results. After reading a few articles about where weirdos on the internet think we might be, I finally find a name.

Sylvie Martin.

God, could my sister actually be living under her given name?

I quickly type her name into Facebook. Scrolling through a few pages, I see a list of Facebook profiles.

I've looked for Stella online before... but I've never tried looking on Facebook. I click the link and cruise through four pages of results before I find someone I recognize. Her face is fuller and rounder, her eyes more grown up than I remember. Her red hair is unmistakable though, a nest of fiery copper curls.

My heart seizes up as I click on her profile. Her page is set to private so there is almost no information to be found… except for her location.

She lives in Nantes, a little more than three hours from Paris.

A million questions enter my mind.

How long has she lived there?

What is she like now?

Is there any room in her life for her surely long-forgotten sister?

I bite my lip, my finger hovering over the button that will add her as a friend. Is that something she would want? If I were her, would I want a big sister reappearing in my life, fifteen years after the fact?

In the end, I bookmark her Facebook profile, unable to bring myself to click on the *add as a friend* button. I stare off into the distance, thinking about the past.

If I could do it all over again, given what I know today, I would do everything differently. Then again, what if doing anything differently resulted in not knowing Lars quite as well as I do now?

That thought haunts me.

I get a text message, which pops up on my computer screen and chimes. I startle a little as I shake my head and check the message. It's from Margot.

Hey, are you still planning on meeting me at the baby store later? I know that I shouldn't be planning already, but I'm in full baby crazy mode. Help!

My lips curve up slightly. I text her back.

It's funny to see you like this, because you were never the baby crazy one of the two of us. I always figured that I would already be married with a bunch of kids by now. You would be the fun aunt and you would spoil my whole brood. And yet... Here we are.

She texts back.

I know, right? I never expected it either. But now that I'm expecting, I can't help it. I spent an hour this morning watching Tik-Tok videos of cute babies and sobbing uncontrollably. There's no helping me.

I chuckle. *I'll be there. Just let me know which store you decide on. And be ready for me to buy you every cute onesie that I see.*

She just replies with the *100* emoticon. I set my laptop aside and stand up, stretching. I looked down at my current outfit, a black sweatshirt and a pair of pink tie-dyed leggings. I'm definitely going to have to reconsider my outfit choice if I'm going to actually go into *Politiken* today.

The very thought of going into the actual office makes my stomach sink a little. I usually love my job, but lately it's been a lot less fun. Mostly because I have this new editor that is all over me, constantly asking what I'm working on and why I am not focusing more on my *insider knowledge* of the palace.

My phone starts ringing, shaking me out of my thoughts. I frown and walk over to answer it, seeing that my editor is calling as though I summoned her.

I take a deep breath and answer. "Freja. To what do I owe the pleasure?"

Her high-pitched voice grates on my ears. "Pippa! I was just wondering when we would see you in the office. I have some story ideas that I would very much like to run by you."

I grit my teeth. "Well, why don't you just run them by me right now? I'm probably not going to be in the office today…" I don't know why the lie just slips past my lips, but there's something about Freja that just gets on my nerves.

She clears her throat. "Well, all right. I guess it couldn't hurt. I have three ideas that are really good. The first one is about you and Margot and how you went to college together…"

I shake my head a little. Who would've guessed that Freja would present such a terrible idea to me? I try to keep this sigh from my answer. "Uh-huh. I don't think that the Queen would really like me taking advantage of our mutual past like that."

"Oh, I'm sure that's not true. Queen Margot seems like a cool person. I think she would—"

I interrupt her. "Let's not get into what she would or would not do and what you personally think would or would not be okay with her. You said you had three ideas. So what are the other two?"

There's a few seconds of awkward silence on the line. I hear the sound of pages flipping as she clears her throat again. "Well, okay. I've got another idea that is about you and Lars and how your relationship first started almost fifteen years ago in boarding school."

I grimace. "Again, I think you are asking me to trade on my personal relationships in order to give an inside look into the personal lives of the royals. And I don't think that Lars would appreciate it any more than Margot would. I think that's one of the reasons that they both respect me is that I may be a journalist, but I'm not always asking annoying personal questions *on the record* when I'm hanging out with them.

We're friends first. I'm a journalist second. Does that make sense to you?"

I can just imagine her pinched face, her look of disappointment complete. "I don't think that you are really getting a full picture of what I am asking you for. It's nothing that couldn't be gleaned from reading the papers…"

I clench my jaw. "I think I've already answered your question. What is the third idea?"

She blows out a breath. "Well, this one is a little more personal and a little more out there, but I was thinking that you could take a vacation with Lars or Margot and record little short video clips of reminiscing on your friendship—"

I make an aggravated noise. "Ja, no. I'm not going to do that. It seems like all of your story ideas center around my friendship with the royal family. None of the other editors have any problem with assigning me stories that are not directly related to my friends. I don't quite understand what the issue is that you seem to have."

"I don't have an issue with you, Pippa. You seem to be the one that has an issue with this newspaper. And to be frank, I don't see how we can keep employing someone that clearly has interests other than the paper at heart. So I would think long and hard about the three stories I presented. I would plan to do one of them. Because until you do, I don't think that you can be assigned another story."

My lips thin and my eyes narrow. "Have you talked to upper management about this? Because David certainly wouldn't like you poking your nose into the royal family any more than I like being asked to do it."

Freja sounds a little happy to deliver the news. "Didn't you hear? David left the paper. We are all undergoing a radical shift right now and reconsidering the terms of employment for all of our writers. So I put it to you instead… Do you think that you can be useful to us? Because if not…"

My mouth opens but no words come out. I am just utterly aghast. "Are you saying that either I do the story that you seem to want or I find another job?"

I can hear her smiling through the phone. "Yes, honestly. I think you have to do some serious consideration of exactly where your priorities lie. I suggest that you take the long weekend and think about whether or not you really want this job."

That's when I hang up the phone on her. I didn't exactly mean to do it, I am just so put off by everything she had to say and how she had to say it. I couldn't listen to another word.

I'm left staring at my phone screen, agog.

Was I just fired from the paper? It certainly feels that way.

I get a notification on my phone that Freja just shared a document with me. I open it up, biting my lower lip. It's a breakdown of each story she has asked me to pursue and how she sees each one ending up. Essentially she has already all but written the articles that she is demanding. I'm just supposed to write down some words and sign my name to this… this *fiction*.

I just can't believe it. As if everything else in my life is just going fine and dandy…. No, it's definitely not. I don't need any additional stress and finding a job as a journalist right now is definitely beyond harrowing.

With my heart still heavy, I start to get dressed to meet Margot as we have agreed. I shower quickly and then I put on a peach silk dress, layering it with a long white cardigan and chunky black heels.

I'm still fuming as I finish getting dressed. How dare Freja even make such demands of me? Someone in the royal press office needs to hear about this in the morning. I kind of hate to fight dirty, but they can exert pressure on the owners of *Politken* when I may or may not have any say in the matter.

I can't be bothered with my hair so I up throw it up in a messy bun and put on just enough mascara and blush to make myself presentable.

Then I look at the time and realize that I am definitely going to be late to meet Margot, even if I hurry. Pulling on my warm winter coat, I grabbed my purse and head downstairs. The cool winter air of the late afternoon catches me by surprise.

It's not that I don't know that it's cold outside, I just didn't expect it to be *this* cold. I pull my jacket tight around myself, thinking that maybe I should catch a cab. I only have to go about ten blocks, but if I catch a cab, I will not only be warm but I will get there faster.

In my haste, I rush by a chic blonde woman in a dark trench coat, bumping her shoulder carelessly. I turn to apologize, my mouth flying open. But when I turn, she is standing still, a tiny smirk on her face.

"Careful, Sylvie."

My eyes widen. My pulse starts racing.

How does she know that name?

"I'm sorry?" I say, pretending that she has the wrong person.

Hell, for all I know, she does.

She arches a delicate brow. She takes off her glove and extends her hand to me, staring at me. "We haven't had the pleasure yet, Sylvie. You can call me Ms. Olson."

Frozen in place, I don't move to shake her hand. "You must have me mistaken for someone else."

I start to turn away, clearing my throat. Ms. Olson steps forward and grabs my elbow, turning me back around. This close, her gray eyes seem like they are filled with a laughing sort of mockery. "Oh, I don't think so. I think you are Sylvie Martin. And I think that you've been masquerading as Pippa Welch for years. Have I got it right, Sylvie?"

Trembling, I jerk out of her grasp. "I don't know who you think I am, but you had better leave me alone."

Her eyes sparkle maliciously. "Unless you want me to tell Prince Lars your secret, you will listen to me."

I shake my head, beginning to walk away. I called back, pointing a finger skyward. "Leave me alone. I mean it."

She calls after me. "You're going to get the opportunity to make yourself a bigger part of Lars's life soon. If you're smart, you'll position yourself to be his future spouse. And when that happens? I'll be in contact."

I stop, glancing back at her. "You're crazy. You don't even know me. You definitely don't know that there's going to be any kind of quote on quote *opportunity coming down the line'."*
I pause, dragging in a breath. "Shit. Why am I even talking you again?"

I start walking away, shaking my head. My hands are shaking with a mixture of fear and anger.

Who is this stranger? And how does this woman know who I am?

I turn the corner, but I can't miss the words that are shouted at my back. "I'll see you again very soon, Sylvie…"

I start to run.

6

———

LARS

I'm sitting at the end of a long, polished conference table, trying not to feel like I'm about to be punished. I lean back in the chair I was given, pushing my cheek out with my tongue.

It's well past eight in the evening. The shadows here in Stellan's study have lengthened. I try not to fidget or show that this little charade of calling me here so late has made me quite nervous.

Inside though, I am drawing a big blank where it comes to guessing what the purpose of this little meeting could be. At the other end of the conference room table, Stellan sits with our very nosy grandmother, Queen Ida, and an older cabinet minister.

Jorgenson. No, Svenson.

Shit, I've forgotten his name.

Stellan looks a little uncomfortable. Momse, as we call the former Queen, looks as pert and pulled together as always.

Her sleek gray hair pulled back in a chignon and her dove gray silk dress hiding her too-demure smile.

It just makes me think of how I've never really gotten on with my grandmother like everyone else does. Momse is controlling and manipulative, always behind the scenes trying to pull everyone's strings like a puppeteer. She was always more interested in Stellan, as he was going to take the throne someday.

I try not think about it too much.

The older cabinet member is short and gray-haired, his piercing black eyes focused on me. He is outright glaring at me, held in check I'm sure by whatever machinations my grandmother has in place. I have no idea exactly why I've been summoned here, but I know that it isn't good. I'm trying not to show it on the outside, though.

Stellan leans forward, running a hand to his dark hair. He shakes his head a little as he looks at me. "I think you have really done it this time, Lars."

My heart beats a little faster. I'm not sure exactly what I've done or how I can be punished for it, but seeing my grandmother here is definitely not a good sign. Still, I try to play it cool.

"You're gonna have to be more specific about what I have done wrong this time." I say it casually, as if I'm just tossing off the first response it comes my head. But underneath the table, my hands are clasped together in my lap, knuckles turning white.

My grandmother tucks an unseen hair behind her ear and smiles a little flatly. "As expected, as I have warned you not to do on multiple occasions, you have violated the wrong young woman."

I squint at the three of them. "Violated? Who are we talking about, here? I definitely never done anything to anyone who wasn't a willing participant."

Stellan and my grandmother both arch their brows, reminding me only now that they are definitely related.

The minister shoots to his feet, pointing at me and unleashing a torrent of invective. "You are lucky that there is still a chance to redeem yourself, you complete waste of space. I for one would have you drawn and quartered for the way that you treated my granddaughter. Ever since you sweet-talked your way into her bedroom, she's been inconsolable. Won't eat, can't sleep, doesn't seem to enjoy anything."

I squint. "It sounds like something your granddaughter has more serious problems than me not calling her after we…" I pause, searching for the right term. "Were together."

He looks like he's about to blow a gasket. "It's only recently that she has admitted that she is sad because you didn't call her! You're just lucky that your grandmother jumped in and offered that you should marry her."

I freeze. "I'm sorry, what?"

He leans close, jabbing his finger at me and roaring. "You are going to marry my granddaughter or I will personally see to it that you are skinned alive. That's a promise!"

I put my hands flat on the table, looking at Stellan. "Please tell me that you don't support any of this nonsense."

He sighs, gesturing to the minister. "Well, did you sleep with his granddaughter?"

I push my cheek out with my tongue. "I have no idea. Probably. This isn't nineteen fifty though. Not everybody that sleeps together has to get married. I definitely am not just going to agree to marry some girl that I barely know. I mean, I'm almost afraid to ask which girl this guy's granddaughter is, honestly."

My grandmother pushes to her feet, running a hand down her dress. "I would think that you would be more interested in knowing the name of your bride to be. Her name is Anna, if you are curious."

I narrow my eyes at her. "Ja, I'm not Stellan. I'm not interested in letting you manipulate me. There's nothing in it for me. What are you guys going to do? What leverage you have? None, that's what."

The old man's face turns bright red. "I'll kill you, you bastard!"

Stellan looks at me flatly. "I'll kick you out of the RAF, for a start. And then I will disinherit you. What will you do then, Lars?"

I look away, at the fireplace crackling on one side of the room. My jaw clenches. The idea that Stellan could take away what I have worked for, the very program that may just send me to space one day… It isn't fair.

Not that I would ever tell him that. With my grandmother and the minister watching, I just say the first thing that floats up to the top of my mind.

"Well, that's going to be pretty hard, since I'm already engaged."

The lie comes to me both spontaneously and smoothly. Before I can even think it over, it's out of my mouth. My words give Stellan, Momse, and the minster pause.

I look back at the three of them at the other end of the conference table and they are all stunned. Well, stunned and disbelieving. Which is totally fair because I am absolutely full of shit.

My grandmother puts her hands on the table and leans in, her gaze frosty. "To whom?"

My heart rate speeds up.

Who?

Uhh...

I say it with only the slightest hesitation. The only person that I know for a fact will back me up no matter what, my best friend in the entire world. "Pippa."

Stellan's eyebrows go up. The minister looks livid. He turns to Stellan, pounding his fist on the table. "He can't do this." He looks at my grandmother, dead serious. "You promised me that my granddaughter would marry a royal! That's the only reason I even walked in here. If Lars doesn't marry my Anna, I'm walking out of this room. And my vote for the treasurer goes with me."

My grandmother fixes him with a glare. "If Lars says he is already engaged, he's already engaged. What do you expect me to do about it?"

The minister actually snarls at my grandmother, making Stellan rise to this feet. He quickly steps between them, looking down on the minister.

When he speaks, his voice is eerily flat. "I think you should leave. Don't make me ask security to escort you out."

The minister seems to shrink back at that, realizing that he has displeased the King of Denmark. He points at me, grimacing, and backs out of the room slowly.

I didn't actually know if my hasty ploy would work, but it seems to have stirred some real emotion in the room. Stellan looks at me, his gaze uncertain. "If what you say is true and you are in fact engaged, then I think the only thing I can say to you is congratulations. But please know that I'm definitely watching you, Lars."

With that, he turns and heads out of the room, leaving me alone with my grandmother.

She folds her arms, pacing over toward the window. "Well, now you have done it."

I push up out of my chair, regarding her as I walk over to the bar. It's just a little mini bar and it only has scotch and champagne for some reason, but I'll take whatever I can get. I pour myself a glass of scotch, probably a little too much, and sigh.

"What have I done, exactly?"

She turns to consider me. "If this engagement is not real, you are going to face some real trouble from me. You had better be serious."

I take a slug of scotch, covering my nervous reaction. "It's real. Everyone has always said that I might as well just marry Pippa because that makes sense for some reason. We got to talking about it yesterday and we just decided to make a go of it."

My grandmother arches a brow. "That's not very romantic. I thought that one of the reasons that you were so against being paired up was that you were waiting for romance."

I lift a shoulder and shrug. "What can I say? Pippa and I have always been in love. A platonic sort of love. We've decided that we should make it more formal, that's all."

I feel her ice blue eyes narrowing on my face. "Have you set a date, then?"

I am halfway through another sip of the scotch and I sputter a little bit, wiping at my mouth. "What?"

My grandmother paces across the room, coming over to me. There is a knowing look on her face. "A date for the wedding."

I feel the back of my neck start to heat. "Oh… no. We just… We got so swept up in the moment…"

She looks like she's amused. "You know, for your sake, I hope that you are really engaged and not just trying to weasel your way out of this situation. Because if you fuck around, if you get caught in the arms of another woman, that's it. You've always been a wild child, never listening to me or anyone else. And now I finally have a chance to have some positive sway over your life. But somehow, you manage to wriggle out of it. If I find out that you are not really engaged, I'll make sure that Stellan kicks you out of the RDAF *and* the royal family."

It's surprising to me how easily I lie right to her face. "You're being too serious about this whole thing. Pippa and I are engaged. I would've told you all eventually, it just so happened that--"

She interrupts me, cutting me off. "You have a month. One month to set a date and plan the engagement party. If not, I'll be all over you. I will use Stellan to bring catastrophe for you. That's a promise."

I open my mouth to respond, but she just takes the glass of scotch out of my hand, throws it back into her mouth, and slams it on the bar as she stalks out of the room. The gauntlet has been thrown down, that much is for certain.

Now all that remains is just the little matter of actually telling my fake fiancé that we are getting married.

I swallow thickly, tightening up my tie.

7

PIPPA

I'm standing in my little apartment in Copenhagen, staring blankly at the peeling bright yellow paint on the kitchen wall. I reach out and trace my fingertips along a seam above the stove, a silent sigh on my lips.

It was a long day at *Politiken*, a day full of finding out with some disappointment that all of the big bosses have been fired. There is no one left to stand up for me. I feel like I've been wrung out and all my mental energy has been drained away. Now I'm just waiting for my little microwave burrito to be heated through so I can eat and pass out.

My phone chimes, stirring me. I look at it. Lars's photo pops up, a dark haired devil with a cocksure grin. It bite my lip.

I am a fool for even thinking about what spending a night in his bed would be like. Being underneath his big body as he growls commands and pulls moans from my lips…

It's forbidden. And yet still, my heart squeezes at the very mention of his name.

I know he's my best friend.

I know I should cherish what we already have.

I know I shouldn't long for him to touch me.

And yet, even getting a text from him excites me beyond reason.

I shiver as I check the text.

I'm coming upstairs.

Goosebumps break out over my skin. I close my eyes and hold my cellphone close to my now rapidly-beating heart.

A few second later, I hear the slide of a key being turned in the lock on the front door. I'm much too tired for any visitors tonight. But Lars has always done exactly what he wanted, exactly when he wants.

This is no exception.

Screwing up my face, I press the pause button on the microwave. Lars walks into my shoddy little apartment, ducking his dark head slightly as he enters. He's so tall that my building's prewar design is really at odds with his height. When he straightens up, he looks at me with his trademark devastating smirk.

I cast a look over his tuxedo, which makes him look ridiculously fetching.

"Hello, Pippa," he purrs.

I swallow, my eyes widening. "Lars." Pushing back several strands of my long, curly copper hair, I watch as he closes the door behind himself. I spread my hands down the skirt of my gray silk dress, drawing a breath. "It's awfully late. Shouldn't you be on a date with some unnamed mystery blonde?"

His smirk deepens, his aquamarine eyes sparkling. "I was in the middle of a date when I was summoned unceremoniously to the palace."

I fidget. "Why are you here, Lars?"

He wanders toward the living room of my cramped flat, leaving me to follow. He looks around the tiny couch and the ancient television that is stacked atop several light blue milk crates.

Every surface is covered with reading material, books and magazines and newspaper clippings. Piles spill into piles; the television screen is actually blocked by a towering stack of literature. I admit that I'm a bit of a mess and I'm ashamed to say that there is nowhere for him to sit.

Wrinkling my nose, I automatically start to clear off the sofa, my cheeks burning. I gather an armful of books, but I'm not sure where to put them.

"Let me just find a place for these…" I murmur, casting my gaze around the small space. I find a spot on the very top of another pile of books, biting my lower lip hard as I turn around.

"Pippa, I don't need to sit down," he says, grabbing my hand. His touch is electric. When I glance up at him, his blue gaze sears me through.

I raise an eyebrow. "What do you need?"

He smirks a bit, pulling me a little closer, making me look up into his face. From this distance, a hair's breadth away from our bodies touching, I feel adrenaline coursing through my veins.

"I need a favor."

My forehead creases. My mouth turns down just a bit at the corners. This is what he does, what he has always done. He uses his charm, knowing quite well how smoothly hypnotic his presence can be. I've seen him do it to hundreds of women in the years that I've known him.

Usually he doesn't use it on *me*, though.

I pull out of his grasp, moving back a half step. My frown grows deeper. "What is it?"

His expression grows intense. "I need you to pretend that I have asked you to marry me and you have said yes."

I swear, I don't mean to laugh. But it bubbles up from deep within my chest and bursts out of my lips, a snort of disbelief and a surprised chuckle all at once.

"What?" I ask, the word coming out strangled.

He squints at me. "I slept with the wrong diplomat's daughter."

I fold my arms across my chest, trying to slow my racing heart. "Again? How many times do you have to get caught before someone banishes you from the whole country of Denmark?"

His gaze tightens on my face. "It's really not funny. Stellan has threatened to strip me of my title and have me kicked out of the RAF. Obviously, I don't want that."

A low throb starts at my temple. I rub it with one hand, staring at Lars. "And this has what to do with me, exactly?"

He steps closer, snagging my free hand and bringing it to rest against the hard wall of his chest. "I need a fake fiancée. Momse told me today that unless I settle down and get married, I'm going to be kicked out of the royal family."

My breath freezes in my lungs. My mind races, immediately going to what the creepy, trench-coated Ms. Olson said.

If you're smart, you'll position yourself to be his future spouse.

Lars leans in, almost close enough to my face for me to think he's about to kiss me. At the last moment, he turns his head, whispering in my ear.

"Breathe, little witch. Don't look so scared."

His breath is warm against my ear, fanning against my over-heated skin.

I won't melt against him. *I won't.*

I push my cheek out with my tongue, forcing my brain to quit pining. Shaking my head, I push myself back and look at him.

"What is stopping you from finding the right girl?"

Someone royal. Or at least someone without the… let's call them *complications* that my history presents. I know very well the list of reasons why Lars can't be tied to someone like me.

I'm a fraud.

I'm a fake and a liar.

I'm not who I say I am.

And someone is already coercing me over an opportunity just like this one.

And that's only the *beginning* of my troubles if anyone finds out.

He gives me a wicked little grin. "You're saying I should sign my death warrant, then? Because that's what being told that I have to get married feels like. I don't want to be tied down. I don't want to be smothered. I just want to keep living like I do now."

I shake my head. "Lars, really—"

He wiggles his brows. "What if I told you that I would bankroll whatever project you asked me to? I know that your work has been a drag lately. So do this: be my fake fiancée for a little while. And in exchange, I'll pump as much money into you starting your own magazine or whatever you want."

My eyes widen. Lars grins at my expression. "You know you want to, Pippa."

I bite my lip. "I don't think it's a good idea, Lars."

He slides his hands down my back and pulls my hips against his. My breath catches in my chest as I gaze up into those pretty blue eyes of his.

This. This feeling, this energy crackling between us?

It's the reason we don't normally allow ourselves to touch, even casually.

I'm *this close* to pushing up on my tiptoes and pressing my lips against his.

Arching a brow, he utters the magic words. "I really need this. *Please*, Pippa? Do it for me?"

And just like that, all my defenses melt away. All the reasons that I can't do it suddenly seem very far away.

Of course I will do it for him.

How can I not?

Lars sees the expression of my face change and knows my answer before I even say it.

"Okay," I whisper. "I will do it. But not forever."

He's already folding his strong arms around me, pulling me into the shelter of his body. "Ahh, thanks, Pips. I knew you would come through."

I sink into the bear hug, my eyes fluttering closed. He's sinfully warm. His smell, pure and clean and masculine, is driving me wild right now.

I inhale a lungful of his scent, feeling like a fool. "That's me. Reliable old Pippa saves the day again."

Lars pulls back. "What do you think about six months?"

I crinkle my nose. "I was thinking a single month would be sufficient."

He gives me a look. "Four months."

I narrow my eyes at him. "Two."

His gaze turns speculative, watching my face intently. "Three months. Surely you can play my fake fiancée for three months."

I look up at him, crinkling my entire face. "Okay. I think I can handle three months."

He grins. "Thanks, Pips. Should we wake the jewelers at Tiffany's up right now? Shit, I should've stopped on the way here and gotten you a ring—"

I push him away, eyeing him firmly. "There will have to be rules. No physical contact, for instance."

He gives me a funny look. "It's going to take a little hugging and kissing to convince my family, don't you think?"

I squint at him. "I meant when we are alone."

He rolls his eyes. "*Ja*, sure. I will behave like a proper gentleman, if that's what you want."

I shake my head, crossing my arms. "No one has ever thought to call you a proper gentleman, I'm fairly certain."

Lars grins at me, his eyes glittering. "If that's what it takes, I'm willing to try."

I shoot him a look. "I'm regretting this already."

He tilts his head, considering me. "Should we go for a drink to celebrate?"

Stepping closer to him, I turn him around and begin marching him toward the door. "We can figure it all out tomorrow. For now, I want to eat something before I pass out."

He chuckles, opening the front door. He catches my hand and gives me a squeeze. "You really are the best, Pippa. You know that, right?"

The corners of my mouth tighten. "Do me a favor. Don't…" I hesitate. "Don't sleep with anyone while I pretend to be your fake fiancée, okay? If this little deception is going to work, you'll have to play along and not be your usual man-whore self for a while."

Lars smirks at me. "You got it, love of my life."

For a second, I can't even wrap my head around that. My heartbeat speeds up. If he had any idea of how long I've waited to hear those words…

But then he turns, showing me his black-clad back as he disappears down the hall. He didn't mean it.

Not like I want him to, anyway.

"Goodnight, little witch…" he calls over his shoulder.

I watch him disappear, slumping against the doorframe when I hear the downstairs front door open and close.

I am in so much trouble.

I know that. I have lied to Lars since the first moment I met him.

If anyone does the slightest bit of digging, I could be exposed.

My life would cease to be my own at that point.

But I can still feel my heart racing, feel the heat of his body pressed against mine. I can sense the excited energy that follows Lars in his wake, everywhere he goes.

Deep in my soul, I know that I shouldn't have agreed to be his fake fiancée.

Oh god.

What have I gotten myself into?

Turning, I close my door and head back to my sad microwave dinner.

8

PIPPA

I WAKE THE NEXT MORNING TO THE INSISTENT BUZZING OF MY phone. Squinting into the early morning light, I groggily reach out across my bed to snag my phone from the nightstand. It's too early for me to really process anything.

I rub my eyes as I read the first text, which happens to be from Margot. *Pippa! What the hell? When were you going to tell me about this?*

For a solid seconds I can't actually connect the dots. I narrow my eyes.

What is she talking about?

I sit up, scrolling through the numerous calls and texts. It's only when I read the words *you're engaged?* from Annika that I put it all together.

The story about my supposed relationship with Lars must be out, then. I assume that Lars himself leaked it, because the whole situation is fake as anything.

He works fast, I guess.

I text Lars immediately. *A warning shot would've been nice.*

He texts back. *And ruin the surprise?*

I shake my head, pushing my copper curls out of my face. Pushing back the covers with a groan, I shower and start getting dressed. When my cell phone vibrates again, I check it and find a message from Lars.

I hope you're ready to go ring shopping. I'll be at your door in five minutes. And just in case you were wondering, I have a horde of reporters on my tail.

Good lord. If I'm going to be on camera, I have to dress for it.

In my black lace bra and slip, I run into my spare bedroom where I keep my racks and racks of clothes. I hunt through the racks, looking for the garment that floats nebulously in the back of my head.

A one piece pantsuit. Lighter in color, maybe pink or tan. Coupled with a long white mohair coat…

I frown as I dig through my clothes.

Admittedly, I am something of a clotheshorse. There is something exciting and elegant about a new designer dress and a great pair of heels.

Add that to the fact that I'm tall and thin, naturally looking as if I just rolled off of a runway…

Designers like the way their clothes look on my body.

I'll admit it. When I first moved here to Copenhagen, my photo was often snapped when I was hanging out with Lars and Stellan. And I used that exposure to convince up and coming designers to lend me elegant clothes.

At this point though, I'm something of a designer darling. I have ten boxes of unopened clothes in my living room, sent unsolicited from the top fashion houses.

I flip through another half-dozen garments before I come to a stop on what is possibly the perfect dress for the occasion. Long sleeves, floor-length, and cut out of this lovely off-white satin. There are little hand stitched magenta roses on it, cascading and multiplying as they spill downward to the dress's hem. The body of it is perfectly fitted and elegant.

It's a dress fit for a princess, I think. Annika and Margot would definitely fight me for it, anyway.

Slipping it on, I add pink rosette earrings, simple black heels, and a gray muslin coat. I'm putting on a coat of dark pink lipstick when the door buzzes. I cast a final look in the mirror, tilting my head at my own reflection.

Somehow, going ring shopping in this outfit *feels* right.

The door buzzes again, making me roll my eyes and stomp to the front door. I press the button and buzz Lars up without even looking to make sure its him.

I'm just gathering my purse when he opens the door, poking his head in. For a second, I falter as I lay eyes on him. He's very tall, impeccably dressed in his steel blue suit, and so handsome that he takes my breath away. He's had a recent haircut; his dark hair is longer and tousled on top and close cropped on the sides.

He swings that sparkling blue gaze my way. When he sees me, his face lights up in a grin.

It's heart stopping, being the object of his attentions.

Well, *fake* attentions. I'll have to get used to that, I guess.

"We are going to have to talk about your building's security," he says casually. His eyes sweep the living room, his mouth turning down at one corner. "Actually, maybe we should move you to a bigger place."

Swallowing, I arch a brow. "That sounds like you would be doing me a very expensive favor. What is my rule about that?"

He rolls his eyes, jerking his head toward the doorway. "I know, I know. That's not allowed. Come on, we can talk about it on the way to the jeweler."

I wrinkle my nose, sighing as I follow him. "All right. But you owe me coffee. Actually, you owe me coffee every single day for eternity. And I mean the fancy kind, too."

Heading downstairs, I emerge from my building.

I'm not expecting the sea of photographers and reporters waiting there, shouting my name. My eyes widen and I freeze.

But Lars smoothly puts his arm around my waist and pulls me onward. He leans in, shouting in my ear to be heard above all the hubbub. "It won't always be like this."

I look up at him, trying to parse what he means. He grins at me. "How about a kiss for the cameras?"

Without skipping a beat, he puts his hands on my waist, pulls me close, and kisses me full on the mouth. His lips feel hot and pliable against mine; his grasp on my waist feels so intimate that I blush furiously. I blink, trying to wrap my head around the fact that this is even happening.

Lars Love is kissing me.

It's only something I've imagined a thousand times over. It's better than the fantasy though.

So, so much better.

Inside, I start to melt.

It takes me a solid fifteen seconds to realize I need to kiss him back. So I reach up timidly, wrap my arms around his shoulders, and open my mouth to him.

As soon as I do, though, he pulls back with a quizzical gaze. I bite my lower lip, feeling embarrassed that I got so wrapped up in everything.

Lars clears his throat, steps back from me, and takes my hand. Only then do I realize that there are still reporters shouting our names and flash bulbs going off.

He pulls me along the street. I shiver, waiting for a break in the reporters shouting at us. But no, as we move along, the crowd's yammer never dies down. I look at Lars, making a face at him. But he just shrugs and continues down the early-morning Copenhagen street.

By the time we reach the jeweler on High Street, I've gone from feeling overwhelmed by the noise of the reporters to being irritated by it. I know I signed myself up for this, but… I'm already over it.

Lars stops at a glass storefront, looking up. It's a high-end jeweler with a few tasteful pieces of jewelry displayed at the front window, diamonds and sapphires, gleaming white gold and titanium.

Lars surprises me by opening the door for me. He never does that; I've actually only seen him open doors for the girls he dates. I arch a brow at him as I step through.

A sarcastic comment is on the tip of my tongue. But it is swept away when a short, balding man dressed in head to toe black approaches us.

"Your royal highness," he says, bowing low. He has a French accent. "Welcome to my shop. I am Etienne."

I curtsy. "Bonjour, Etienne."

Lars just nods and gives a curt smile. "The royal press office said that you were the jeweler to come see."

"Oui, monsieur. Please, come right this way…"

Lars puts his hand on my lower back, gently nudging me forward. My eyes widen at his touch.

He usually doesn't touch me, even casually. Etienne shows us into a back room, which is well-appointed with a pair of heavy, dark wood couches and several tall, thin mahogany chests of drawers.

"Please, make yourselves comfortable," Etienne waves to the couches. "Would you like something to drink? Water, coffee, a latte…"

"No, thank you." My answer is automatic.

Lars slides me a look. "You don't want coffee?"

My cheeks turn pink. I do want coffee, but I don't want to put Etienne out. So I shake my head. "I'm fine."

Etienne purses his lips. "Very well. If you'll both have a seat, we can get started."

Running a hand over my dress, I find a seat on the couch. Lars does too, unbuttoning his suit jacket and leaning back, throwing his arm over the back. He looks like he owns the place, which makes my mouth turn down just a hair.

Etienne picks up a black velvet-lined tray, walking over to us and displaying his wares. I'm not sure what I expected to see. Maybe a selection of new and untouched rings in the latest styles or something.

But instead, Etienne holds a tray of gleaming antique-looking rings, varying in precious metal and stone. They are, on the whole, not especially stunning. When I think of a jaw-dropping engagement ring, I think of some huge, sparkly diamond.

These are much smaller stones, much less glittery than I had imagined. My surprise must be written on my face when I look up, because Etienne offers me a smile.

"Her royal highness, the former Queen Ida, suggested that you might like to choose a ring that is already in the family."

I lick my lips, darting a glance at Lars.

"I see." I don't know quite what else to say.

Lars frowns at the selection of rings. "These are all hideous. Do you have something…" He squints.

"A little more modern, perhaps," I suggest.

Etienne bows his head. "But of course."

With that, he takes the tray back to the dresser, swapping it out. When he presents the new selection, I arch a brow. These may be a little newer, but not much.

I glance at Lars, taking a deep breath. He pulls a face. "Can I see the tray that Stellan and Margot chose their ring from?"

"That won't work," I say. "If I recall correctly, Stellan already had the ring. Margot didn't get to choose."

Lars sighs. "Oh. Well… can we start with the newest rings and work our way back?" He pauses. "You know, Pippa, if we don't find anything you like, we can always keep looking."

I shoot him a look, willing him to remember for a second that this is all fake. There is no need for a fancy ring. After all, I'll only have to wear it for three months.

Etienne steps back. "Yes, your royal highness. Allow me to try again."

As soon as Etienne's back is turned, I mouth *be nice* to Lars. Lars just smirks, shrugging one shoulder. I scowl at him.

When Etienne returns, he holds out a black velvet tray filled with twenty four of the biggest, shiniest rings I think I've ever seen. My jaw drops as I take in the array of white gold, rose gold, and platinum settings. There is no way that these rings aren't worth half a million pounds or more.

"Oh. I think we've gone too big," I say quickly. One ring in particular catches my eye, an enormous square cut diamond with two smaller sapphires on each side, all set in white gold. My fingers itch to touch it.

Lars reads my expression and nods to the tray. "Which one? You want to try it, I can tell."

I shake my head, looking at Etienne. "These are… they're beautiful, but they are too much. I want something simpler."

Lars shoots me a glare. Etienne bows his head, disappearing and reappearing with yet another tray.

This one has rings that are more affordable, that's for sure. As I will only be wearing it temporarily, I point out the first ring that I see that just seems… reasonable.

"May I see that one?" I ask.

Etienne smiles a bit. "I do apologize, mademoiselle. His royal highness may pick up any of the pieces that he chooses…"

Lars shoots me a smug smile as he leans over and plucks the ring off the tray. "Your hand please, my dear, sweet Pippa."

I wrinkle my nose, turning to Etienne. "Would you excuse us? I promise, we are not going to steal any of these rings or anything."

Etienne ducks his head, smoothing a hand down his tie. "Of course, mademoiselle. His royal highness does own them, ma'am."

He has a point. He leaves, shutting the heavy door behind him. I turn to Lars.

"Quit it," I warn.

He gives me an innocent look. "What?"

"Behave."

"Make me," he says, grinning.

I roll my eyes, holding my hand out. He takes my fingers ever so gently, which makes my pulse pick up. I swallow as he looks me dead in the eye, slips the ring on my finger, and gives me the cockiest grin ever.

"Now you're mine," he tells me.

My face heats, my heart beating embarrassingly fast. "No, I'm doing you an immense favor because you asked me very nicely. And by the way, I meant it about our fake relationship only lasting for three months."

A dimple flashes in his cheek. "I was thinking of pushing it out to a year."

I pull my hand from his grasp, putting a little more space between us. "And I was thinking of changing my mind and saying that I couldn't possibly be bothered for longer than a month."

"Six months," he fires back.

My eyes narrow on his face. "Three."

He looks me up and down, as if considering my offer. "Four months. And you let me move you into my place temporarily."

I open my mouth to argue, but he stops me with a gesture. "There is no more haggling. It's four months. And at the end, you will have your magazine funded. Yes?"

I frown. Four months isn't a breeze, but it seems doable. I don't like that he sees my terms as being flexible, though. Alas, that is very typical of Lars.

I clench my jaw. "Fine."

"Great." His eyes twinkle. "Now are you sure about this ring?"

I look down at the ring, my mouth twisting. It's two sizes too large and not the right shape at all. If this little deception was real, if I had to wear this ring forever, then no way. But it's just a prop.

A very expensive prop, but fake nonetheless.

I nod, taking a breath. "*Ja*, I'm sure."

He grins at me, dazzling me with his smile. "Good. Now come on, wife to be. I think we should tell Etienne together."

Getting up, he offers me his arm. I rise, taking his arm, a sigh on my lips. "Lead the way."

9

LARS

I'm waiting anxiously at the swankiest hotel in Copenhagen, trying not to freeze my ass off while I wait by the front doors. Pippa's my New Year's Eve date. Actually, we have had this planned out for weeks.

It just so happens that now I have just added a ton of weird pressure by making it our debut as a couple. And royal couple at that.

I'm genuinely a little worried. Pippa was pretty grumpy all of yesterday, fueled in part at least by our brand new arrangement.

And I get it. She is doing me a huge, immense favor, getting me out of a less than savory situation.

So she gets to be a little grouchy, I guess.

When her limo pulls up and she emerges, I'm beyond relieved to see her look for me and then smile.

Then I allow myself to breathe a little... and to take her in. She's wearing a huge fuzzy floor length white coat, which she sheds the second she walks in the door. What she reveals actually makes my mouth water. She's wearing a floor length, long sleeve gown made of what looks like molten silver. It hugs every tantalizing curve and only enhances her fiery copper curls, which trail down her back.

She turns for a second, handing her coat off to a waiting attendant, and I see that the dress is cut very low in the back, emphasizing her amazing skin. Looking at her right now is making my tuxedo pants a little tight. I feel like ripping off my bowtie. I'm stifled, looking at her silver-coated curves.

She floats over to me, a smile curving her lips. "Don't you look dashing."

I drag my gaze away from her, refusing to be thirsty. "I was just thinking the same thing about you."

She touches my arm, looking up at the hotel's second story. I follow her gaze up to see several people taking pictures of us surreptitiously.

But when Pippa leans over and kisses my lips ever so carefully, it still takes me by surprise. Worse than that, when she pulls away again, I'm left aching.

God, this is going to be a long night.

A long four months, really.

I shouldn't have chosen the girl I'm in love with to fake an engagement. I'm kicking myself over the choice now.

I clear my throat. "Shall we?"

Pippa smiles, seeming in good spirits. "Lead the way, your highness."

"Don't start with that shit," I say, rolling my eyes.

I usher her to the escalator and we ride up to the second floor. I spend the whole time looking at Pippa's ass and speculating whether or not she's wearing any panties.

My guess is no.

On the way off the escalator, I stop and look around. Tonight, my favorite hipster bar has taken over this floor and they've really gone all out. The doors to the grand ballroom are thrown open, revealing some extremely hip black and white decor. To our right, there is a bar set up, the stylish bartenders in their black shirts and denim aprons busy mixing drinks. And to top it all off, there are uniformed waiters walking around with trays of drinks and appetizers.

Pippa pulls away, heading for one of the waiters. I follow, noticing that people are looking at me oddly.

Pippa hands me a glass of champagne, nodding subtlety to a group of girls who are gawking at me. "What do you think is going on there?"

I lift a shoulder in a shrug. "If I had to place odds, I would wager we are watching my pool of dating prospects drying up."

Her eyes twinkle as she takes a sip of her champagne. "How will you ever survive?" She laughs. "Just remember, you were the one who pushed for four months of faking your engagement."

Before I can come up with a good comeback, Margot peeks her head out of the ballroom. "There you two are!" she says, beaming. "Come on, we have a table waiting."

Pippa throws a look at me over her shoulder, heading into the ballroom. I follow her, entering the dimly-lit space. Electronic music courses through the whole place. The ballroom's high ceilings and classic parquet floors are enhanced by the white tables and futuristic white decorations hanging from the ceiling. Margot waves us over to a corner where Stellan is sandwiched in with Erik and Annika. I repress a sigh, pulling up a seat at the end of the table.

Stellan shoots me a look, like I've already done something wrong. Then I look up and realize that Pippa hasn't sat down yet. I don't like my brother reminding me of social customs, but he's right. I stand, pulling Pippa's chair out and deftly moving it right beside my own.

Pippa smirks at my gesture. "Thanks," she says, taking her seat. Turning to Annika, she smiles. "I love this dress. Actually, I love Margot's dress too. A part of me is definitely envious."

Ja, I could definitely use a drink. One of the reasons that we chose this party, of all the parties going on tonight, was that it promised the liquor would be flowing. The other was that I felt that there would be plenty of ladies around, looking for their next one night stand.

I guess that isn't in the cards tonight, though.

Looking around, I spy a waiter and signal him to come over. I don't even have to ask Pippa what she wants to drink.

"A French 75 and a whiskey neat. If I don't ever see the bottom of either glass, there will be something extra for you, okay?" I tell the waiter.

He rushes off like his life is at stake. I smirk and watch as Pippa catches up with Margot and Nika.

I cast a gaze over to Erik, who is giving me a funny look. "What?" I ask.

He slides a look to Stellan. "You just cost me a hundred pounds. I bet Stellan that you would never settle down. Especially after telling me just a few days ago that Pippa is basically your sister—"

I glare at him. "Shut up."

He shrugs, looking elegant in his tuxedo. "I'm just wondering why you completely flipped your story, that's all."

I casually put my arm around Pippa's shoulders, arching a brow. She blushes, pulled away from the conversation. "What now?"

I lean over to kiss her full on the mouth, adding a little tongue in for good measure. She freezes up, resisting at first. Then she seems to remember that she agreed to this, relaxing in my grip.

Her mouth is hot and her lips plump. Her eyes close a little. Then she opens her mouth for me the barest inch...

My eyes close involuntarily as I gently slip my tongue into her mouth. Damn, she tastes good. I've imagined this moment a thousand times over, my very first time French kissing Pippa.

But it's so much better and deeper and more complex than I'd imagined. She makes a soft sound, curling her fist against my lapel, pulling me closer.

God, I can smell her delicate floral perfume, taste her minty mouthwash overlaid with a splash of sweet champagne fizz.

"All right, all right!" Erik shouts. "We get it, you guys are in love..."

Pippa pulls back, her eyes a little wide. It looks like I'm not the only one who got a tiny bit carried away. Pulling from my grasp, Pippa flushes and turns to the rest of the table.

"Sorry," she apologizes. "You know how it is, I would guess."

Annika leans in and covers Pippa's hand, giving her a secretive smile. "I promise, we all do. Congrats on finally deciding to sleep together."

I grin. "Actually, I don't know if you saw Pippa's hand, but we are engaged."

"I know!" Margot says. "Let me see the ring!"

Pippa lifts her hand to Margot, her cheeks burning bright red.

I smirk as my gaze slides to Stellan. His eyes narrow on my face, suspicious as ever. Of course, he has every right to be suspicious; there is no relationship between myself and Pippa except friendship.

Really good friendship.

The kind of friendship that is a once in a lifetime find. Not worth risking, not for any price.

I drop my gaze, reminding myself of that very important fact. The waiter delivers me a fresh whiskey and I pound it, not even pretending like I'm too classy. Getting drunk is more important.

Several drinks later, Pippa is red-cheeked and grinning around the table. That's Pippa's drunk face, which is sort of the opposite of mine. I generally get more scowl-y the more I drink.

Annika stands up, drunker than I have ever seen her, and pulls Erik out to the dance floor. Margot and Stellan are right on their heels, Margot grinning and laughing even though she's dead sober.

Pippa glances at me, biting her lip. "I know you don't dance, but I think you should make an exception. Come on."

She stands up, pulling me along with her as she heads out to the dance floor. The music slows down a good bit, changing tempo to something nice and easy to dance to.

I can actually ballroom dance. It's just the whole dancing alone and looking like a fool thing I'm not good at.

I beckon to Pippa, putting my hand out. She takes it, an uncertain smile on her lips.

Then I pull her into my arms and dip her. When I pull her back up, she's laughing. "Lars! I didn't know you could dance."

I tuck her snugly against my body, feeling cheeky. "I can slow dance."

I slide my hands down the sides of her body, making her shiver. As I suspected, she isn't wearing a bra. Bracketed in my big hands, her waist seems impossibly slim. I wonder if I were to let my hands wander down further if they would find a thong or not.

God damn, this woman in my arms is so hot.

"Hey!" Pippa's voice breaks through my reverie. "Do you mind?"

...and I realize that I'm staring right at her tits. I look up at her, my neck heating. "Sorry," I say with a shrug. "They were just right there…"

Pippa shoots me a glare and tries to pull away. Because I'm so much bigger than her, I just hold her a little tighter. She scowls at me, leaning close.

"Let me go," she whispers, looking fierce.

I bite my lower lip, my eyes sinking to her lips. "I don't want to."

She grips my forearms. "Seriously, Lars? You're drunk."

I scoff a little. "You're drunk too. Stop being melodramatic. We are supposed to be engaged. I'm just acting like an engaged guy who is super horny for his fiancée." I cock my head. "Hell, maybe we should just sleep together. Call it an experiment."

Her face turns red. In a second, all the teasing vanishes from her tone and body language. "Get off of me."

Shit, I crossed a line. I immediately let go, stepping back. "I was just kidding," I add lamely.

Pippa takes a deep breath in, looking me dead in the eyes. "Tomorrow, we are establishing better boundaries."

Then she turns, zeroes in on a waiter carrying a tray of champagne flutes, and grabs two. She upends both of them, poring them down her gullet, and then wipes her mouth.

"Take it easy with the booze," I say. "You throw up pretty easily."

Her mouth twists. "Don't worry about me."

My brows rise. That's impossible. I've always been looking out for Pippa's best interests, even when she doesn't know what they are.

Pippa makes a show of dancing with Margot and Nika, getting more and more drunk. With a sigh, I slow down my intake of alcohol.

One of us has to be sober enough to get us both home.

When the DJ turns the music down and tells us it's almost midnight, I pluck two champagne flutes off a waiter's tray and wade over to find Pippa. She is really drunk now and she screams with excitement when she sees me, throwing her arms up.

"Dance with me!" she says, bouncing up and down.

I roll my eyes. "You have had a lot of wine, haven't you?"

She just laughs and hugs me, snagging one of the champagne flutes that I brought over. "You want to know something?"

I crack a smile. "What is that, drunk Pippa?"

She beams at me. "You look really handsome in that tux. Like… really. You know how to… to… work it. If you were anyone else, I would have already tried to come onto you."

I roll my eyes at her drunk compliment, but I can't help grinning. "Thank you. You look quite sexy in that dress."

She opens her mouth. Before she can respond, the DJ comes over the mic. "All right, everyone! It's fifteen seconds now until the new year. Let's all count… ten! Nine! Eight!"

Pippa grins up at me, counting along. "Seven! Six! Five! Four!"

I squeeze her tightly. "Three! Two! One!"

Everyone shouts happy new year. That, I was prepared for.

But the hot, wet, drunken kiss that Pippa lays on me… the one that has me pulling her closer, and her grabbing my face… the one that goes for almost half a minute…

This is unexpected.

When she pulls away, my cock is hard, my breathing coming out in pants. I look down into her eyes, trying to make sense of that kiss.

What was that supposed to be for? She holds my gaze for a second, gazing back up at me. I press her body closer and try to read her expression.

"Do you—" I start.

Which is when she turns away, delicately putting the back of her hand against her lips and dry heaving.

Aww, shit. I hustle her toward a bathroom, grabbing an empty ice bucket as we go. She immediately throws up in the bucket.

I switch from party mode into medic mode, getting her into the bathroom and helping her kneel down before the toilet.

Then I try not to get too grossed out for the next twenty minutes as she wretches, throwing up over and over again. All I can do is hold her hair and feel bad.

After all, I'm pretty sure that she wouldn't have gotten so drunk if I hadn't come on so strong earlier.

I end my night by calling for a royal limousine and bundling her inside. Erik, Stellan, and their respective women are nowhere to be seen.

"Just take us to my apartment, please," I tell the driver.

I sit back, letting Pippa lie in my lap, and feel very tired all
the sudden.

10

———

PIPPA

I WAKE UP IN THE EARLY HOURS OF THE MORNING, BEFORE THE sun has even thought about rising. Opening my eyes a crack, I realize a couple of things pretty quickly. First, I am so completely and utterly hungover, it's ridiculous. I think I remember being sick… but when I think too much about it my head really starts throbbing.

And second, I am in Lars's bed. I have no memory of coming here. In fact, the last thing I remember was…

Ah. Getting absolutely plastered at New Year's Eve. That tracks.

I'm not wearing the slinky silver dress from earlier. Somehow that has been replaced by one of Lars's plain white tees. I can't help but sniff it and rub it against my chin. It's old and soft, washed so often that it almost feels fragile. I stick my hand down the covers, hoping against hope that I'm still wearing my little black thong.

Somehow I am. Thank god for that.

God, I'm so thirsty and I really, really have to pee.

I throw my heavy blankets off and stand up. My mind is still foggy as I stumble to the en-suite bathroom. Lights seem too bright for the moment. So I just close the door and use the light from the window as I try to put things right.

I pee, use a little toothpaste to do a quick rinse of my mouth, and halfheartedly try to tame my curls. There is no point in the last one; with my mane of red curls I look like a lioness, and not in a good way.

This is one of many reasons I don't spend any nights over here at Lars's place. No frigging hair products and nothing to even comb my hair with other than my fingers.

I feel vaguely silly when I drink straight from Lars's elegant tap but the water tastes pure and so, so good.

At last I yawn, leaving the bathroom. My brow furrows as I take in the spectacular view of downtown Copenhagen. Lars showed me this view once when he first moved into this place. How many bedrooms have such a spectacular view?

Wait a second…

My eyes widen. I glance over at the bed, where Lars himself is stretched out on the bed. It looks like I stole most of his heavy comforter for myself some time during the night… leaving him with the barest edge to cover himself with. My jaw drops.

He's perfect. At first all I can stare at are his abs, which seem like they are carved from frigging stone. Then I notice his long arms and legs are splayed out, covered in a fine layer of soft, sparse fuzz. His dark head is resting on a fluffy white pillow. And as I tilt my head to one side, considering how he's only covered his thighs, one of his eyes cracks open.

"Pips?" he asks. He pats the expanse of bed beside him. "Come on, come back to sleep."

My cheeks heat. I tug down the hem of his old tee shirt, conscious of my bareness. "I… uh… I didn't think I was in your bedroom."

He eyes close briefly. "I didn't exactly put you in here. You found your own way."

Lars pulls at the comforter, covering himself more. I'm at once terribly glad that he did and also sort of sad. It's not very often that I get to admire… well, so much of Lars. Visions of him will populate my fantasies for years, I'm sure.

"Pippa!" he snaps.

My eyes widen. "What?"

"Will you please stop being so fucking weird? Get back in the bed. We're adults. We can share a bed for a night, surely."

I lick my lips. Do I say no?

Or should I—

"Get the fuck back in bed," he growls. "And try not to snore this time."

Reacting to his tone, I tiptoe over to the bed and avert my eyes as I lie down. Lars throws the covers back on top of me. I freeze, unable to look over at him. He's naked under the comforter and… well, I just don't trust my hands not to… wander.

Haven't I dreamed of just exactly this moment happening? I'm absolutely sure of it.

I look up at the high ceiling, swallowing. For a few seconds, I wonder if he has just gone back to sleep. Curling my hands into fists, I will my heartbeat to slow down.

He sighs and adjusts next to me. "I can actually feel your brain growing hot from too much thinking."

I bite my lip, turning my head toward him. How did I get out of my dress?"

He makes a vaguely amused sound. "I don't know. I brought you back here to my apartment. You made a beeline for my bathroom. A few minutes later, you said you needed a tee shirt. I didn't think it wise to ask any questions."

"Oh god." I cover my eyes, blushing furiously. "Did I really snore?"

I peek at him. He chuckles, nodding. "Yes you did, little witch."

I groan, which makes my head throb more insistently. "Happy engagement."

That pulls a genuine laugh out of him. He turns over on his side toward me, tucking a bit of the blanket in around his hips. I only let my gaze drop there for a second before the internal red light starts going off.

Danger! Danger! Not a good idea! Do something else with your eyes!

So I drag up gaze upward, up his flat stomach, past his amazing abs, above his stellar pecs. I look at his face, which is mostly obscured by shadow.

Lars is staring right at me when I get to his eyes, startling me. I don't say anything but my eyebrows do fly up.

He finds it funny, letting out a rumble of laughter. "You are something else, you know that?"

I feel my face grow hot. "Am I?"

"Yes," he affirms.

I cock a brow. "At least I wear clothes when I sleep."

"Pfft." He rolls his eyes. "As if that is worth bragging about."

I turn on my side, facing him, and stick my tongue out at him. "One of us has to be the adult here."

His laugh rumbles again. "Would it truly be so terrible if we were both naked?"

I frown. "Well… yes."

He shakes his head. "Why would that be bad? Hmm? As I said, we're both adults."

I squint at him. "That's probably the line that you use to get girls to play strip poker or something. And it won't work on me."

He shifts forward, so that I can see more of his face. He's smirking, which makes me want to hit him.

"First off, you *wish* I was asking you to play strip poker. And second, you would one hundred percent fall for a line."

I scrunch my nose up. "I would not."

"You would," he says, grinning. "You definitely would. Here, let me try out a line on you."

I snort. "Go right ahead."

Lars looks thoughtful. Then he pulls his comforter up, wrapping a corner of it around his body like a toga. He lifts his chin, smirking at me with a knowing look. He reaches over the side of the bed and pulls his shirt onto his stomach. Then he looks at me, his eyes sparkling with mischief.

"Feel my shirt."

I crinkle my entire face. "What? We just established that you are all but naked."

"Come on, play along. Feel my shirt."

Shaking my head, I reach out, smoothing my hand against the hardness of his chest through the thick comforter. "Feels… um… nice?"

He covers my hand with his, trapping it at the same time he pins me with his gaze. "Ja? You know what it's made of?"

It feels like someone has sucked all the air out of the room. Lars's skin against mine is hot. I lick my lips, shaking my head a little.

"No, what?" I ask. My voice sounds a little breathy; I blame it on the late hour, though.

Or is it early? It's hard to tell.

He meets my eyes, grinning broadly. "It's made of boyfriend material, sweetheart."

It's impossible not to crack up at that. For some reason, that strikes me as the funniest thing I've ever heard. "That's terrible!"

He smirks at me, wiggling his eyebrows. "You doubt me, but it's true."

I can't stop laughing. I ball up my fist, hitting him lightly. He acts like I've just killed him, groaning and turning onto his back, using my hand to pull me nearer. He wrangles my hand so I'm all but toppling across his chest.

"You murdered me! I'm dying!" he cries, trying not to laugh. "You've done it now, little witch."

I grin at him, biting my lower lip. "You deserve it for that terrible pun."

"Hmm," he says, flashing that wicked grin again. "It made you forget about being awkward, though."

I realize then that Lars has pulled me so that I am pressed up against him. Only the thick blanket separates our bodies. My breath leaves me in a huff. A shiver of anticipation skitters down my spine.

I look up, right into Lars's deep blue eyes. I swallow, my tongue darting out to wet my bottom lip. My gaze slides to his mouth.

Lars's eyelids close halfway as he moves in toward my mouth.

I can feel the kiss before it even happens. He moves closer. I close my eyes, my lips parting ever so slightly. His breath against the sensitive skin of my lips makes me shiver.

There is no room for softness in this kiss. Lars cups the back of my head and brings my mouth against his, searing me through. His lips are hot against mine. I open my mouth more and he takes full advantage, growling low in his chest. He moves his tongue against mine in a rhythm as old as the ages. I can barely help myself, curling my hand around the warm back of his neck and pulling myself closer. He tastes of clean mint and smells like aftershave; it is beyond me how he can smell so good while he's asleep.

His free hand comes down to the notch in my waist. I feel small compared to his much bigger body, almost dainty.

That's a new sensation for me. I may be slender but I am still tall.

When his hand slides up to cup my breast, all the breath leaves my lungs in a rush. I suck in a breath and a moan escapes my lips.

Yes.

God, yes.

Lars is touching me.

I nip at his full bottom lip. He slides his hand down my waist and hip to my knee, pulling my leg onto his hard, hot body. I can feel my body tightening, my breasts growing heavy, my pussy growing wet. I lean into him, rocking my lower body against his. I want him to touch me everywhere, but my clit is actually so hot it's almost achy.

I'm on fire for him.

Only him.

He stops kissing me for a second and rolls away, opening his bedside table. My brain takes a second to process the crinkling sound. But he holds a condom up in the air.

"Got it," he says.

My face contorts. It feels like I've suddenly been drenched with a bucket of ice water. I wasn't expecting to actually have sex with him...

"Umm... hold on." I murmur. Sitting up, I pull the blankets up over my chest.

Lars looks a little puzzled. "You don't use protection?"

I frown. "We were just kissing. I mean…" My face grows hot. "I think I'm still drunk, Lars. I don't want to… do more than that."

The words spill from my lips, unbidden. Lars frowns and looks away. "Oh." He clears his throat awkwardly. "I mean… of course."

Oh god, I can tell from his facial expression that I've hurt him. He clears his throat, trying to pretend away his awkwardness.

I reach out, my fingertips falling on his forearm. "I'm sorry, Lars."

He tosses the condom off the bed, shaking his head. "No, it's… I mean, I shouldn't have… assumed…"

I drop my hand. "We shouldn't… I mean, what we have is already so special."

He takes a deep breath, pinning me with his aquiline gaze. "Seriously, it was just… a lapse. I was on autopilot or something."

My eyes widen a bit that. The fact that his autopilot involves condoms is just…

It hurts my soul.

Before he can puzzle out my wounded expression, I turn onto my back and pull the covers up to my neck. "It's for the best. Like I said, I'm still drunk." I bite my lower lip, desperate to change the conversation. "I can't believe you let me drink so much."

I feel him roll onto his back beside me, sighing. "I didn't let you do anything, little witch."

Silence stretches between us for half a minute. "Can we just not talk about this ever again?"

"Sure," he says, a little too quickly.

I roll away from him, facing the Copenhagen skyline instead. "Um. Night, Lars."

He just grunts, shifting a few times. Then I assume he just goes right to sleep.

Not me.

No, I lay here and go over things again and again in my mind. Like how amazing the kiss was. How into it I was.

And how he definitely ruined my mood by completely assuming that I would just fuck him. Like it was that easy.

Like it wouldn't have effects on our friendship.

My mouth twists.

If I thought there was the remotest possibility of that, Lars and I would have gotten naked and sweaty together ages ago.

At some point, my eyelids drift closed. I don't remember falling asleep. But when I wake up, it's mid-morning.

I roll over to find Lars's side of the bed has been made. And a handwritten note on the pillow.

P —

Had to work out early.

There's coffee in the kitchen.

See you later.

— L

GROANING AT HOW CASUAL HIS NOTE SOUNDS, I PULL THE blankets over my head. I definitely learned one lesson for the fiftieth time in our friendship. It sucks to be in love your best friend.

I roll over, squeezing my eyes shut, and try to pretend last night didn't happen.

11

PIPPA

THE NEXT COUPLE OF DAYS ARE HELLISH. LARS SEEMS TO handle me with kid gloves, being very courteous while at the same time keeping me at arm's length. Nika is angry at me for some slight I made when I was drunk.

And to top it all off, I have a lingering remnant of a headache that just won't go away. I blame the champagne for it.

Actually, I blame the alcohol for a lot of things. Like French kissing my best friend, for instance.

After running all my errands Friday evening, I finally arrive home. I have to be careful when I carry my grocery bags upstairs because my entryway is absolutely bursting with thousands of dollars' worth of clothing. I skirt the boxes and let myself into my flat, only to nearly drop the bags when I get the door open.

A small, dark-haired figure in a belted trench coat stands at the window. She turns and quirks an eyebrow at me.

Ms. Olsen is here, in my fucking flat.

I drop my bags unceremoniously, backing out the door. I trip on the boxes behind my feet, trying to get my cell phone out of my purse.

"Pippa, dear," Ms. Olsen lets out the tiniest smirk. "I let myself in. I hope you don't mind."

"Of course I bloody mind!" I yell, looking at my phone screen. "Listen, whoever you are. I'm dialing the authorities right now!"

She steps forward, her lips quirking. "You can, if you wish. But I wouldn't."

I shake my head, pressing the call button. "You're insane. You know that? Just totally daft."

The phone starts ringing. Ms. Olsen smiles coolly. "Do you not care about Lars's wellbeing, then?"

I glare at her. The operator picks up. "Emergency services. What is your emergency?"

I flush. "Yes, hi. I just came home to my apartment and there is an intruder," I say quickly.

"What is your address, please?" the operator asks.

Ms. Olsen arches a brow. "We will tell him your secret." She pulls out her phone, showing me a flash of a photo. In the photo is the same girl that I found on Facebook, my little sister Stella. "And we will hurt your sister, if we have to."

I open my mouth, but that gives me some pause. My eyes slide over to Ms. Olsen's face, which is both smug and superior.

Is she serious?

I cover the microphone. "You should leave."

Ms. Olsen tilts her head. "You should hang up the phone, my dear."

"Excuse me, what address?" prompts the operator.

Ms. Olson scrolls through six or seven pictures of my sister, obviously taken when she was leaving the grocery store. I automatically reach for the screen, curious. She yanks the phone away from me, her tone threatening.

"Hang. Up." Ms. Olsen looks serious now.

"Uhh… never mind. I thought it was an intruder, but I… was mistaken?"

The operator replies. "Are you sure?"

Ms. Olsen checks the elegant silver wristwatch she wears.

"Yep!" I blurt. "Sorry."

I hang up the phone, a scowl on my face. I don't know how to even approach this subject. How should one act when being blackmailed?

"What do you want?" I ask at last.

Ms. Olsen's expression lightens. "For now? Not a thing."

"Why are you here? Why are you waving these… these creepy photos around?" I ask, gesturing wildly.

She shrugs a single shoulder. "Those are questions that I do not have the answers to. I'm just here to ascertain if we believe that you can be loyal or not."

I ball up my face. "What are you talking about?" I shout, exasperated. "Can you leave my flat?"

Ms. Olsen gives me another cool smile as she looks me up and down. "I think I'll tell my bosses that they had better keep Lars and Stella under observation for now."

I shake my head in disbelief. "Just wait until he hears about this."

She gives a tiny yap of laughter. "If you tell him, if you tell anyone, we will expose you. No one will even remember the story you tell because they will all be focused on the story of Sylvie Martin. And oh, what a story it is…"

I lift my chin. "I don't know what you are talking about. Please, leave my apartment!"

She purses her lips. "We both know that isn't true, Sylvie."

Tears prick my eyes. "I mean it. I will call emergency services back."

She sticks her hands in her pockets, moving forward slowly. I can't step back so I stand my ground. Her eyes twinkle for a moment as she pulls one of her hands out, revealing a basic flip phone. She reaches out to me as she comes to stand in front of me.

"We will be in touch. Take care of Lars, Sylvie."

My beat beats like a jackhammer in my chest. "I don't want your phone."

Ms. Olsen navigates around me, heading down the stairs. "Keep it close."

As I look over my shoulder, she raises down the stairs and out the front entrance of my building. Glancing down at the black phone in my hand, I realize that I am shaking.

Who is Ms. Olsen?

What does she want?

Staring at the phone, I can't come up with a single answer that makes sense.

12

LARS

"Try not to look as though the car in front of you has done something to personally offend you," I whisper into Pippa's ear.

She blinks a few times, blushing as she looks at me. She clears her throat and runs a hand down her light pink dress, licking her lips. "Sorry," she whispers back.

"And this car is the very first automobile to have rubberized wheels!" the older man leading our tour says. "You might think that the wheels look the same as they did in the last model, but I assure you they are not."

Pippa looks around the massive white tent where we have been learning about Denmark's part in the automotive boom. I check out Pippa while she isn't looking, finding the way that pink fabric clings to her ass much more interesting than the history of cars.

We've been extremely awkward since she spent the night in my bed last week. I've been kicking myself for blowing my one chance with the woman of my dreams.

And Pippa has seemed wrapped up in something else altogether. I guess it's better that way.

"Now if we move on to the next car, you will see that the shape looks a bit different…"

Pippa glances at me. I raise a brow. She leans close. "Please don't make me listen to any more. I'm begging you, Lars."

I can't help but smile. "What, you're not riveted to our guide's dissertation on how some old cars were made of wood and…" I pretend to fall asleep, snoring mid-sentence.

She rolls her eyes. "Come on. If anybody asks, I'll tell them I am not feeling well."

My lips curve upward. "You deceptive little minx. Lead the way."

One corner of Pippa's mouth tugs down but she just sighs silently. Turning on her heel, she spins and makes her way toward the tent's exit. I follow her as she weaves her way around half a dozen more old cars, then duck out of the tent into the bright sunshine. There are even more cars parked here, rows upon rows.

And these cars are much newer, much sexier, and much sportier than anything parked inside. Pippa glances back at me, arching a brow. "Isn't this one of the cars that James Bond drove in the 1960s?"

I wander towards the baby blue Aston Martin, feeling cooler just by being near it. I run my hand along the door, whistling. "Yes, I believe it is."

She wrinkles her nose. "You boys and your toys." She steps closer to me, bringing her hand up to my neck to straighten my tie. "At least you look the part."

My stomach sort of flip flops when she touches me. I play it cool, not reacting outwardly. "What? Devastatingly handsome?"

Her snort of good humor warms a little of the frost I've been feeling coming from her direction. "I just meant you were wearing a suit."

I put my hands behind my back, twisting my spine to survey the other cars. "Bond is known for wearing a tuxedo, if I'm not mistaken."

Her lips tip upward. "Tell me about this James Bond. I'm afraid I'm not familiar with him, seeing as how he is only my country's most famous fictional spy and all."

There it is. The banter that I've so greatly missed for the past week seems to have returned. I roll my eyes, taking a deep breath. "Who do you imagine I have to charm and dazzle to get the keys to one of these cars?"

Pippa pulls the ends of her pink cardigan closer, shivering. "Maybe that gentleman?"

She points behind me. I turn and spot a blond man in a dark winter coat approaching. He doesn't seem to recognize me until he's only a few feet away. Then he slows his pace, his gaze sliding between me and Pippa.

We've been splashed across the front page of every tabloid for a few days. His expression grows tense as he approaches.

"Your royal highness," he greets me. "Do you have a question about one of the cars, sir?"

Taking a step toward Pippa, I grab her around the waist. "My fiancée here was wondering if we might test drive one."

Pippa shoots me a flat look, elbowing me in the ribcage. I grin at her.

"Oh, I'm not sure… I mean…" The man grows red-faced. "Let me ask."

I nudge Pippa. "See?"

She shakes her head at me. "You are so spoiled. You know that, right?"

I wink at her, enjoying holding her close for a moment. "If you don't complain about it, I will let you drive a bit."

She wrinkles her nose. "I can't drive."

Nodding to the returning employee, I disagree. "He's got the keys right there."

"No, I mean—"

I cut her off, raising a hand to the dark-jacketed man. "Toss them!"

He looks vaguely nervous but he does toss a set of keys high in the air. "Here you go, your royal highness. I didn't realize that this car collection belonged to your father, sir."

Pippa glances at me, her eyebrows rising. "Wait, really?"

I shrug. "It's okay. Tell me, which car do these belong to?"

He gives a tiny bow. "The lime green Porsche, sir."

My eyes land on it, a few rows away. There is certainly no mistaking it for anything else. I grin. "Oh, that'll do nicely."

Jerking my head toward the car, I wiggle my brows at Pippa. She scrunches up her face as she follows me over to it. I go to the passenger side door, getting in.

"Lars!" I hear Pippa complain. "Seriously, I can't drive. I don't know how."

"And I heard you the first time. Get in. There is no time to learn like the present."

I pat the leather seat beside me. She huffs but reluctantly climbs in the car, sitting in the injection-molded seat. She glances around, the keys still clutched in one hand.

"Are you sure that this is okay?"

I point to the ignition. "Yes. Put the key in."

Scrunching up her face, she does. She turns the key, as if expecting the car to start up.

"It's a manual transmission, little witch," I tell her. "Look at the gas pedal."

She bites her lip, looking down. "I see three pedals."

I lean over, touching her leg. It's very little contact, but still enough to make my pulse race. "Look, the one closest to me is the clutch. The gas is in the middle. The brake is on the far side."

She arches a brow. "Why don't they make it simpler?"

I smirk a little at her. "Why ruin the fun?"

"Okay." She wrinkles her nose. "What now?"

"Push down on the clutch and hold it down. The one near me. Ja. Now the key should turn."

She does it a bit clunky, pressing down the clutch and the brake all the way to the floor. When the engine turns on, she looks at me. "Did I do it right?"

"*Ja, ja.* I mean. You got the thing running, at least. Ease up on the clutch. It only takes a light touch…"

She lets up completely and the car dies. She looks at me, panicked. "Oh god!"

I wave my hand. "No big deal. Do it again. Only don't stomp all the way to the floor. And don't let up on the clutch completely."

Her brow furrows as she does it with a tiny bit more grace this time. Then she looks over at me, awaiting instruction.

"The next part is tricky," I say, moving a bit closer. "You have to press the brake a little, keep pressure on the clutch, and shift into first."

I tap the gear shift. To my great surprise, she does it right the very first time, as if she has been doing it forever.

"Is that it?" she asks.

"Yep. Now comes the hard part. You have to press the gas pedal while you ease completely off the clutch. It's a smooth, even transfer, like this." I mime the pedals switching positions.

"Okay…"

Pippa lets go of the clutch too fast and the engine dies. She howls with frustration, hitting the steering wheel. "Stupid car."

"Come on, come on. Try it again. After you manage this, you can drive."

She makes a little grr sound but she does try again. And again… and again.

On the fourth try, she nails it. The car lurches forward a few feet. Pippa is so surprised that she takes her foot off the gas.

The engine dies.

I expect her to groan but she doesn't. Instead she turns to me, eyes shining with excitement, and throws her hands up. "I drove!"

She hugs me, doing a little dance. I freeze for a second, only relaxing when I force a laugh out. "You did. Well done."

She pulls back, her expression radiant.

Ah. That face she is making, the way her eyes are shining, the cheerful glow in the apples of her cheeks…

I live for that expression.

It doesn't last long, though. She sighs, rolling her head on her shoulders. "I think that's rather enough for one day, don't you?"

I look at her, completely serious. "It's whatever you want Pippa. We only go on your word."

A flush rises in her cheeks. She gives me an odd look. "Well, I think I'm done. I'm also freezing. Come on, I think I saw hot cider being poured in the refreshment tent."

She hops out of the car. I lean over and pluck the keys from the ignition, then follow her.

As I head toward the tent once more, I repress a sigh. For the millionth time, I am reminded of just how deeply in love with Pippa I am.

But at the same time, how much she means to me as a friend. If anything were to happen to our friendship, I would be…

Well, it wouldn't be good, at least.

Pippa turns, tucking a bit of her red hair behind her ear. "Are you coming?"

I nod. "I am."

Wishing I had found anyone else in the world to have a fake relationship with, I head into the tent.

13

PIPPA

I GLANCE AT LARS NERVOUSLY, SUCKING MY FULL BOTTOM LIP into my mouth and abrading it with my teeth. He stands stiffly beside me, his eyes turned forward to the open balcony doors. I slip my hand to his elbow and rest it on his heavy black jacketed arm. He doesn't seem to notice.

I draw a breath and smooth a hand down my frost blue heavy winter coat. Lars looks over at me, his expression lightening a bit. "I can tell you are stressing too much," he says. He reaches over and fusses with the white lily that is pinned to my coat. "We are just pretty background decoration, I promise. We won't be expected to speak." He rolls his eyes. "This is Stellan's show."

I wrinkle my nose. "I just assumed I would watch the King's speech from the massive audience gathered outside."

He tilts his head to the side. "That's Pippa Welch talking. You have to forget about yourself and remember your role. What the palace is expecting is the future Duchess of Marion. I find it is easier to deal with it all if I know to put Lars Love away and bring out Prince Lars of Denmark."

I nod, pensive. "I suppose so."

Two of Lars' brothers, this and that, make their appearance. They stand just behind us in line, coming after Lars in line for the throne. I peer around them to Nika and Erik, who currently have their heads close together, whispering about something.

Behind them are Lars's silvering father, his mother in royal blue, and his scary but always elegant grandmother.

The whole family is just waiting on the King and Queen now.

There is a commotion behind us. I turn my head and see Stellan and Margot arriving with a flock of secretaries and assistants. I must say, they do look rather royal. Stellan is outfitted in a dark suit and a dark overcoat similar to Lars. Margot is wearing her signature light pink color in her coat and dark heels.

If I didn't know them as people, I would still think that they made a stunning King and Queen of Denmark.

Margot shoos away one woman who is trying to put a final touch on her hair. She stops for a second to squeeze my forearm and wiggle her eyebrows. "We'll talk after the speech."

My lips curve up. "Sure."

But even as I answer, she is hustled past me to stand at Stellan's side. The balcony doors are swept open by two footmen. The audience begins cheering as Stellan and Margot step outside, smiling and waving.

"Your royal highness," a palace secretary says, beckoning Lars forward.

Lars clasps my hand in the crook of his elbow and steps forward. I fall into step almost automatically, wincing a little as the sheer wave of sound overtakes me. I step forward and look out at thousands upon thousands of people, cheering and holding signs. It's freezing outside, but the Danish people don't seem to care.

"Wave and smile," Lars shouts in my ear. "And don't forget to breathe."

I lift a hand, plastering a smile on my face. He guides me to our prominent position beside Stellan and Margot. We continue smiling and waving as the rest of the family finds their places. The crowd continues to cheer, especially when Annika steps out with Erik.

She's always been the people's favorite princess, so no surprise there. Stellan takes the microphone and coughs into it; the noise dies down as he begins his speech.

"Welcome," he welcomes the crowd. "As you undoubtedly already know, on this day in 1953…"

My brain blanked out whatever he is saying. Not that it's not important. But I'm too fascinated by looking around at everyone clustered on the balcony on this cold, bright morning.

I look up at Lars, biting my lower lip. He's focused on a spot in the crowd. I follow his gaze to find that several young girls are holding posters with my picture pasted on them. They say "Pippa + Lars 4Ever" and "Team Pippa!"

I have to admit, I don't even know who I am playing against in whatever team sport that young girl is so pumped about. I glance at Lars again and he looks at me, giving me a secretive smile. He nods towards Stellan, reminding me that the King is still speaking.

I yank my gaze to Stellan, who speaks for some length of time about the country's values and how proud he is to be Danish. I smile and sort of check out for a while, coming around when the crowd starts to cheer once more. I applaud, looking around at Lars's brothers.

Everyone seems to politely clap. No one has even a note of boredom on their faces.

Interesting. I know that Annika has not even the vaguest hint of interest in what Stellan was talking about. Yet I look at her pretty blonde features and she looks engaged.

That must be something learned over time, I guess. I've watched a thousand royal events as a member of the audience; it wasn't until today that I really got to see the other side of things.

"Pippa," Lars says, putting his hand on my lower back. He guides me back inside, following Stellan and Margot. As soon as we step inside, we are enveloped by warmth and the sound of cheering is immediately dampened.

I take a deep breath as Lars leads me down the stairs in the procession to the formal dining room. The dark wood room has a single long table in the middle with an elaborate and decorative place setting. As we step through the doors, footmen wait for our coats. Lars has his off in a flash, revealing his suave black suit beneath. He smiles at me as he helps me take my coat off, his chilly bare fingers touching my nape for long enough to raise goosebumps.

A server approaches with a tray of champagne. Lars picks up two glasses, just assuming that I want one.

I accept it from him and look around at everyone milling about near the window. "So now what?"

Lars shrugs a shoulder and sips his drink. "Stellan will probably give another speech about how we are all lucky. Then we'll have dinner."

I raise my brows. "Is that it?"

"Pretty much, ja." I see him wrinkle his nose slightly. "Fuck. My grandmother is looking at me like she expects something."

His hand instinctively finds mine. I blush as his grandmother comes marching over, leading several aunts and uncles in her wake. It's very difficult not to fidget as his grandmother looks me up and down. Her mouth turns down at the corner.

It's hard not to take that personally. Nevertheless, I greet her formally, curtsying. "Your royal highness."

Those bright blue eyes of hers pierce me. She's wearing a blue skirt and a cream top that make her eyes seem to pop. "Pippa, I presume."

"Momse," Lars cuts in. "You promised to be nice when I let you meet Pippa."

She touches the back of her silver hair. "Did I?"

He lets go of my hand. Before I can do anything else, he slides his arm around my waist and tugs me into his side. "Do we have to do this fifth degree business? Can't you just be happy for us, Momse?"

Momse raises her chin. "How are we to know that she is really the girl for you, Lars? If she's really your fiancée, that is."

Lars bristles. "She is what I say she is."

I cut in, trying to lessen the tension. "We went to the palace jeweler and got a nice ring." I lift my left hand, showing the ring off.

The expressions mirrored back to me are confused. One tall, gray haired gentleman clears his throat.

"It's very… nice. Very tame," he allows.

I frown. This man, who probably has never worked a full day in his entire life, thinks my ring is too small?

"The diamond costs what a new car would cost. I don't need or want anything larger."

Lars's grandmother shoots us an unreadable smile. "Very sensible of you."

Lars squeezes me close. "Pippa is nothing if not sensible."

Momse narrows her gaze on us, not impressed. "So it's to be a marriage between friends then, is it?"

My eyebrows fly up. "What?"

"No, we… we love each other," Lars declares, his hand on my waist flexing.

I know suddenly what I must do. Turning to Lars, I smile sweetly.

"They want to see us kiss, darling," I say.

There is a flash of puzzlement across his face before it's replaced with resolution.

"Ah." He smirks at the crowd. "You want a show?"

Without warning, he dips me backward, pulling me into position for a kiss. My hands come up to his chest and I am about to protest.

But before I can utter a word, Lars zooms in and presses his lips against mine. For a second, I am lost in the sensation of the kiss.

His lips are hot. My whole body tightens at that. When he opens his mouth to me and I do the same to him, he tastes like clean mint and a hint of champagne.

My hands curl in his lapels. My eyes drift shut. I wish it were possible to get closer to him; if we were alone, I would definitely quantify the feeling I have as distinctly horny.

Lars slides his hands down from my waist to my ass, making me giggle. I open my eyes, staring deep into his…

He grins at me, a smile that promises naughty things to come.

For a relationship that is fake, this is starting to feel dangerously real. Every time he so much as touches me, it's the kindling to my body, lighting the match to my soul. Even while I know in my gut that it's not fucking real, it feels too good to be fake.

I stare into his eyes, trying to find a similar emotion in those cool blue depths. What does he feel?

Someone across the ballroom drops a glass, making me cringe. And that's when I remember that the rest of the world still exists. I redden, looking at the people watching with wide eyes. Momse clears her throat and shifts her stance.

"Yes, all right," she says, waving a hand. "I'm satisfied for now, Lars."

He is quick to physically separate us, laughing a little. It sounds fake to me, but then again, I'm in on his big secret.

The sound of a glass being gently rung with a knife cuts through all the noise. "Everyone!" Stellan calls out. "If you would find your places at the table, I'd like to say a few words."

Momse shoots Lars a last look before turning away and moving toward the head of the table. I exhale a shaky breath. Lars grabs my hand, giving it a squeeze.

"What do you say we try to sit far away from my grandmother?" he asks.

I nod, moving away from that end of the table. "She's very direct and intense."

His lips quirk. "Indeed."

We find two seats at the end, far away from his grandmother, and listen to Stellan talking about how lucky the people gathered here should feel.

And I do feel lucky, more so than most of the royals. But I watch Lars out of the corner of my eye, wondering.

Was that kiss merely for show?

It didn't feel like I was faking anything.

Then again, I'm really in love with him, so... maybe that's why it convinces people.

Blowing out a breath, I drag my gaze away from Lars, trying to focus on literally anything else.

14

LARS

Pippa looks over at me from her seat in the chauffeured limousine, giving an aggravated groan. "Three days! It's been three days of nonstop royal visits and parading ourselves around to prove that we are really engaged. Does the palace just assume that we have nothing better to do with our time?"

I straighten my tie, sighing as I adjust my seat. "Yes. Traditionally, we are in positions that put us at the palace's beck and call."

She scrunches up her face. "I'm so unbelievably done with being a fake royal right now."

"Oh Ja?" I ask, raising a brow. "Try doing it twenty four hours a day, seven days a week for twenty five years."

Pippa picks at a bit of lint, flicking it off of her slinky black dress. "I honestly had no idea. No wonder you loved going to boarding school so much."

One corner of my mouth turns up. "I did love St. Matthew's. I was all but forgotten while I attended. I don't know if you remember, but I campaigned to be allowed to remain at school through winter and summer breaks."

She smiles a little at the memory, tucking a bright copper stand of her hair back. "Of course I remember. You were upset because the school refused. So you invited me home for the winter break as a sort of rebellion."

I chuckle. "I did. Of course, my mother and father barely noticed. If I hoped to grab their attention by bringing home an orphaned scholarship student, I failed miserably."

"Ja, sure." Pippa's cheeks warm and she looks away. That's usually her reaction to hearing herself described as either orphaned or disadvantaged.

A muscle in her jaw flexes. She looks out the window, her brow furrowing. "If you'd told me then that I would be here now, faking an engagement with the prince of Denmark, I wouldn't have believed you."

My lips twitch. "Same."

Out my window, I see the familiar-looking gates of the Air Base Karup looming. The whole base is ancient, a repurposed medieval fortress with a load of airplane hangars and landing strips surrounding it. All of it is neatly encircled by enormous iron gates.

"Is that the place we are going to?" Pippa asks, leaning over to look out my window. She's let her hair down today and the magnificent copper mass looks amazing. One particular curl seems to stand apart from the others; my fingers itch to smooth it down.

I swallow. "Ja. Ja, this is our last stop for the day."

She straightens, huffing a sigh. "At least you will know the people here." Her brow wrinkles. "Or does that make it harder? Since, you know… we are lying."

The limousine driver pulls up to the base's gates, rolling down the window. I watch him talk to the guard, distracted.

"I hadn't given it that much thought," I say, shrugging a shoulder. "We won't be the starring attraction anyway. There is some sort of show being put on today that a lot of the soldiers have been talking about. It's like a tame form of burlesque, I think."

She nods, looking ahead. The limo is waved through the gates and soon we pull up to the fortress. I run my hand over my uniform one final time, preparing myself.

"Ready?" I asks Pippa.

She nods. "After your grandmother's questioning, I feel like the military will be a breeze."

I grin as I get out of the car and escort Pippa into the actual building. It's gloomy inside the formal reception area. As soon as we step inside, a group of high ranking brass marches through, on their way from one area of the building to another. I pull Pippa toward the wall and salute them; one of the generals gives me a stiff nod as they pass.

Pippa cranes her neck to watch them go. "It's crazy that in the palace this morning, everyone was bowing and scraping and calling you royal highness. Yet here, that doesn't seem to matter at all."

I nod to the receptionist and pull Pippa along, resting her hand on my inner elbow. "The RDAF runs on their own rules. Everything here is decided by rank and merit."

Pippa smirks a little. "I see. You aren't seen as a prince here. I can tell by your tone that you like that."

I nod to another group of lower ranking cadets who stop and salute me. "Yes, I've been allowed to thrive here. It's a lot like St. Matthew's, in a way. Whatever you are outside these walls, once you step inside, it all falls away."

A jet takes off outside as we continue down the corridor. Pippa looks around, taking it all in. "I expected that the Royal Air Force would have done more remodeling. It basically looks in here as I imagine it looked a thousand years ago. There's absolutely zero soundproofing in here. Plus it is so…" Her mouth twists. "Well, it's a bit dank."

I smile at her. "That it is, Pippa. We like it like this." I turn a corner, pulling her to a stop. There is a line of uniformed men slowly filing into the fortress's big auditorium.

I pull her along, going with the flow as we squeeze through the double doors. The space we step into is truly awe inspiring, with a very high ceiling and smooth concrete underfoot, reminiscent of an airplane hangar. There is a ton of light in here from skylights cut into the ceiling; at the far end of the room, a stage has been assembled, a microphone stand the only decoration.

Pippa takes it all in with wide eyes. "What a space," she breathes.

"Come on," I say, taking her by the hand. "Let's get a place up front. We will be accepting some award or the other on behalf of the palace, but I assume that will be after the main show."

As I lead her forward, elbowing my way through the crowd toward the stage, a uniformed officer taps the microphone. "Good afternoon, Royal Air Force Base Karup!"

There is an immediate wave of loud applause and wolf whistles. The officer refers to a piece of paper. "Please welcome the Dusseldorf Dance Troupe!"

Loud rap music starts booming over the sound system. I manage to squeeze myself and Pippa up near the left side of the stage. Ten people parade out wearing a very bastardized, hot pants version of the same dress blues the Royal Air Force is known for. There are seven women and five men dancing. My eyebrows rise as I watch the spectacle. They separate into two rows, one moving forward and going down to their knees. They move quite deftly to the rap music, as I suppose you would expect a dance troupe to move.

I am deciding whether or not to be offended by their take on our uniforms. Everyone around me whistles and cheers, though. They don't seem to mind.

I frown.

Pippa leans in close with a secretive grin. "What do you think?"

I shoot her a glare and lean my head closer. "I think they are very close to mocking us with those uniforms—" I stop mid-sentence, because several of the dancers shed their uniforms for bikinis or speedos. My jaw drops.

One of the dancers edges near the area of the stage where I stand. She casts her gaze around and makes eye contact with me. All the while, she gyrates and grinds, shooting me naughty expressions.

I tilt my head, trying to decide if the blonde is sexy or if I'm still offended. Pippa squeezes my arm.

I glance at her. She doesn't look entirely pleased with me.

"What?" I ask.

Pippa leans her head in close. "At least act like you're in public with your fiancée," she hisses. "That is part of the deal. No making me look bad."

I roll my eyes. "Calm down. I'm not doing anything but looking."

Her cheeks flush. She pulls away from me and gives her head a little shake. Then she turns and starts threading her way through the crowd, heading toward the exit.

Fuck. I didn't mean to make her mad.

I glance back at the stage, guessing that I have plenty of time before I have to be onstage. Elbowing my way through the crowd, I heave a sigh.

If I wanted to deal with stuff like this, I would've just proposed to the minister's granddaughter. I push open the heavy double doors, spotting Pippa as she hurries down the hallway.

"Pippa!" I call.

She stops, turning with a frown. "What?"

"You're being ridiculous," I say, walking over to her. It's only when I get up close that I can smell her rose perfume and see the unshed tears in her eyes.

"You promised me that you wouldn't sleep with anyone else while I am pretending to be your fiancée," she whispers. "You could at least try to hide it a little better."

I reach out for her arm, tugging her closer. "I didn't do anything, Pippa. I was just standing there."

A tear breaks away from one of her eyes. She wipes it away angrily. "I saw your face. Everyone could see you making eyes at that dancer."

I shake my head. "Honestly, I wasn't. I was trying to decide if I was offended by her uniform." I take a deep breath, looking down into her face. "I think you might be overreacting a little bit."

She pulls out of my grasp. "Stop telling me that. Stop telling me what I'm supposed to feel. I hate that!"

I raise my hands up, backing up half a step. "Whoa. Okay."

She wipes at her face again, looking miserable. "You asked me to be your fake fiancée. Which is a lot. It's fine, but… a lot to ask another person. And all I asked in exchange is that you don't make a fool out of me by fooling around behind my back." She grows tearful. "It's not a lot to ask, Lars."

I don't know what else to do, so I enfold her in a hug. "I know, Pippa. I know." I murmur into her hair. "I'm sorry if it seemed like I was…" I pause. "Whatever you thought was going on. I assure you, there is no reason to feel jealous."

She looks up at me, her face contorting. "I'm not jealous. I'm just… I'm trying to tell you how other people perceive you!"

I narrow my eyes on her face. I could challenge her, but I want to calm her down. And that isn't the way, knowing Pippa as I do.

She is the only person in my entire life that demands so much of me and doesn't treat me as if I am special; but at the same time, she doesn't hold herself apart from me, either.

There's no way I'm about to risk that over something so small and dumb.

"I'm sorry," I tell her. "Really, I am."

She hangs her head with a sigh. "Okay."

My mouth twists. "You know that I will eventually have to go back to living my life though, right? You can't be all up in arms about me making eye contact with other girls forever."

She shoots me a glare. "I know that, thank you. I'm just trying to preserve some small amount of dignity. In two months, you can eye fuck anyone else that you want."

I repress an eye roll. "Fine. We'll deal with that when we get to it. For now, can we go back in the auditorium?"

She sniffs. "Fine."

I wave a hand toward the doors. "Fine. Lead the way."

As I follow her though, I can't help but turn the whole situation over and over again in my mind.

15

PIPPA

"OKAY. WAIT HERE FOR JUST A SECOND. DON'T LOOK!" LARS says.

I keep my eyes covered and shiver against the cold air. Lars has brought me somewhere an hour and a half north of Copenhagen, saying we need a break from everything. I listen as his boots crunch across the snowy ground.

"Where the hell are we?" I ask.

"You'll know in about thirty seconds," he says with a laugh.

Wrinkling my nose, I kick at the ground beneath my feet. I can tell it's been freshly shoveled, but I don't dare peek out from behind my hands just yet.

I hear something scraping the ground. Lars comes back and leads me forward a few steps, standing right behind me.

"Okay. You can look."

I drop my hands and see an enormous modern cabin before us, the door open wide, the heat escaping it in clouds. I look at Lars, extremely surprised.

"Where are we?" I ask again.

He grins and grabs my hand, leading me up the front steps and into the foyer. "I rented us a cabin for the next few days. It's sort of my way of saying I'm sorry for dragging you to three days of royal events."

I look around the cabin, if it can even be called that. One of the walls is made entirely of glass. Just outside, the landscape drops dramatically away, making for a breathtakingly snowy vista.

A living room is set up immediately in front of me, all the cozy white furniture arranged around a wrought iron fireplace with a chimney going up to the ceiling. The kitchen gleams from across the space, all dark stone and stainless appliances. Between the two is a charming cedar table set for six.

"Well?" Lars prompts me. "What do you think?"

I turn to him with a slow smile. I point out the skis hanging on the wall in the entryway. "It's amazing. But why here? As far as I know, we've never skied or done anything remotely woodsy."

He shrugs, closing the door behind him. "Well, maybe it's time we tried. Hmm?" He shoves him dark hair back off of his forehead. "I think I've put us in a high pressure situation. So this is me trying to release some steam that has been building up."

My lips quirk. "Ah. You're talking about how I lost my cool at the Air Base Karup, I'm guessing."

He shrugs. "I mentioned to Erik that we needed a break. He suggested a cabin in this area. Now here we are."

I turn around, giving him a soft hug. "Thank you. It's very thoughtful. Maybe I could use a break, now that you mention it."

The hug lingers for a second too long before he steps back, clearing his throat. "Want to try skiing? Or better yet, we can snowboard."

I laugh. "Sure. Let me just change into more layers. Then we'll try whichever you want." I pause, tilting my head. "As long as I make myself clear. I think that too much exercise is for people who secretly hate themselves."

He grins. "Come on, get dressed."

The next few hours are fun, if not productive. Lars trying to snowboard and failing. Me trying to ski and ending up on my ass, over and over. Both of us laughing as we hold hands and sled down the huge hill behind our house on a big double raft.

By the time the sun starts to dip behind the trees, I'm completely done for. I wave a hand, stuck in a snow drift with my skis askew.

"I give up!" I laugh. "I am not any better at skiing than I was a few hours ago."

Lars frees himself from his snowboard, which he's actually annoying okay at. He walks over and grabs my hands, helping me up.

"Ja, I'm ready to call it a day. I'm also so hungry at this point that I could eat a bear."

I follow him to the cabin, my eyes dropping to the spot on his ass where he's landed enough times to make his pants damp. "Mm," is all I have to add to the conversation.

We head inside the cabin, shedding our clothing before the snow that clings to it melts. I head into my bedroom, just upstairs. Digging fresh clothing out of my suitcase, I change into a loose, flowy white dress.

I guess I don't fully understand that our bedrooms are connected by a bathroom. Because I step into the bathroom, my mind on my hair. And I see Lars with no shirt on, just buttoning a pair of dark, low slung jeans.

He turns around and catches me looking at him. He smirks as my cheeks grow red.

"Don't let me stop you," he jokes. "By all means, little witch. Take all the time you want. Stare away."

I shoot him a glare. "Ha ha." I clear my throat and drag my gaze to the big mirror in the shared bathroom. He pulls a white tee shirt on as I try to futz with my halo of insane curls. I try not to notice that he fills up almost the entire doorway with his sheer height.

Lars leans in the doorway, his biceps gently bunching as he crosses his arms. I won't let myself notice.

Just because he's unspeakably hot and I have wanted him forever doesn't change anything at all. First, I am a fucking liar. I have been since the week we met.

And there is the fact that our friendship is more important than anything else. We can't forget that, can we?

"What are you thinking about?" he wonders.

I blush, looking at his reflection in the mirror. Ja, I'm not answering that one.

"What's for dinner?" I ask instead.

He smiles slowly, pushing off the doorway. "The oven is heating up for a frozen pizza. I also think there is a salad."

I turn. "I'm starving. Let's go raid the fridge while we wait."

We eat pizza and talk about inane things for the next hour. Up here, in his jeans and tee shirt, Lars is imperceptibly more laid back. His smiles are more frequent, his jokes are mostly terrible. There is none of the posturing and bravado that usually follows him around. He's just… happier.

I realize that he probably needed a break from everything almost as much as I did. That thought comforts me a little bit.

Lars eventually opens a bottle of wine and pours us each a glass. I swirl the contents of my glass gently, looking at him as he settles on the couch. He quirks an eyebrow at me.

My lips quirk. "Yes?"

He spreads out on the couch and shrugs. "Nothing."

I narrow my eyes. "I know you too well for that. What is it?"

He takes his time sipping his wine before he answers. "I was just wondering what it would be like if we lived very different lives."

I tilt my head. "In an alternate universe? We wouldn't know each other, probably." "Maybe. But I was more thinking of a world where we knew each other. I wonder what would have happened if we had just met in our twenties."

My brows rise. "Oh?"

"Ja. Imagine if we had not been largely ignored by our respective families growing up. If we were both just normal, well-adjusted adults when we met."

I wrinkle my nose. "I can't picture it, honestly. We wouldn't have any history."

He chuckles a little. "No. I wonder if we wouldn't just date each other."

My heartbeat instantly speeds up. I lick my lips. "You think we would be an item?"

He shrugs a shoulder, picking up my feet and putting them in his lap. I bury my toes under his thigh, enjoying his warmth. He shoots me a secretive smile.

"Maybe. I mean, you are definitely not my type. But maybe in this alternate world, you would be."

Oh god. I blush a little bit.

"I've seen your blonde supermodels come and go like a revolving door," I answer crisply. "I'm really not interested in being your type, I think."

That's a lie. It feels false even as I say it.

He finishes his glass of wine and sets it aside, rubbing one of my bare feet with both of his thumbs. He goes right to a spot that feels so good, digging into the pad of my foot.

"Oh, little witch," he sighs. "There is no denying that we have both found each other attractive."

My brow descends. "Ja. It's all the other pieces about you that I find problematic. For instance, the fact that you've slept with half the pretty, young blonde girls in the city."

He smirks. "What if I was well-behaved? Hmm? Would that make you happy?"

One corner of my mouth bends downward. "Hypothetically?"

He pins with his sapphire gaze. "I don't know, Pippa. Do you want us to be discussing things hypothetically?"

No.

God, the way he is looking at me just now. The way he is smirking at me. The way he touches my feet.

My hormones want him to stop talking and kiss me. Hell, they wouldn't mind if I jumped him.

I lick my lips again, taking in the expression on his face. "Are you actually suggesting that we sleep together, Lars?"

He pauses, pushing his cheek out with his tongue. "I could be. I mean, you think I'm hot. I think you're hot. We could just… take it to the next level."

I frown. While I obviously want him more than anything, I don't want to destroy what we already have.

"I… I don't know, Lars. We are best friends. And to me, that is more important than some little fling."

He bites his lower lip. "So we'll just… keep it casual."

I shake my head. "I don't think that's a very good idea."

Lars narrows his eyes on my face. "Kiss me."

I shoot him a look. "What?"

"Kiss me," he says, moving closer. "Just one time. Kiss me for real. And then if you still feel like it's a risk to our friendship…" He reaches up to my face, brushing back a curl. "Then we can pretend it never happened."

I swallow. My eyes are on his, trying to gauge how serious he is. I suck in sips of air and notice how his eyes slip down to my neckline. My nipples pebble at the very thought of his lips touching my overheated skin.

God, my heartbeat is so loud in my own ears that I am afraid he will hear it.

He puts my feet down, moving so he's only a few inches from my face. He licks his lower lip, reaching out slowly to cup my jaw with his elegant fingers.

"Pippa?" he murmurs.

I can barely breathe. "Yes, Lars?"

He brings his face closer, feathering a kiss over the corner of my mouth. I open my mouth, sighing silently. I can feel a storm gathering inside me.

Lars kisses my cheek, grazes his lips over my earlobe. "All you have to say is yes," he whispers.

A dam breaks in me. I move my head, catching his lips with my own. He is surprised for a split second. Then he takes control of the kiss, cupping my jaw and teasing my lips apart.

He's sweet and salty and earthy, his tongue working against mine. My hands come up to grab his shirt, forming fists as I drag him closer.

He pulls back and nips at my lower lip. I can't help it. I let out a little moan.

"Is that a yes, little witch?" he whispers.

I nod, struggling to draw a breath. "Yes." He moves in to kiss me again, but I pull back.

"There have to be rules," I say, looking in his eyes. "To protect us both."

He looks puzzled. "Like what?"

I draw in a long breath. "We are friends first. Okay? We just… we don't do anything that would hurt that." I reach out, grabbing his hand and pulling it over my heart. "Promise me."

He frowns. "Of course, Pippa."

I lick my lips. "Okay. There are probably more rules—"

He cuts me off with a kiss so dominating that all thoughts of rules are driven from my mind. My hand fists in his shirt. He moves effortlessly to scoop me up off the couch, not breaking the kiss.

And then he starts carrying me upstairs.

1 6

PIPPA

LARS PRESSES HIS LIPS TO MINE, BENDING ME BACKWARD. MY hands touch his face and then creep around his strong neck. He picks me up. My legs go around his waist naturally. I moan as he walks us both backward, toward the bed.

God, is this really happening right now?

As he lays me back on the bed, I shiver. He breaks off the kiss only to move his mouth lower, to my jaw and my neck. Scorching a path to my pulse point, he buries himself there. I feel the sting of his teeth for a second before he kisses the sensation away.

I had no idea that his mouth could be so *hot*. His lips against the pale column of my neck causes my breasts to tighten and lift. I realize that he is already pressing himself between my legs, falling there naturally when he moved us both on the bed. I am suddenly aware of the place between my thighs where I ache, the feeling more and more insistent the longer I'm with Lars.

His hand trails down to cup my breast through my shirt, pinching my nipple through my bra. Everything he does feels amazing, like a fire burning through a drought-parched land. He pinches my nipple again, sending shivers of electricity down my spine. I gasp at how connected my breasts seem to be to the slit between my legs, the slit that is growing damp now.

I have some ideas for what would feel good right now, most of them centered on the bulge in Lars's jeans. Pressing my hips up against his, I make a sound of pure need.

Lars pulls back, desire flaring high in his eyes as he meets my gaze. When he speaks, his voice is rough as gravel.

"Tell me what you want," he murmurs. "Tell me that you want me half as badly as I want you, little witch. Make me believe it."

I suck in a breath. Do I want him? With every single molecule of my being, with every breath in my body.

"I want you, Lars," I whisper, looking into his eyes.

He smirks. "Are you sure, Pippa? Because I want you so damn much it hurts."

I bite my lip and nod, my eagerness overcoming my shyness. He kisses me again, his hands drawing my tee shirt dress up and over my head. Just like that I am bare before him, wearing nothing but my bra and leggings.

Lars looks at me hungrily, his eyes dipping down to my breasts. He takes a second to unlace his boots.

I watch him, my heart beating in my throat. Then he strips off his shirt, leaving me half-drooling at his hard muscles. His abs. His pecs. His biceps…

Everywhere I look is ridged with muscle. The exercise regimen that he's been on is no joke, it seems.

He returns to me, unbuttoning his jeans. He leaves them zipped, cradling my face as he kisses me. My heart is a humming bird, fluttering in my chest. A moan emerges from my mouth as he takes me back onto the bed, trailing his hot kisses down my neck and across my chest.

He kisses his way down to my breast, pulling one strap of my bra down and baring my nipple.

The breath seizes in my lungs. Then he fastens his wicked mouth on my nipple. I cry out at the almost electric sensation. It makes the ache between my legs spread a little wider.

He releases my breast, his face utterly dark as he reaches behind me to unclasp my bra. I take a little bit of initiative and draw my bra off, tossing it aside. Then I'm bared before him, my hard nipples jutting proudly between us.

I hear his harsh intake of breath. It makes me flush.

"You are so goddamned beautiful to me," he whispers, reaching out to cup one of my breasts. "It's killing me, I swear."

My cheeks flood with heat. Reaching out a hand of my own, I touch his neck and trail my fingers down his arm. "You're a Greek god, in case anyone was keeping score."

That makes him chuckle, his eyes crinkling. His humor is infectious and I find myself smiling softly.

"What?" I say.

"I never know what you're about to say, that's all. I find you surprising, continually." His eyes wander down my body.

He runs his hands down my sides, finding the fullness of my hips between his two hands. He kisses me again, firmly and passionately, making me gasp with want. I hardly realize that he's stripping off my leggings until they are gone, until I am left with a skimpy pair of black lace panties as my last layer.

He leans down and presses his face close to my mons, inhaling. "Fuck, you smell so good. It should be illegal to smell like this."

He starts to touch the tiny triangle of damp fabric between my legs, running his fingers down from the hem to the vee of my thighs. I let my eyelids flutter closed as his clever fingers begin trailing closer and closer to my aching slit. God, even this much friction is incredible.

He kisses me, his lips and tongue every bit as clever as his fingers. I'm shamelessly excited by him, by what lies ahead. I know nothing except how those fingers and that tongue make me feel.

Soon my panties too are gone, slid down my legs by his hasty hands. I look up at him as he spreads my thighs wide.

"Fuck," he says, running his hands down my inner thighs. "You're shaved smooth. Fuck!" He swallow, his eyes dark with excitement. "You have the prettiest pussy I've ever seen, little witch."

He brushes his fingers along my slit. I groan, trying to stay still.

"Ah, fuck," he murmurs.

I'm wet for him, excited beyond measure, unsure that this is really happening. He traces the line of my slit, gathering the evidence of my excitement of his fingertips. When he draws his fingers to his mouth, glistening with my wetness, my mouth falls open.

He closes his eyes briefly, moaning a little. Has anything ever been sexier than watching Lars lick my juices off of his own fingers?

Then he lifts himself up, his fingers going to his waistband. I watch, wide eyed, as he begins to unzip his pants. His cock springs free almost immediately, unencumbered by any underwear. My eyes zero in on it. It's long, thick, and perfectly pink.

My mouth starts to water.

He's going to fucking stretch me out with that perfect cock of his.

I shouldn't be surprised to find out that Lars is well endowed, but my jaw does drop a little anyway. He shoves his pants down and steps out of them completely. Now he's naked before me, his thighs and hips as taut with muscle as the rest of him.

There is even that little vee of muscle at his hip bone. I shiver when I see that. My fingers reach out to touch that vee, without my ever having consciously thought about it. He moves closer, allowing my inspection.

And why not? He's certainly got nothing to hide.

My heart in my throat, I know that this is it. I'm going to lose my heart to Lars, right here and now. Once he has sex with me, spends the night making me call out his name, that will be it for me.

I'm already in love with him. By touching me, by exciting me, by fucking me… he's going to ruin me for everyone else on the planet. He's going to shred my heart.

And yet, I can't stop. I won't. I grip his hip, looking at him with a pleading gaze.

"Touch me," I whisper. "I'm on fire for you, Lars."

When he finds my pussy with his fingers again, stroking up and down the slit in rhythmic caresses, his gaze latches onto mine.

In his clear blue eyes, I see an expression of pure want. As his hand works a little faster, I make tiny mms and ohhhs of pleasure.

He leans down, his cock pressing against me intimately. My mouth opens to kiss him when he gets closer, but he surprises me by murmuring in my ear.

"I want you so badly, little witch. You've cast a spell over me, I think," he breathes, his words tickling my ear.

I flush. My mouth is suddenly dry. I lick my lips, unable to move my body away from his clever fingers. "Yes," I say. "I want you, Lars. I need you to fuck me."

"Are you on birth control?"

I just nod again. His mouth curls into a grin. He kisses a spot on my neck, sucking it hard enough to pull a moan from my lips. "I'm going to rock your fucking world, Pips."

He surprises me yet again by pulling away and sinking to his knees. I sit up partway, alarmed, but he pushes me onto my back with steady hands against my stomach.

"I've been waiting a lifetime to do this to you," he whispers, bringing his hand up to part my pussy lips. "Your pussy smells so good. I am going to make you come apart with just my tongue, little witch."

Then he touches the tip of his tongue against my exposed clit, the part of my that has been throbbing for so long. It feels like a lightning bolt, straight to the pleasure center of my brain. The breath leaves my lungs for a minute as his tongue works around it in steady circles.

Soon I'm burying my hands in his hair and moving in time with the rhythm he sets. It's so good that my whole body is on fire. He seals his lips around my clit and sucks. I'm on a precipice, holding onto my connection with reality by a thread.

Then he groans into my flesh, sending a tidal wave straight to the heart of me. With a shudder and a low moan I come apart, gripping at his hair. He's so good that I tremble and groan, calling out his name softly.

He continues to lick and kiss my clit gently until I stop him with my fingers.

I pull him back up to my head, kissing him hard. He tastes like ozone and something a little sweet. With a start, I realize that that's my unique flavor that I'm tasting on his lips and tongue.

He pulls me under him, kissing me soundly. I groan as his hard cock brushes the sensitive folds of my pussy. I'm still feeling the aftershocks when he fists his cock, bringing the head to my entrance. I'm slick from what he just did with his mouth, but when he starts to push his cock inside, even the smallest amount stretches me out. My body is resistant even though I want him.

He's just so fucking *big*.

There is a moment of genuine pain, bringing tears to my eyes. And then he is thrusting all the way in, making me forget the pain. Our bodies merge. I cling to him, my mouth open, my eyes closing. I'm enraptured.

I relax into the thrust of his big cock. I start to feel something building, a vague pressure from far away. It is different than the burning desire I felt before, more like a spring slowly tightening.

"Open your eyes, Pippa," he grits out.

So I do. I stare up into his gaze, feeling the coil of my desire tightening, inch by inch. Raking my nails down his back and meeting his thrusts with my own, I feel I have never been closer to another person than I am to Lars right now.

"Fuck," he mutters. His expression says he is either in pain or ecstatic, one of the two. "You are so goddamn beautiful."

Watched by those dark blue eyes, I start to shatter once more, spasming as I come. He is right behind me, fucking me frantically, finding my hand and gripping it so hard that I am honestly afraid that it will break.

He comes with a shudder, pounding into me relentlessly. I can actually feel his cum inside me, but in the next second I forget that I was even thinking about it because he kisses me, long and with tongue. For several seconds, it's just me and him, no one else even existing in the entire world. My heart beats erratically, in time with Lars's, and it just feels so *right*.

Everything that I was worried about… how he's a player and out of my league… it just melts away. All that is important is the here and now, his body against mine.

Eventually of course he does roll away. He turns onto his side and takes me with him. Kissing me again, slowly and meaningfully, he sighs against my lips.

"I need ten minutes to recharge, sweetheart," he says, kissing his way to my ear. "Then I can make us both come again." I shiver as he nips my ear. "But while I'm waiting…"

His hand slips down my belly, tracing its way between my thighs, teasing. I open my mouth and a gasp comes out as he parts my lower lips and finds my clit.

"Oh, little witch," he murmurs. "You're already wet for me…"

I kiss his lips, desperately wanting this moment to go on forever.

17

LARS

I FUCK PIPPA TWICE MORE BEFORE WE FALL ASLEEP, SWEATY and exhausted. The last thing I remember before falling asleep is the sound of her steady breathing and the feel of her lying on my chest.

I open my eyes to find myself alone in my bed. Pippa's clothes are gone from my floor. Her side of the bed has been straightened. There is no sign that Pippa was even here other than the wrinkled sheets.

It's early in the morning but I can hear her moving around downstairs.

After a quick shower, I head down to see what she's up to. Clattering down the stairs, I find Pippa in the kitchen, cooking eggs in a loose light blue dress. She turns to me, blushing a little, and points to the French press on the counter.

"Coffee."

I pad over to the French press and find a mug. As I take a sip of the steaming brew, I eye her. She is using a spatula to stir the eggs and making a concerted effort not to look my way.

"You're being weird," I say.

She sets the spatula down and pushes back her copper curls. She turns, wrapping her arms around herself and resting her hip against the counter. "I feel pretty weird," she admits. "I just spent the night in my best friend's bed. I'm not sure where to go from there."

I take a deep breath, tilting my head. "Do you want things to change drastically?"

She looks down, frowning a little. "Not really."

I shrug a shoulder. "Then they won't. We'll just be friends who occasionally fuck each other's brains out."

She bites her lower lip. "Won't that complicate our fake relationship?"

"Why would it?" I nod at the pan of eggs. "Those are going to burn if you don't stir them."

Two spots of color appear in her cheeks. She stirs the eggs then pushes some toast in the toaster. Her expression is unreadable.

"You're overthinking things," I say, taking another sip. Her expression remains puzzled.

"It doesn't seem like we should just be able to do this," she says, shaking her head.

The toast pops up. She dishes the eggs out into plates and adds the toast.

I stop her as she's about to pick up the plates. Turning her around, I put my hands on her shoulders and look down at her.

"We can do whatever we want," I say, looking intently at her expression.

There is a little fear in her blue eyes. "I don't want anything to come between us and ruin our friendship. You're basically the only family I have, Lars."

My heat thumps in my chest. "I promise that won't happen."

She looks at me, her expression almost begging. "You swear?"

My lips tip upward. "On my life, Pippa. And I will abide by your rules — that is, not seeing anyone else while we're… choosing to be intimate."

She chews on her bottom lip. "Are you sure?"

I huff a laugh. "Ja, I'm quite sure."

She exhales a deep breath. "Okay."

I pull her into the shelter of my arms, kissing the top of her head. She smells faintly of vanilla.

"One thing that will probably make it easier is the fact that we have a planned escape hatch," she murmurs.

Pulling back, I raise a brow. "Oh?"

She smiles lightly and moves away, picking up the plates. "Ja. I mean, we are supposed to break up in a couple of months anyway. So that will be a good time to think about… ending things."

I grab our coffee mugs and follow her to the table. "You already have that planned out, huh?"

She sits down, shooting me a little glare. "Look, some of us don't live like you do. We don't base jump or race yachts just because we like the rush of adrenaline. Some of us are plotters and planners."

I pull a plate of eggs over to me, digging in. "You had better eat fast."

Her brows rise. "Why?"

"Because," I say, picking up my toast and taking a bite. "After this, I will be sufficiently recharged."

Her expression is questioning. "Are you talking about skiing again?"

I pin her with a heated gaze. "No, Pippa. As soon as I'm done eating, I'm going to drag you over to the couch and fuck you senseless. So hurry the hell up."

Her eyes widen. She blushes furiously. "Oh!"

I notice that she doesn't exactly protest, though. Instead she just wolfs down her breakfast, finishing it with sips of coffee.

18

PIPPA

We fuck.

We nap.

Then we fuck some more.

"Like what you see, little witch?" His voice is still groggy, but oh so beautiful.

"Yes. I suppose that I shouldn't be staring while you're asleep though, huh?"

He reaches a hand up to my face, brushing my hair from my eyes and tucking it gently behind my ear, fixing me in place with his piercing eyes.

"It's okay. I like you looking at me. Like seeing you looking at me more."

"Even then, it's rude to stare at a sleeping person." I avert my gaze and focus on my knee instead.

"Pippa, you can stare at me all you want. As long as it's me you're staring at like that, I'm happy. Fucking ecstatic, actually." He cups my chin so that our eyes meet, still not moving to hide any part of himself.

"It's okay to be curious. Hell, I'm fucking honored to be the one who gets to indulge your curiosity." The way he is looking at me, practically naked, eyes hooded and dark with desire, relaxed about his exposed body... it had to be the single most erotic thing I'd ever seen.

My breath hitches at his words, but I wasn't feeling shame anymore at being caught. It is amazing how comfortable he made me feel, how at home, how wanted.

He is still looking at me with desire, waiting for my reply. I have no words as I start tracing the lines of his chest, then the ones on his arm and all the way to his hand. Next, I trace the muscled lines of his stomach down to his hips. His breath hitches. His cock twitches, begging for my attentions.

I trace my fingers down his stomach and toward the elastic of his boxer briefs, it jumps again. "I'm really trying to let you do your thing here, little witch. But you're really fucking killing me."

I am killing him? That seemed impossible, but yet, the evidence is right in front of me. A shiver of excitement runs up my spine and I can feel dampness seeping from my slit.

"Fuck," he breathes as I run my hands over the outline of his hard cock over his boxer briefs. "I can't fucking wait to get inside of you."

He flips me onto my back and presses his body to mine, kissing me deeply and tracing the neckline of my tank top as he runs his other hand up and down my thigh. I moan as he reaches the edge of my shorts and grasps at the fabric. He rolls my shorts over my ass, down my legs and then kicks them off the bed without breaking the kiss.

"Pippa," he said softly. "Look into my eyes for a second." I open my eyes and he drinks me in, running one hand up and down my side, leaving goosebumps in his wake.

"I'm trying to go slow here, little witch. But you're making it very, very hard for me." He reaches for my hand, pulling it to the bulge in his boxer briefs. "See what you do to me?"

I look into his eyes and slowly nod.

He kisses my neck. "I need to hear you say it, Pippa."

"I see," I breathe softly. I shape his cock inside his boxer briefs and he lets out a soft moan.

"Oh, little witch. You are such trouble." He kisses down my neck, planting soft kisses and nips between his words. "I can't wait to taste you again."

He looks up at me, one hand tracing my nipple through my shirt. I bite my lip, unable to form words because of the sensations he is eliciting in my body.

He is still teasing my nipples, planting soft kisses on the exposed skin on my stomach.

I barely manage a nod. My skin is on fire everywhere he touches me, aching for more. Each stroke on my nipples causes my pussy to clench and I am pretty sure that by now, my panties are drenched. I would be embarrassed, if I could bring myself to think that far, but all my thoughts are completely wrapped in what he is making me feel.

His hands slide my panties down and my tank top disappears over my head. I am now completely naked in front of the most gorgeous man on the planet.

If this were anyone else, I would be trying to cover up. But the way that Lars is looking at me, his blue eyes dark with lust, makes me feel sexy, desirable and beautiful.

He drinks me in with his eyes, growling softly as his fingers stroke my dripping slit.

"God, Pippa. You're so fucking wet." He brings his glistening fingers to his lips and licks my juices off the tips of his fingers. He closes his eyes and lets out a low moan as he tastes me on his skin. "Fucking delicious, little witch. So sweet. I can't wait to taste you."

All I can focus on is his fingers that are now playing with my clit, teasing my seam.

He kisses me deeply, hungrily. I can feel his rock hard cock digging into my hip. I moan loudly, still unable to form any words.

"Fuck, Pippa. I've never cum from just sounds before, but if you keep that up, that might change. Breathe, little witch…" His voice is husky, low.

I follow his advice, taking a deep breath to clear my ridiculously, pathetically aroused mind enough to whimper, "For fuck's sake, Lars. You're killing me. Taste me! Or fuck me! Do something, anything…" I beg.

He lifts me as if I weigh nothing at all, moving me up the bed. Then he drops his whole body down low, kissing his way across my stomach and making me writhe.

He licks slowly but hungrily along my seam. Up and down, sucking in my lips, darting his tongue into my pussy, before starting all over again. He let out a low moan again. "So fucking sweet, Pippa." He groans before taking my sensitive clit in his mouth, sucking lightly, his tongue flicking against my bud.

His tongue reduces me to a shivering, moaning maniac. I try to buck my hips against him, unable to contain myself any longer, but his strong hands on my hips keep me in place. He licks and sucks until I see nothing but stars and fireworks, feeling like I am about to fly away if it wasn't for him anchoring me down.

Far too soon, the pressure that had been building up inside me releases into a ball of light, my mind shattering in every different direction possible. I scream his name, digging my fingers into his shoulders and tugging at his hair.

He keeps licking until he wrings every last drop of pleasure from my body. He crawls up and kisses me as he slips his boxer briefs off. I can feel the tip of his cock against my entrance, positioned perfectly to slide into me. He doesn't though, he kisses me hard and I can taste myself on his lips. Somehow, it just arouses me even more. I moan into his mouth and hear a low sound at the back of his throat.

"I want you inside of me," I say, my voice coming out in a breathy whine. "Please, Lars."

He lets out a low growl, but doesn't say any more. I can feel his hard cock gently pushing against my entrance. He slides in slowly, watching my every facial expression, seemingly gauging my every move.

"Fuck, so tight," he breathed as he edged in, still very slowly. He's so fucking big but the delicious fullness and pleasure of having him inside my outweighs the discomfort. I cling to him and run my hands through his hair and down his back.

When he is all the way in, he stops, driving me crazy. His muscles are taut, eyes blazing with need, but he doesn't act on it. He is huge, but I need to feel him move already.

"Okay there, little witch?"

"I'm fine, Lars. I need to feel you!" I manage, my voice breathy. "Fuck me, Lars."

At that, it is as if his resolve breaks and he starts moving.

Slowly at first, but it is the most incredible feeling I have ever experienced. Pleasure fills my body, taking over every inch of me. The entire world has disappeared and all that exists is the feeling of him in me, his body on mine, breathing deeply and softly growling and moaning into my ear, kissing me and whispering to me.

He rocks into me with perfect rhythm, with just the right amount of depth. I can feel the pressure building again. His breathing is ragged now and I can feel his muscles start to shake as he thrust into me more forcefully, but still taking care not to hurt me. He is nearly there, and I am right there with him.

A final thrust and my world is shattered into a million pieces again as the knot that has been building inside me releases. All those things I'd ever heard and read about mind-blowing orgasms could not compare to this. To him.

He nips at my bottom lip as his eyes roll back, his muscled shoulders flexing and thighs quivering as he fills me. I feel his orgasm pour into me, his cock twitching deep inside of my body. And it is the most exquisite thing that I've ever felt.

He presses his lips against mine and pulls me into a long, deep kiss.

19

LARS

ONCE I CONVINCED PIPPA TO FUCK ME, SHE WAS INSATIABLE. We would fuck for hours and hours, catching a quick nap or a bite to eat before tearing into each other again. It felt like something that had been brewing between us ever since I laid eyes on her.

For as long as I have known Pippa, I've been half in love with her. And now I had her in my sights. Hell, I had her in my bed, screaming my name.

I was not eager to let her go again.

The only thing that came close to marring our time together was Pippa's mysterious, unspoken boundaries. If I held her for too long after sex, she would squeeze out of my hold and act skittish about it.

But when I dangled the carrot of fucking in front of her again, she was on board. On board… and hungry for more.

For three days, I canceled my royal duties and just focused on Pippa. Even I am pushed to my limit, operating on almost no sleep.

I'm still sad to leave that little cabin, though. Even for this tour of the European Space Agency's facilities here in Denmark, which is pretty exciting.

As I place a hand on Pippa's lower back and rush her up to the European Space Agency building, she glances at my dark blue uniform. I shoot her a questioning look.

"What?" I ask.

She wrinkles her nose, plucking at the hem of her dark dress. "You look handsome in your uniform. That's all."

I grin. "You're having lustful thoughts about me while walking into what is sure to be a big boring meeting?"

Pippa sticks out her tongue at me. I laugh and hold the door open for her. Inside the building, everything is steel and glass, ultramodern in style. We are greeted right away in the lobby by a young woman who bows her head. "Your royal highness."

I nod. "We are here for a tour of where your astronauts work and train."

The dark-haired young woman blushes. "Yes, your highness. I'm Ingrid and I'll be showing you around today." She curtsies to Pippa, who squeezes my hand hard. She smiles at Pippa. "Ms. Welch. It's my pleasure to show the future princess around our facilities. If you two will just follow me?"

She turns and opens a door. Pippa and I follow her. Pippa shoots me a wide eyed look.

"The future princess?" she mouths silently. "Oh my god."

I shake my head, smothering a yawn. Pippa sees me do it and is immediately triggered into a yawn of her own. Ingrid looks back, catching Pippa's yawn.

"Would you like some refreshment, ma'am? Perhaps some coffee or water?"

She swipes her identification badge and unlocks a set of doors. Pippa smiles at her. "No, thank you."

Ingrid ushers us deeper into the building, showing us several pristine laboratories and a room devoted to 3D goggles.

"The young woman training in there right now is in a space simulator of the international space station's tiny food prep area. It's one of many such exercises that we have our astro-nauts-in-training run through."

I nod. "I imagine you have a simulation for almost every scenario."

Ingrid blushes, seeming uncertain what to do with her hands. "Yes, your royal highness."

I chuckle. "Please, call me Lars."

Pippa rolls her eyes. Ingrid tucks her hair behind her ear and gives me a shy smile.

"If you both will follow me, we'll go down to the spacewalk tank. I believe we should see someone using it…"

I wiggle my eyebrows at Pippa. She shoots me a filthy look.

"What?" I whisper, following Ingrid.

Pippa brushes back her hair, shaking her head. "You just can't turn it off, can you? Just let the poor girl do her job."

I smirk. "I don't know what you mean."

She drops her voice to a whisper. *"Oh Ingrid, please, call me Lars. I'm so charming and elegant and royal."*

I grin at her. "Is that jealousy I hear?"

Pippa looks irritated. "What? No."

"Are you sure about that, little witch?" I ask.

She shoots me a glare and pushes her shoulders back, hurrying after Ingrid. I press my cheek with my tongue, trying to decide just what to make of that.

Is Pippa really acting jealous? I mean, we did have four amazing nights together. But… she knows that it's going to come to an end.

…right?

We meander through the rest of the tour. I keep a close eye on Pippa, but she just seems irritable for most of the time. After the tour is complete, I shake hands with several generals and scientists that oversee the space program. Everyone is smiling, but I can sense an edge to Pippa's cool smile.

She also pulls out of any embrace I initiate after a few seconds.

By the time we finally get out of the building and into the chauffeured limo, I level her with a look. "You are pissed off at me?"

She licks her lips and looks out her window. "No. It's not… I'm just tired."

"I've known you for more than half my life, Pippa. I've seen you tired. I have never seen… whatever that was back there."

She puts her hands over her face and sinks lower in her seat. "Sorry."

I grab her elbow, slowly pulling one of her hands away from her face. "If we were trying to put on a happy front to the world today, we failed."

She squints. "*Ja. Ja*, I'm sorry. You, uh… you hit a nerve, I guess."

My eyebrows lift a little. "Wait, I did?"

"Oh god. This is so embarrassing." She sinks lower in her seat, her cheeks burning bright red. "You called me jealous. And a little voice in the back of my head knew you were right. God, how much of a child am I?"

She closes her eyes, shaking her head.

I pull at her hand, easing her onto my lap. "So… you got jealous. You didn't feel that way on purpose, did you?"

Her light blue eyes open just a slit. "No."

I run my fingers down her arm, enjoying how pale her skin is against mine. "It didn't hurt anyone, did it?"

She wrinkles her nose. "No. But… that's such a ridiculous thing to feel. I mean, we just basically hooked up one time. Like… that doesn't give me the right to feel jealous. Especially not just because you were flirting with some tour guide."

She lets out an exaggerated exhale.

My lips curve up. "I have to say, I didn't really expect jealousy from you. But as it turns out, green looks pretty damn good on you."

She eyes me. "I embarrassed you."

I let out a sharp bark of laughter. "Hah! No. I can't be embarrassed. I have an immunity."

She sighs again, sitting up. "I'm sorry, Lars."

I am tired of this conversation. So I change it by kissing her full, lush lips.

And she doesn't exactly seem to mind or protest…

2 0

PIPPA

I SWALLOW AS I WATCH THE PALACE GROW CLOSER AND CLOSER out the window of my limousine. Momse, Lars's grandmother, called me and personally invited me to a soiree she is throwing to celebrate our coming nuptials.

She barely let me get a word in edgewise about the party tonight. She just spent most of our brief time talking about what I would wear. At the end of the call, she said she'd just 'send some dresses over'.

Which is how I came to be wearing a very expensive, very fine strapless ballgown made of ivory silk. The dress itself is absolutely gorgeous. But as I try to adjust it while the limousine pulls around to the grand entrance, I remember all too well that the dress is very heavy.

Keeping that in mind, I touch the back of my hair, which has been piled up on my head. The car comes to a stop. I take a deep breath as the car door is opened for me.

Then I smile and get out of the back seat, only wobbling a little bit. This dress almost forces me to have perfect posture as it trails behind me. I hug my wrap, made of the same silk, and smile at the palace guards as I head inside.

A red carpet leads me up the stairs. My heart races thinking of all the people that I am going to lie to tonight.

At least no one would dare stop me and ask for my identification now. I'm a princess-to-be.

Or that's what everyone thinks, at least.

As I climb the stairs in my extravagant dress, I feel a few beads of sweat break out across my forehead. This dress may look like a fairytale, but it is hot and heavy.

As I come to the last stair, I see Lars waiting rather impatiently for me. He looks so dashing in his tuxedo that it actually takes my breath away.

He turns his head and spots me. A huge smile appears on his face. He walks towards me, his eyes taking me in. "Fuck, Pips. You look…" He shakes his head, biting his lip.

I flush a little. "Like the topper for a wedding cake, maybe?"

He offers me his arm, arching a brow. "I was going to say hot, but that's not quite it. Maybe… beautiful? Radiant?"

My neck heats. "Thanks. I'm glad that you find this dress acceptable. I think you're hot too, obviously."

He nods toward the ballroom. "Ready?"

I nod. "Why would I not be eager to enter a ballroom full of people that I plan on deceiving? Let's go."

He walks me in, a smirk on his face. I can hear the murmur of the crowd from here. When we step through the double doors, everyone immediately turns and ceases their conversations. All eyes are on us.

I can't help but swallow nervously. Lars is great and all, but at this exact moment I'm wishing that I had never agreed to his little plan.

"Lars!" His grandmother says. "I thought perhaps you two were not coming. After all, it is quite late…"

Lars rolls his eyes. "We're here, Momse."

His grandmother rushes up to us, taking our elbows and wedging herself in between us. She beams out at the crowd, which is relatively packed. "Every dignitary in Denmark is here right now, every military general and every polished socialite."

They are all looking at us, judging for themselves how Lars and I fit together.

I hate it.

Lars's grandmother clears her throat. "It is my pleasure to announce that Lars and Pippa have set a date for their wedding. It will be held in June, at the Royal Palace. Isn't that wonderful?"

I blink rapidly, my gaze going straight to Lars. His expression is questioning too.

Not only did we not set that date, it's also actually the first time I've ever even heard it and mentioned at all. Everyone in the audience applauds politely as Lars and I shower the room in our confused smiles.

Momse moves forward, glancing at both of us. She doesn't seem worried that she just announced a random date that we are supposed to get married on. "I'm so happy for both of you. Come, I have some people for you to meet."

Behind me, Lars finds my hand and gives it a squeeze.

For the next hour, I plaster on my smile and murmur *thank you* in response to everyone's well wishes. At one point, Lars is so antsy and ready to leave Momse's company that he keeps sighing. I look at him, my eyes begging him to take me with him. So he does the unthinkable: he just tells Momse flat out that we want to mingle alone.

"Pippa and I are going to take a turn around the room by ourselves, Momse. I'm sure you have a lot of people to talk to. Don't let us get in the way of that." He grabs my elbow, pulling me close.

Her eyes narrow. "Surely you can allow me this one night to celebrate you both."

He smiles lightly. "You got your hour on the arm of the new Prince and Princess. You've declared a wedding date. I think you've done enough."

Momse's eyes open quite wide. "I don't appreciate how you're talking to me right now, Lars."

He removes her hand from his arm, shaking off her grip. "Ja, I'm not Stellan. I'm not interested in politics or in whatever weird power play you're trying to pull right now. So Pippa and I are going to go over there and talk to our friends. And when we are tired, we're gonna leave. So…" He shrugs. "There you go."

With that, he takes my arm and pulls me away toward Stellan and Margot. I glance at him, my eyes wide. "What was that?"

He rolls his eyes. "Momse has some idea that we are going to dance to her feet now that we are supposedly engaged. It's better for both of us if we just don't let her boss us around, not even a little. Because if she is given an inch, she'll take a mile. Trust me on this."

He rakes his gaze over me, smiling a little sadly. I don't know what exactly he is talking about, but I lift my hand to touch his cheek, the gesture intimate enough to let him know that I hear what he's saying.

He slows down, turning to face me. Then he truly totally surprises me by sliding one hand around my waist and cupping my jaw with the other. He bends me back a little and kisses me so deeply and firmly that I forget everything else in the world.

For just a few seconds, it's just Lars and me. Just two bodies, all alone in the universe. His taste is on my lips, his scent in my nose, his hot hands on my sensitive skin…

I almost forget that we are not actually in a relationship, that we are not the real Prince and Princess. When he breaks away, I look up into his handsome face, my heart beating fast, my breath all but gone. Lars looks at me, a smile tugging at the corner of his mouth.

"Should we go talk to our friends, then?"

At this moment, he is irresistible to me. I nod slowly, grinning at him still.

Lars takes me by the hand and pulls me along toward Stellan and Margot. Stellan looks like a much more uptight version of Lars, all dark and tall and buttoned up and brooding. Margot still looks like a little pixie, although she has only recently stopped bleaching her hair. Instead, I see that she has had her hair professionally dyed, and it falls around her shoulders and face just so. She looks at me with genuine delight, raising her arms to embrace me.

I let go of Lars's hand, hurrying into Margot's embrace. I hug her hard, inhaling her cotton candy sent. "I have missed you so much. Where have you been?"

She pulls back, looking at me. "Where have I have been? Where have you been? I've been right here, trying to get the king to relax a little during the holiday."

Stellan frowns at us both. "Someone has to do the work around here. Keep the lights on, that sort of thing."

Lars beckons to Stellan, drawing him away. I have no idea what Lars is telling his brother, but I am glad for a little alone time with my bestie.

"What are you drinking?" I ask Margot.

She sighs, hooking her arm in mine. She lifts her cup, showing me the contents. "It's some blend of ciders or something. I asked for something hot and something nonalcoholic and this is all that they could come up with other than coffee." She wrinkles her nose. "One of the less amazing things about being… in the condition I am in."

I smirk. "Are you two still not telling people?"

"No, we decided to wait another month. Well, I decided. Luckily my husband is willing to bend on the issue at hand."

"Well, you let me know the second you can go shopping for baby necessities without causing a national crisis. Because I will be there with all the bells and whistles that I can carry."

She smiles up at me. "I'm really very glad that we are friends, Pippa. I mean, looking back five years, would you have imagined that we would be standing right here, with these men as our partners?"

A flash of guilt runs through me. I look away, frowning at an imagined sight on the other side of the ballroom. "Is that Annika?"

I feel bad for lying, especially to her. But I am completely certain that she wouldn't be able to conceal the truth from Stellan, and Stellan would come down hard on Lars. So I have to lie to her, for everyone's sake.

Her brow wrinkles as she searches the crowd. "I thought Annika and Erik were on some tropical vacation or something. I think you might've seen someone else."

I nod. "It's entirely possible."

Margot sighs. "I think I have to pee again. Will you excuse me?"

I look around as she slips away through the crowd, sucking in a deep breath. To my left, I can see Lars's grandmother talking to a group of people and sizing me up. I definitely don't want to be trapped talking to her, especially not after what Lars said to her earlier. So I take a sharp right turn, almost plowing into a gorgeous, very thin blonde in a hot pink, skintight dress.

"Oh! I'm so sorry," I apologize.

She laughs daintily, as if I have just told a funny joke. When she answers, her accent is clearly German or Austrian. "Oh, excuse me. I am so clumsy sometimes." She sticks out a hand. "I am Gretchen."

I grip her palm, shaking my head at the same time as I shake her hand. "It was all my doing. I'm Pippa, by the way."

She arches a brow. "Oh, I know who you are. I think everybody in this room knows who you are. It's nice to meet you, Pippa."

I blush. "Yes, I keep forgetting that I am engaged to the second most famous man here. It's all pretty new still."

"What's new?" Lars asks, coming up from behind me. His hands land on my waist and he pulls me a little closer to him, kissing the top of my head. I blush again, feeling like that gesture is something intimate and private, usually just kept between the two of us.

I look up at him, shooting him in a look. "Our engagement. I was just telling Gretchen here that I keep forgetting why everyone knows who I am already even though I don't know them."

He squeezes me a little. "*Ja*, it's true. She is still pretty starstruck by being engaged to me."

Without thinking about it, I actually glare at him and hit him on the shoulder. Gretchen titters at us.

"Look at the two of you. Aren't you just made for each other?"

GRETCHEN BEAMS AT BOTH OF US. I SLIDE MY GLANCE OVER TO Lars, expecting... Well, I'm not exactly sure what I was expecting.

Perhaps he would be looking at her in a certain way that indicated interest. Or laughing at what she just said even though it wasn't really a joke. Or if my own experiences being true of his style, he might even touch her wrist or slide his arm around her waist.

But instead, I look at him and find him staring directly at the dark and space between my breasts. He isn't even remotely listening to Gretchen. He isn't staring at her, even though she is tall and blonde and extremely thin and gorgeous. Not to mention she is wearing a dress that would shame the devil.

Lars doesn't even seem to notice her. He looks up at me, cocking a grin, and my cheeks flame scarlet. I can't do anything but give him a secretive smile. His intention is just so all-encompassing that I sink into his eyes for a long moment, forgetting that Gretchen even exists.

I bite my lower lip. He pulls me in closer, smirking a little. His fingers tighten on my waist.

I know that he is not actually mine. And I know that just because he's paying attention to me right now doesn't mean he will be in the future. But it feels so good to be looked at in this way, by this man, at this moment.

"Well, I can see you two are busy… If you will excuse me, I have to find the ladies room…" Gretchen says, smiling and wandering off.

I look up at Lars, wrinkling my nose. "Was that rude? It felt rude."

He shrugs a shoulder. "I couldn't care less. If I had to make a list of all the people who I was rude to in a day, I would never do anything else."

I quirk my lips. "As long as you're not rude to me, I suppose I don't have anything to say about that."

He draws me close, raising my chin with his finger. The press of his lips against mine is brief and not nearly deep enough for my liking. But we are in a ballroom full of people and we should probably be on our best behavior.

Lars sighs. "I have to catch Stellan again before we leave," he says. He frowns a little. "I think I actually know something that will help him in negotiations with the minister of Belgium. Do you mind if I just…?"

I smile. "Of course not. I'm actually going to step outside for a minute and just get some cool air. You wouldn't believe how hot this dress is."

Lars looks me up and down, a grin spreading across his face. "Oh, I believe it. You know where it's gonna look even better than it looks on you right now?"

I pull away from him, rolling my eyes and smiling. "If you say on your floor, I am going to revolt. And you should take that seriously, Prince Lars."

I waggle my finger at him, heading away toward the big balcony doors that open up into the night. A few people cast questioning glances at me as I pull open the door and let myself out into the chilly night. I shiver even as I sigh with relief. Hopefully no one is able to tell that I am as hot as I am. Under the full skirts of this dress, I'm wearing a lacy slip and a thong and both are plastered to my skin. I walk a few feet away from the doors toward the balcony, glancing down.

"Hello, Sylvie."

I freeze at the sound of Ms. Olson's voice. Turning my head, I find her looking in the shadows, talked away behind a stone pillar. My heartbeat races as I glance behind me nervously. "What are you doing here?"

Ms. Olson emerges from the shadows, showing off her slim figure in a bright red ball down. She gives me a cold little smile. "Visiting you, of course. I see that you took my advice and accepted Lars's proposal. Clever girl."

I gather my skirts, fisting the fabric. "You can't be here. You just… I don't even know who you are, but you need to leave. You are bothering me."

Ms. Olson gives a bark of laughter. "Bothering you? You should be thanking me. My organization made you and Lars happen."

I pause. Part of me wants to scream at her, tell her that there is no *me and Lars*. But the other, smarter part makes me fold my arms across my chest. "What is it that you want? I'm very close to calling a security guard, so I would make it quick if I were you."

She smirks at me. "Oh really? I don't think you're going to do any such thing, Sylvie. Not if you want to keep that precious sister of yours a secret, anyway."

I shake my head, turning to go inside. "This is crazy. You're crazy."

"All I'm asking is for a few questions to be answered. Surely that is worth your secret being kept, no? Because otherwise, I will go straight to Queen Margot and tell her who you really are."

I slow. "I don't know what you think I can do for you. I don't know anything. Lars is not the head of state or anything. He's just…"

"Just the brother of the king. And that's fine. I just have a couple of questions. Specifically, I would like to know what Lars's position in the Danish Royal Air Force is and whether or not he has much contact with Colonel Ahmad."

I cock a hip and cross my arms, turning to glare at her. "I don't know the answer to that. How would I even go about finding out the answer to that question?"

Her smile is staid. "I also want to know if the younger Løve brothers have girlfriends or boyfriends. Is there anyone on the horizon for either of them?"

I scrunch up my face, disbelieving. "What? I don't know."

"Well, I would make it your business to find out. When you do, you can dial my number in the prepaid phone I gave you. I won't answer, but you can give the message to whoever picks up the phone." She smiles again. "That's all I really require at the moment."

I shake my head. "You're insane. Just… Don't contact me again. I don't care what you threaten me with. It can't be worse than thinking I am plotting against the country of Denmark."

"Oh, Sylvie. Do me a favor before you go telling anybody about these little meetings of ours. I would check my phone first." She whirls on her heel, heading back into the shadows. I shiver against the cool breeze that picks up, turning toward the balcony doors again.

I slip inside and immediately start searching the room for Lars. The need to be near him, to be protected by him, is intense right now. Or maybe it's the other way around and I feel like I'm protecting him? Either way, I have to find him.

After looking around for him for a few minutes, I finally find him talking to Stellan just outside the ballroom doors. When he looks up and sees me heading his way, his eyebrow rises. "What's going on?" he asks.

I smile at Stellan, putting my hand on Lars's arm. "Do you mind if I just borrow him for a second?"

"Be my guest," Stellan says, waving his arm.

Looking both ways up and down the hall, I lick my lips and pull Lars toward the first room that seems unoccupied.

21

PIPPA

I flush, looking over my shoulder as Lars hustles me out of the room. He's right; his grandmother is glaring at me now.

I turn around and hurry after Lars. I glimpse Stellan talking very intently with two of the palace staff just outside the doors. Lars quickly heads the other way, trying not to draw attention as he opens another door.

He hurries me inside what looks like an ill used study. Light pours in the window, spilling across several large pieces of furniture that have been draped with protective white cloth.

Lars looks around, one brow raised. "I don't think I've ever even been in this room before."

I walk over to a cloth-draped desk, lifting the corner to peek at the massive oak shape below. "We are honestly just lucky that you chose this room and not a mop closet."

"You are right about that," he agrees. He looks around the room and then shrugs. Taking a seat on the cloth-covered couch, he coughs a little from the dust released.

I wrinkle my nose and plop down beside him. A plume of dust rises, landing in a fine sheet over both of us.

Lars shakes his head at that, sipping his champagne. "Now you've done it. We are both ruined. If we go back to the dinner, we'll both look like we rolled around in a pile of ashes."

I scrunch my face up. "Maybe that's what I was going for."

He flashes me a smirk. Slipping a finger under his necktie, he loosens it. "Might as well get comfortable, then. Once everybody has had a few glasses of wine, they are less likely to notice a pair of sewer rats in their number."

I laugh at that. Lars grins; he's always trying to make me laugh and only sometimes succeeding.

"Okay. Well, I'm taking off my heels. They are absolutely killing my feet."

I stand up and take my shoes off, letting them fall on the ground. When I sit back down, I realize that I am close enough to Lars that our knees knock together. Instantly I start to get up again, thinking to give him some space.

But Lars grabs my wrist. "Where are you going now?"

Heat sizzles along my skin. I look up at him, blushing.

"Nowhere, really."

He leans closer to me, giving me a delicate sniff. "You smell good. I mean, you always smell good. You smell of roses right now, though."

I give an awkward titter. "And what do you smell like?" I sniff his chest. "You smell like pine trees and…" I give another sniff. "What is that called? Like right after it rains?"

He throws me another smirk. "Petrichor."

I nod, leaning back. "Of course you know the name for that smell."

He grins. "Well, Ja. It is a natural phenomenon."

I pull a face, sipping my wine. "Sure."

He seems amused. "I see you're back on the champagne then. I could swear you avowed never to drink again after New Year's Eve."

I squint down at my glass, shrugging. "Well, I definitely thought that I was going to die on New Year's day. Which, by the way, you conveniently disappeared for."

He smiles. "I thought I would just do us both a favor and get dressed. And then I had time to think about how I should work out…"

"You didn't just want to avoid me, then?"

He shoots me an innocent look. "No. Why would I?"

I blow out a breath. "Because… we made out the night before?"

He rolls his eyes. "I make out with a lot of girls, Pippa. It's perfectly natural."

I tilt my head at him. "Is it?"

He arches a brow. "For two people who are as close as we are and as attractive as we are to kiss? I would say so, yes."

My cheeks redden. I bite my lip, playfully eyeing him. "You think I'm attractive?"

He scoffs. "Oh, please. It goes both ways. Don't think I don't notice you staring when I take my shirt off."

I squint at him. "Do not."

He sets his glass aside, leveling me with a look. "Look. It was just a kiss. I can kiss you right now. It doesn't mean anything."

Before I know it, he's grabbing me around the waist. My heartbeat skyrockets. I try to bring my hands up to block him, but he captures both of them and brings his lips down on mine.

He tugs at my waist, pulling me into the kiss. I soften against him, under the heat of his lips pressed firmly against mine.

My cheeks feel hot as I let my eyelids slide closed.

22

PIPPA

LARS LEANS DOWN, CUPPING ONE BREAST AND PULLING THE nipple to his mouth. I immediately groan at the sensation of his hot, wet mouth on my flesh. He rolls it around with his tongue, then bites it very carefully, almost like he's testing me.

"Ahh!" I gasp. "God, that feels so good."

He smirks, looking up at me. "Everything I do to your body should feel that good."

Then he elbows me aside, lying down. I look at him a little quizzically, but in the next second he lifts me onto his body, so that I'm straddling him. He angles me so that he's planted face first between my breasts, and my bare ass is in the air. I'm a little shocked at how easily he picked me up, but he clearly has other things on his mind.

He licks the skin between my breasts with his tongue, then pulls one nipple into his mouth. I moan as he bites it and sucks it, alternating pain and pleasure for me. His hands wander down to my hips. He runs his hands over my ass, groaning as he shapes my body.

He releases my breast with a wet pop, looking up at me. *"Fuck.* Do you know how turned on I am?"

I blush, slowly shaking my head. "Uh uh."

He pushes my hips down until my pussy is pressed directly against his cock through his unbuttoned jeans. We both groan as he bucks up against me. He runs his hand through my hair, fisting it, and uses his hand on my hip to guide me just where he wants me.

I gasp silently as he lifts his hips and bears down on me, his denim-clad cock almost touching my clit. He starts kissing and licking my neck. He sucks the spot where my neck meets my shoulder, bucking his hips up, and my eyes roll back into my head.

"Fuck!" I cry. "Lars—"

He's not satisfied with that, though. He releases me, pushing me off of his lap. I'm left breathing hard. He gets up and starts to peel his jeans off.

I'm taken aback for a moment by the image of Lars, completely naked. He's all muscle, his cock juts proudly out... and right now, he's looking at me like he's going to consume me.

He climbs onto the bed, dragging me down to lie beneath him, and he starts kissing my neck again. I wrap my arms and legs around him, pulling him closer. I can feel his hardness against my thigh, long and hot and throbbing. He sucks at my neck, my breasts, and then he moves lower.

I don't know if I can even handle his mouth on my clit, but he passionately kisses my thighs and my knees. His five o'clock shadow tickles me in the best way. I open my legs wide for him, spreading my thighs. He makes a growling sound as he kisses my clit, and my whole body is suddenly alive with electric sensation.

"Oh my god!" I cry out, my hands burying in his hair.

Already, I'm bucking my hips against his mouth, desperate for more. He closes his mouth around my clit and sucks on it in long pulls, each one sending ripples of sensation up my spine. My toes curl as he brings his hand up to my pussy and introduces one thick finger. He ever so slowly pushes his finger inside as he circles my clit with his tongue.

I come suddenly, clenching and crying out. His tongue slows, helping me ride out my orgasm. Soon though, he climbs up my body, kissing me hard. I taste the faint flavor of my own juices on his tongue and shudder.

He pulls back a little bit, grasping his cock and positioning himself just so. The blunt tip of his cock presses against my pussy, and I still for just a second. I'm busy looking at his cock, biting my lip with anticipation of how he's about to stretch me out. He pushes inside the barest inch.

I gasp, feeling so full of his hot cock.

Lars glances down at me, biting his lip. "You're so tight, Pippa."

I'm honestly not sure if that's a good thing or not, judging by his face alone. He looks like he's trying to defuse a bomb or something. I wrap my legs around his hips, pulling at him a little, urging him onward.

He closes his eyes and pushes himself inside, inch by slow inch. I feel like he's stretching me out, little by little, filling me up and touching every single part of me. It's uncomfortable, even though I'm wet, but I push for more. When he is finally inside me to the hilt, he opens his eyes, staring down at me with the most intense aquiline gaze I've ever experienced.

I look him right in the eye, remembering that I'm in love with him. I don't care that his dick is so big that it hurts a little; I'm too busy being stupidly, dumbly in love with Lars.

I reach up to pull his mouth down to mine, tenderly kissing him. He kisses me back, starting to move his body, withdrawing his cock and then thrusting back in.

"Ahhh, that's so good," he mutters, raising himself up so that he can see our bodies joined together. "Fuck, Pippa. God, you're so damned beautiful."

He grabs my wrists and pulls them up above my head, working his thick cock in and out of my pussy. I dig my heels into his upper back as he starts kissing and biting my neck again. I start to forget the discomfort, focusing instead on the pleasure of his lips on my skin, the wonderful weight of his body against mine.

I moan as he releases my hands in order to palm my breasts. It feels natural to wrap my arms around him, to lightly rake my fingernails down his back.

Lars suddenly withdraws from me, flipping me over. He guides me to my hands and knees, positioning his cock at my entrance before he plunges back inside.

"Ohhh!" I cry out, feeling my innermost muscles clench.

"Your pussy feels so good," he grits out. He takes my hand and guides it down to my clit, rubbing it in gentle circles. "I want you to come. Show me what a good girl you are. Make yourself come for me."

His words send a shudder of pleasure down my spine. He lets go of my hand and grabs my hips, thrusting his cock into me again and again, as hard as he can. I call out, an insensible sound, as I start to touch myself.

The way he is fucking me now is rougher, coarser than before… but for some reason I like it more. A lot more. I close my eyes, rubbing my clit, and feeling the brutal way he handles me, ramming into me over and over again.

An invisible spring tightens deep inside me with every thrust, feeding my craving. My fingers help me along, but it's really Lars's cock that makes little ripples of pleasure swell and burst across my body.

He's touching some spot deep inside me, a spot that I seem to be able to angle my body just so to encourage him to hit over and over again.

"Yes," I groan desperately. "Yes, right there… I…"

And then I'm calling out his name, screaming it, as I go over the edge, falling into a deep ocean of pleasure. He stiffens and growls, filling me with three single, brutal thrusts. I can feel him pulsing inside my pussy.

He slows at last, half-collapsing on the bed with me. He turns me over, kissing me tenderly.

I curl up against his chest, completely satisfied, and feel like a warm glove has been wrapped around my body.

23

LARS

"MOVE THAT STACK OF BOXES RIGHT OVER HERE BY THE DOOR," I say. "Be careful."

"Sir." The mover hauls the last of Pippa's boxes into the huge main room of my loft apartment and sets them down.

I smile at him, passing him a fat wad of cash as a tip. "Thank you. And remember, Pippa and I are really not telling anyone that we are moving in together yet. So if by chance someone tells the newspapers about us living together, I'm going to blame you. I'm going to blame your company. You don't want to know what kind of legal headaches that will entail for you guys. Okay?"

He swallows, nodding. "Yes, sir."

He hurries off down the hall, pressing the elevator button insistently. As soon as he is in the elevator and the doors are closed, I turn around and look at my messy apartment. There are boxes on every surface and I've given up two entire closets to Pippa's enormous clothes collection. But I did actually convince her to move in… At least for the time being.

Pippa sticks her head out of the bedroom, brushing back her magnificent curls. "Is that the last of the boxes?"

"It was," I say, smirking a little as I sauntered towards her. "You're officially a resident now."

She rolls her eyes, a little flush rising in her cheeks. "I'm not officially anything and you know it. This whole moving in business is just to further your little deception. Let's not forget that."

I sidle up to her in the doorway of my bedroom, leaning against the frame and leaving only a few inches between us. "I hear you talking, but I don't see your point." I look down at her loose black tank top and black leggings, running a finger down her shoulder and into her cleavage. She giggles, embarrassed, and smacks my hand away.

"I am busy unpacking!" she protests. She can't help but grin as she says it though. "Look, I'll make you a deal. We will unpack a whole room and then after we're done with that, we will take a break together. Does that sound okay?"

I pull a face. "You're no fun. Didn't I offer to have people sent here from the royal palace to unpack your things for you?"

She shoots me a look. "This is what normal couples do. They move in together and they are messy and they don't have servants to attend to their every need. People all over the world do this exact same thing. Whether they're in a real relationship or not."

I groan and roll my eyes. "*Ja*, whatever. Just promise me that when we finally get naked, you will let me do that thing I brought up last night."

She glances at me, wide-eyed. "Are you talking about… *anal?*"

I wink at her. "I may be. Have I ever done anything to you that you didn't like?"

She gives her head a tiny shake. "No."

"Then start unpacking somewhere. Pick a room." I frown. "A *small* room. Let's get this show on the road."

She looks around with a sigh. Pursing her lips, she heads toward the second bedroom. "I might as well start in the closet. I can't think of the last time that I even looked in your spare bedroom…"

She pads down my hallway and disappears inside the second bedroom. I follow her with a frown. It's not that I don't trust her, per se. It's just that there are several boxes tucked away in the walk in closet that are full of my personal things.

Childhood mementos, long distance use sportswear items, and some heavy jackets that have been long forgotten about. Blowing out a breath, I turn and head out of my second bedroom and start grabbing the heavier boxes. Pippa may be mostly disorganized, but she is on top of her packing and moving game. Every box has a tag with specific components that can be found within the boxes contents. *Dress shirts, summer.* Or *books, not for rereading.*

I sort through the boxes, starting with the heaviest ones, and figure that I should bring her the clothes into the closet she'll be using first. It turns out that Pippa has a million different boxes of clothes, at least forty percent of what she owns.

So for a little while, it's just a lot of moving boxes into the spare bedroom. I stack them all neatly by the wall and figure that she will just find the ones that she needs. After I move things for a while though, I get curious about what Pippa is up to.

I stick my head into the walk in closet, finding Pippa up on her knees, sifting through a box of my stuff. A knot forms in my stomach. She wasn't supposed to be looking at any of my old stuff. She's just supposed to be making room for hers.

But when she turns her head and looks at me with the biggest, brightest grin, the knot loosens a little.

She raises a picture of all of the Løve siblings, taken when I was probably four years old. We are wearing matching naval uniforms and all looking bored. "I didn't mean to find this," she swears. "But look at how serious you were as a child. Look at your face!"

I sigh. "*Ja*, I like the fact that we are all wearing matching outfits. Somebody thought that was a good idea, apparently."

She wrinkles her nose. "I think it's kind of cute actually." She takes the picture back from me, sticking it back in the box full of mementos. Just underneath it is a plastic binder that I vaguely recognize. I step in the closet and reach down, pulling the binder loose.

My lips curl up. "Ah. So, I remember this well. My English tutor as a kid was a failed poet. So we all had to learn about poetry." I laugh a little, flipping through the pages. "Here's the very cutesy poem that I did about a ladybug."

Pippa gets to her feet, coming over and peering over my arm. "The ladybug has tons of spots, which should go on and on, red and black…"

She looks at me, touching my arm. "You're adorable. I mean, you were adorable. But also, that you are now."

I hand her the sheaf of papers, clearing my throat. "I'll have you know that I did the best out of all my siblings on this specific subject, according to the would-be poet. So there you go."

She grins, returning the paper to the box and tucking it inside before closing the flaps. "You mind moving this over there?" She points. "I'm trying to make space."

I grunt and move the box for her. She sort of sighs. "It figures you would be good at that. You're good at everything. When we were in school together, I was often jealous of the fact that you were just effortlessly talented at everything."

I cock a brow. "It is hard to be in the presence of perfection, I can only assume."

She shakes her head, continuing as if I hadn't spoken. "God, remember how we both got really into photography for a while there? You were so good at it. It drove me nuts."

My lips twitch. "Ja, I think when we were around fifteen years old. I had a dark room installed in the royal palace, as I remember. I spent many hours there for about three months and then…" I shrug.

Her lips curl up. "I think that was right around the age that you discovered how to drive. Another thing that you are just so stupidly good at. Ugh, was there anything that you weren't naturally good at?"

I roll my eyes. "Well, it helps that I came in second to Stellan at basically everything. Not only at being the crown prince, but almost everything else as well. I only look good to you because you aren't witnessing how badly I was beaten in every competition on a regular basis."

Her eyes narrowed a little on my face. "What? What competitions were you and Stellan part of?"

I turn around, shaking my head. Walking out of the door, I yell back at her. "Anything and everything. Stellan was groomed to be the king from an early age. And I was always kept as his backup. It was fucked up, looking back at it. I didn't know that at the time, though."

I walk out into the main area of my apartment, pursing my lips. My eyes roam around, trying to decide which box to pick up next.

Pippa follows me out of the bedroom, a frown on her face. "Give me an example."

I shrug. "I don't know. When we were in school together, before I was sent to St. Matthews, we would often go head to head over spelling or naming the world capitals. Or really *any* subject. And it seemed like Stellan, for only being a year older than me, easily had the answers to everything. It wasn't fair, or didn't seem that way at the time."

Her lips press into a thin line. "That sucks. I'm sorry."

"My entire life growing up I was compared to Stellan, told that I was the second choice. You know, until Stellan reached eighteen, I wasn't allowed to do anything fun. Nothing dangerous, nothing risky, nothing that could possibly put me in harm's way."

Pippa tilts her head a little. "I remember there being a long list of things you were supposed to do, yes. I also remember that you and I did most of them anyway." She smiles a little. "Remember when we climbed up that mountain and all the teachers at St. Matthew's were looking for us for hours? God, we caused much trouble."

I smile at that. "I remember that we both forgot to wear sunscreen on that trip and we got back to the school and had the worst sunburn ever. I just remember that I couldn't sleep because I was so sunburned."

Pippa sidles up to me, catching my wrist and pulling me closer. I grab her around her waist and lift her up, my lips lifting as well. "I thought we are supposed to be unpacking things."

She wrinkles her nose and presses a kiss to my lips. Maybe I was hasty, deciding not to take advantage of the helpers that you offered. I forgot that unpacking things is just so boring."

A deep rumble slips from my chest. "You know what's not boring?"

Her eyebrows raise a little bit. "What?"

I wiggle my eyes brows at her. "I'm so glad you asked."

I carry her into my bedroom, kicking the door closed behind me, and she giggles with glee.

24

LARS

"Just keep going," I say aloud to myself. "No matter what, just keep going."

I'm jogging on a treadmill hooked up to the space agency's many machines, measuring my heart rate, pulls, oxygen level, and of course speed. I've been running for almost twenty minutes now and I'm starting to feel some serious fatigue.

That really is the point of this test; what happens when I feel fatigue?

Sweat rolls down my brow, soaking my shirt. I'm aware of a tiny bit twinge in my left foot, just above the heel. But I don't let myself be distracted by it. Instead, I look straight ahead and count to myself. Someone a long time ago told me that counting to thirty would give me the purpose needed to run any length of time. And I have kept it going since then. I just count to thirty then start over again.

The clock to the right of my field of vision hits twenty minutes, blinking in bright red letters. I slow my pace on the treadmill, breathing hard. I'm used to running ten miles every day as a regular course of affairs, but I'm rarely running flat out as I am now.

I spend about half a minute slowing my pace, coming to a halt finally. I'm winded, sucking in deep long pulls of air, leaning on the treadmills arms as I press the stop button.

"Very good," the older doctor says, stepping in front of me. He smiles at me kindly, motioning for me to get down off the treadmill. "Please, come down. We can remove all your guide wires now."

I breathe out. "How did I do?"

The doctor smiles lightly. "You did well, I'm very sure."

"*Ja?* How did I do in comparison with the other candidates?"

He gives me a cool little smile. "I'm sure you did well."

He removes the guide wires and the bits of plastic stuck to my chest then steps back. "That's all we need right now. Have a good day, your royal highness."

He motions toward the locker room, bowing again.

"Thanks." I pick up my water bottle and drink from it as I walk out into the locker room. It's late in the day, past six o'clock. Still light outside, but because it's the weekend there is almost no one else in this locker room.

I power through showering and changing, heading outside to the cool stone corridor of the Royal Air Force Base. The second I step outside of the locker room, I see Erik leaning against the wall, obviously waiting for me. I arch a brow.

"How did you know that I would be here??

He gives me a little smirk. "The secretary at the royal press office was feeling especially chatty today. She said that you were doing an endurance test for the space program. I figured you might want to grab a bite to eat when you got out of the test."

I run my hand through my dark, damp hair, nodding. "Ja. As it happens, Pippa is eating dinner with Margot and Nika tonight."

He rolls his eyes, smiling. "I know that. That's why I came to find you."

I squint. "Oh. Maybe I need to eat more than I thought I did. It's proving hard to think right now."

He claps me on the shoulder and turns me toward the base's exit. "Come on, I want to go get a steak. Have some real manly food." He will wiggles his brows, teasing

I let him drive me to a place not far from the base, a little hole in the wall that serves steak and potatoes and cold beer. We walk into the dimly lit restaurant, looking around at the four plastic tables surrounded by a clutter of chairs. Two of the tables are occupied so we take the farthest one back. I laugh a little as Erik chooses between two small chairs, which is only funny because Erik is the only person that I know that is taller than me.

We sit down, my stomach rumbling. One waitress comes out of the back with a platter of sizzling steaks, rushing towards one of the other tables. I groan a little bit. When the waitress drops off the steaks and comes by, I make sure to order a steak and two potatoes and a giant glass of cold beer. Erik orders the same, but he adds an order of cheesy bread as well. I cock a brow at him, but he just shrugs.

"I ran ten miles this morning. I can carbo load all I want."

The waitress comes back quickly with our beers and an order of bread and we dig in. The beer is nice and frothy, the bread hot and cheese melty. I nod, voicing my appreciation.

"You're right. This is pretty much heaven after exercising so much."

His lips twitch. "I'm glad. It seems like it's been a really long time since we have had a chance to catch up. It's been what, almost six weeks?"

I nod. "*Ja.* At the same time though, it seems like it's only been a week or something. It's funny how life becomes so busy."

He slides me a sly glance. "Ja, I bet it has. I heard that you moved in with your new fiancée."

My head bobs. "She moved in this week. It's been... Well, a lot of fucking, frankly."

He snorts into his beer. "That I am sure of. Things are going well for you two otherwise, I guess? I mean, at least neither of you has Queen Ida on your back. I'll tell you this right now, she really caused a lot of tension in the early days of me and Nika."

"Truth be told, I don't think that I would've asked Pippa to marry me if it wasn't for my grandmother butting her nose in. It was that or I would probably be engaged to some older minister's granddaughter. Take your pick."

That seems to have been the wrong thing to say. Erik shoots me a look that isn't happy. "Wait, you asked Pippa to marry you because your grandmother put pressure on you? That isn't very romantic."

I purse my lips. Taking a second to have a swig of my beer, I shrug one shoulder. "My reason for the engagement really has nothing to do with my relationship with Pippa. The engagement is really just for show."

His eyes narrow on my face. "Are you trying to tell me that you and Pippa are not an item?"

I shake my head. "No, we are an item. Or… we are something. But we definitely got engaged just to pacify my grandmother. Without Momse, we would probably still just be two very attractive people, not looking to settle down at all."

He squints at me. "I thought you had been in love with Pippa for a thousand years or something."

I shoot him a glare. "It's a lot more complicated than that. Besides, I've never said that I was in love with anybody at any point."

Erik pulls off another piece of bread, pointing it at me. "No, you'd never admitted it. But if you think I didn't know what was going on, you're crazy. That's why I kept bugging you about getting together with her."

I roll my eyes. Looking around, I wave the waitress down. "Two more beers?"

I turn back to the conversation, sighing aloud. "I'll admit to you, Erik. I'm as unlikely now as I was then to listen to you tell me about how perfect Pippa is for me."

He raises his brows. "Really? Name one way in which she is lacking."

I shoot him a glare. "Don't say it like that. She's not lacking. It's just… You know, I'm supposed to go to space at some point…" I purse my lips. "And there's… There's this wall that she has…"

He tilts his head. "You're gonna have to be more specific. You mean like Hadrian's Wall or the Great Wall of China or…"

I wave off his silly answers. "No, no. Like there is this wall between me and her. This like wall that blocks off a certain part of her from… I don't know, being intimate I guess."

He frowns. "How does that happen exactly?"

I suck in a breath, finishing the last of my beer. "Well, it's like… We will be lying in bed, just after we finished fucking. And will be like… looking in each other's eyes or whatever. And then I suddenly will see a little bit of fear run across her face. And then I just like come up against this wall. It's like one second she's there, the next second she's rolling over and burying her head under the pillows. She just doesn't want to be that close to me, I guess."

He looks thoughtful. "I see. I mean, I don't really see? But I can imagine. I've never gotten that close to Pippa, honestly. But I can see that you are frustrated."

The waitress brings a fresh round of beers and I take a sip of the refreshing brew. I nod my head a little bit. "Ja. So between that and the whole *I might be going to space* thing… It's not perfect, is what I'm getting at."

He picks up his beer, regarding me over the rim. After a long swallow, he sets his glass down. "It sounds like she knows about you going to space, right?"

I nod.

"Then it sounds like she's sticking around for the long haul. So I would definitely bear that in mind."

I push out my cheek with my tongue. "Ja, she has already set a deadline on this whole wedding business. We're supposed to pull the escape latch when it's been four months."

He frowns. "Pull the escape latch? What, from your relationship? Are you serious? How are you gonna do that?"

My neck heats and I give him sheepish look. "I hadn't thought that far, honestly."

"She's crazy, if that's really what she intends to do. Because I will bet you more money than either of us has that she loves you as much as you love her. It's obvious enough if you spend two minutes with the two of you."

I roll my eyes. "She doesn't love me. She's just playing along because I begged her to do this as a favor for me."

He looks unimpressed. "I say that she's doing it for love. Those are the facts, man. She loves you. She's known you for half of your life and yet she still loves you like crazy."

"If she does love me, which I doubt, she has a funny way of showing it. I'm telling you, this wall of hers is impenetrable. There is no getting through it. And when her wall is up? It's useless trying to get around it."

One corner of Erik's mouth curls up. "I think that's your challenge, my friend. No one said that love was going to be easy, did they?"

I exhale a long breath. "I think there is a difference between loving someone from a distance and really falling in love with a girl. Right? I mean, I've loved the person that Pippa is for a long time. But it's almost easier in a way to love someone as a friend because all those little imperfections and quirks… You can just let those go. That can be okay because you are friends. But loving someone in a deeper, more meaningful way?" I shake my head and take a sip of my beer. "That isn't for everyone."

Our steaks arrive, sizzling and smelling absolutely amazing. We dig in, the conversation naturally sliding onto easier topics. But Erik's words ring through my head for hours afterward.

Could Pippa really love me? Or more to the point, could I really be in love with her?

That idea unsettles me as much as it excites me and I can't get the thought out of my head.

2 5

LARS

Finn takes off his shirt and cracks his neck, standing up straight. He passes his gaze around the small locker room, biting his lip. "Thanks for inviting me here, big brother. Ever since I got back from climbing Mount Kilimanjaro in Kenya, I've felt like my whole system is out of whack or something. I think what I need is really a good long soak."

I shed my T-shirt, standing up. "No problem. After all, how often do we get the chance for a little bonding time? You're always out of the country."

Finn smiles, pushing his hand through his dark wavy hair. At the moment, he is letting his hair grow out a little, so it is hanging down in his eyes in the front. Not my style exactly, but it does let me know what I would look like if I ever decided to grow out my military style haircut. His eyes twinkle a little mischievously.

"I can't believe I asked Kalindi and she actually agreed to come. I figured that she would say that she was too busy or something."

I cock a brow at him. "*Ja?* I always thought that she kind of liked you, at least the few times that Nika has brought her around. I figured that she just had better things to do than to waste time with either of us. I mean… We're not even the *good* royals."

Finn cracks a smile at that. "You are right about that. We are the second and third string of the royal family, for sure." He wrinkles his nose. "I don't know, I kind of like it this way though. I mean, Stellan is so consumed with being king. I am not consumed with any particular thing except for whatever passing fancy I might have. It's pretty great, I'm not gonna lie."

I shake my head. "You won't hear any argument from me. Come on, let's go out to meet the girls."

I slip on my sandals and head out to the natural hot spring, shivering at the cold air. We're outside here, surrounded by several natural steaming pools and steely gray skies above.

I look around and don't see Pippa or Kalindi, so I take a spring at random, dipping my toe in. I'm satisfied with how hot it is, so I walk to the bench and slip off my shoes, noting that there are fresh towels hanging on a towel warmer above the bench.

I turn around and check what Finn is doing but he is off looking into the distance, doing whatever it is that Finn does. So I climb into the hot spring, making a funny face at the incredibly hot water as I slide in.

I breathe out for a minute, circulating a little. The water is a little higher than my bellybutton, with some stone benches on one side of the little pool that I'm in. Finn joins me soon after, making the same face that I did when he gets in.

"Woo, this is really *hot*."

"That it is, little brother. I'm starting to like it though. Especially if you duck down and sit so that the water covers your shoulders? That's pretty much where it's at, as far as I'm concerned."

I swim over to the other side of the pool and sit on the stone bench, breathing a sigh of relaxation. That's a moment at which I hear Pippa talking, laughing a little as she coaxes Kalindi outside.

"Come on. Seriously, there's no one out here…" Pippa steps out, gesturing to a hidden person. My eyes dip down from Pippa's curtain of glorious hair to her barely there bikini. I can see practically everything, her boobs, her hips, her ass…

When she turns to face me, I can see her nipples standing out from the tiny black triangles of fabric over her to it. I bite my lip appreciatively. She sees me and sees the look on my face. She makes eye contact with me and reddens, laughing.

She turns back toward Kalindi. "Okay, you may want to bring a towel out or something. Granted, it's only our men that can see us but…"

Finn settles then on the other end of the bench, about ten feet away from me. Pippa finally manages to coax Kalindi out of the changing room. Kalindi is small and dark-haired, a young British girl of Middle Eastern descent. Her arms and legs are shapely, I'll give her that. But if there is more to see, I have no idea. Because she shuffles out to the pool, clambering in and removing her towel inch by inch as she does.

Not my Pippa though. She kicks her shoes off and smoothly descends into the water, her smile bright. "Oh, this is nice. How have I never been here before?"

She wades over to where I'm sitting, taking a seat beside me. Kalindi looks a little lost and out of place, her gaze starting from the empty seat between Pippa and then to the empty pools around us.

"Are you sure that we are not each supposed to get our own pool?"

"You are welcome to get another pool if you want. But that will require getting out of this pool, which I assume will be freezing cold. So make your choice carefully." Pippa winks at her.

Kalindi eventually settles into the last seat on the bench, glancing at Finn like he is about the most attractive thing in the world. I roll my eyes. Finn is a daredevil like I am, but he also loves to travel and seems very worldly. He attracts a certain kind of girl, and apparently Kalindi is one of those. Not that I particularly care, because I have a hard time paying attention to anyone that isn't Pippa.

"This is so nice," Pippa sighs. I can't wait to get my hands on her. So I beckon her over.

"Wait until you have been massaged while you are in the water." Turning her around with gentle hands, I start rubbing her neck and her shoulders. Pippa makes the most contented sort of sounds. That in itself really fills up some missing part of me that is been empty for too long. I'm not getting any gratification from this exchange other than the amazing feeling of a very wet Pippa under my hands. But it still gives me an unadulterated kind of joy when she tips her head back and lets out a breathy little moan.

We hang out for a little bit, Finn and Kalindi talking, Pippa and I mostly just enjoying touching each other innocently. There is a moment when Pippa puts her hand on my knee. I can't help but get excited whenever she so much as touches me like that. She gives me a naughty smile as she caresses my inner thigh, teasing me a little.

That's when I start to get hard under the water. At the same time, Kalindi and Finn are getting a little too hot to stay in the spring anymore. Finn turns to me, standing up. "We're gonna go ahead and go inside and get changed for the next little while. I think that this place offers food so we are going to try to grab a little smorgasbord to bring outside. Okay?"

"*Ja*. Thanks. I think we will stay outside for a little while longer." My eyes slide to Pippa. I cock a brow. "Right?"

Her face is already quite flushed from the heat of the pool but she turns even redder under my gaze. She nods. "That sounds great."

Kalindi seems to struggle to get out of the other end of the pool. Finn splashes over and jumps out, pulling her out of the water with both hands. For second, my gaze is riveted on Kalindi's body.

For being such a slight person, she has a huge ass. And her jiggly breasts are just incredible. Even buried in the rather modest black bikini she is wearing, she's definitely worth looking at.

Apparently I stare a second too long because Pippa smacks me on the arm, sounding a little angry when she calls my name. "Lars! Seriously?"

I look over at her and she is wearing a look of anger and disappointment, her curly red hair slicked back and her cheeks rosy. "You don't have anything to say for yourself?"

Not really knowing what else to do, I get defensive without really thinking about it. "What, I can't look at another girl?"

Pippa levels me with a glare. "Not like that you can't. You're just lucky that she wasn't looking. If she had been, she probably would have been horrified. At the very least, it's embarrassing. To her, but also to you."

I narrow my eyes at her. "I'll be the judge of what I find embarrassing, okay?"

Pippa smacks me on the arm again. "I want you to apologize."

"To whom? You just said that Kalindi didn't see me."

She makes an aggravated sound. "To me, you... you *caveman*. As if I didn't already have enough to worry about."

I give her a puzzled look. "What? What do you mean?"

She pushes a hand through her damp red curls. "Lars, I live in a world where I worry all the time about whether or not you will still find me attractive if I gain a pound or get a little older. I worry about that all the time. And for you to stare at Kalindi like that, so openly, just... It undermines all the work that I've done to reassure myself. I tell myself that I am being crazy worrying about these things, but this doesn't help me feel that it's true.

My mouth opens, but no words come out. Usually I don't hear Pippa say things like this out loud and to hear them now, said in anger, is just a little shocking.

Before I can say anything or disagree, she pushes away from me, making a disgusted sound. She starts to climb out of the pool. But I'm not about to just let her run away from me after lobbing a grenade like that.

"Oh no you don't," I say, grabbing her by the waist and pulling her back into the water. "We need to talk about this."

She spins in my arms, looking up at me with anxious eyes. "Maybe I was a little too honest there," she says very softly.

I pull her against me gently, wrapping one arm around her lower back. She looks so lovely right now, so open and honest, so alluring. I touch her bottom lip, cup her jaw, slide my fingers into the mass of her hair.

"I don't want you to think that I am some shallow young princeling," I utter, scanning her face. "If it wasn't already obvious, I like you for a lot more than your looks."

Her eyebrows go up just a little. "Really? You're not just…" She swallows. "You're not just sleeping with me?"

"Oh, little witch…" I sigh. "I am very much in this for more than just your body. Okay? I mean, don't get me wrong. I fucking love your body. Every inch of you is absolutely incredible. But I like you for more than the sum of your parts. The fact that you didn't know that already makes me think that I am doing something wrong."

She puffs out her cheeks for a moment. "Are you going to apologize for staring at Kalindi?"

I nod very slowly. "I apologize. Especially for making you feel less than you are. Because you are incredible. That's an absolute fact.

She gives me a tiny smile then presses up on her tiptoes, catching my lips with her own. I respond in kind, dominating the kiss, grinding my lower body against hers. Backing her against the wall of the spring, I trap her and enjoy her soft sighs of pleasure. And before I know it, we are lost in each other for some time, forgetting the entire world exists.

2 6

PIPPA

"And so I told him, why don't you just buy both houses? I know it's the most basic rich girl thing to say, but honestly. I was just tired of hearing about it. Lake house, ski lodge, who cares?"

Nika throws her arms up in the air, looking frazzled. I walk down the sidewalk beside her, peering at Margot to see her reaction. Margot does in fact look a little bit puzzled, even though she's by far the richest one among the three of us.

Her face wrinkles. "I assume that Erik set you straight. Normal people don't go around buying houses left and right, you know."

Nika shoots her a look. "He said something similar, as a matter fact. I told him that it didn't matter to me which house he bought or whether he bought any house at all. We can live on an abandoned oil freighter for all I care."

I snort. "I don't think that Erik took you very seriously, Nika. Of the three of us, you are the one who was raised with unimaginable wealth."

Nika sighs. "I know, I know. I just couldn't hear one more word about where we were going to vacation. It's like… rent a house, buy a house. I really don't care. Just don't bother me with it." She pulls a face. "Anyway, thanks for letting me vent. I know it's silly."

Margot leans over and brushes a fleck of dust off of Nika's long wool jacket. Her breath fogs a little in the air.

"It's quite all right. We all need to vent about the man in our lives now and then. Don't we?"

The last it is definitely directed at me, which she lets me know by pointedly staring at me. My cheeks flush and I look ahead on the street, not really wanting the conversation that Margot is seeking from me. "Um…"

"Oooh! Look!" Margot pulls her attention away from the conversation, pointing across the street. Where she points there is a large shop with a beautiful glass display case, filled with wedding dresses of every style imaginable. My eyes widen but Margot already has her begging face on.

"Oh, please, please! I know that you'll probably get your wedding dress designed by someone famous, but please say you'll let us pick out a silhouette together? It's basically like the perfect moment to do it, and I do still love playing dress-up."

I open my mouth to say no, my mind reeling. The last thing I want is to be plied with gorgeous white dresses right now. After all, the girls still don't know that the whole engagement is completely fake. But before I can say a word, Margot yanks me across the street, a determined look on her face.

"That's what we have to do," she mutters. "We have to make sure that Pippa falls in love with the dress and the wedding as much as anything else. That's how you can trick someone who's both a clothes horse and a commitment-phobe into planning their wedding with you."

"I really don't think…" I tried to butt in. But the two women shushed me, pulling me into the fancy shop.

A bell tingles as we walk into the store. My eyes widen as I take the shop in at a glance. I have there are ten mannequins all done up in their wedding dresses and gorgeous veils and pretty stands of pearls. I'm attracted to the first one I lay eyes on, a skintight lace number that feels good underneath my fingertips. My lips twitch. It's not the dress for me, but I could definitely see myself wearing it somewhere else.

Then again, where else you need a full length lace wedding dress?

A plump blonde woman looks up from sewing the hem on a dress mannequin. It only takes a second for her to recognize Margot, the Queen of Denmark. Her dark eyes dart over Princess Annika… then they land on me. She quickly realizes that I must be the one marrying into the royal family. A look of pure, unadulterated joy comes over her face.

"Ladies!" She curtsies awkwardly. "Or should I say your highnesses? I'm Brigid. Welcome to my shop. Please, come in and make yourself comfortable. Tell me what I can do for you."

Nika and Margaret obviously each have their own dresses in mind, because they start talking at once, at full volume.

"I was thinking something like strappy top and full at the bottom…"

"I think Pippa needs something simple, something with no sequins or anything shiny…"

I roll my eyes. Brigid seems unfazed by the girls talking over each other. She hustles us to a large fitting room area, with several seats surrounding a runway of sorts with a three way mirror at the other end.

"Please, sit. Would you like some champagne?"

"Sure," I say, relieved to at last be presented with something that I can say yes to. Nika and Margot immediately decline, causing me to raise my eyebrows.

When Brigid is off getting my champagne, I look at Nika. "Is there reason you're not drinking?"

Nika flushes. "Nothing so exciting as that, I'm afraid. I just have a dress fitting next week and I am trying to maintain my figure, that's all."

I look at Nika's perfect, petite body and I pull a face. "Well, all right then. I guess I will drink alone."

Bridgid returns with my champagne and askes for what I am looking for exactly in a dress. I wrinkle my nose delicately.

It's not as if I have not dreamt of exactly what my dress would look like. I'm a very girly girl and I'm into fashion already. But it just seems wrong to even talk about that when I know that I won't be wearing any dress.

She sees the hesitation on my face. She leans over, pats me on the shoulder, and says, "Should I just pick some things out for you? We can go from there."

My cheeks flush. I nod a little. "That would be great, thank you."

I sit back, sipping my champagne and looking at Nika and Margot. Margot is eyeing me, trying to figure out what I'm feeling so weird about. She peels off her white woolen coat and straightens the hem of her pink skirt.

"What's going on with you and Lars? I sense that there is something that you aren't telling us."

I take another sip of champagne as I decide how to answer that. "What do you mean?" I finally settle on.

Margot leans forward. "I've seen you two together. It's obvious that you are both in love with each other. But you aren't excited about trying on wedding dresses? That's not the Pippa I know."

Nika shoots me a smirk. "Wasn't it just yesterday that we were sitting together at a fashion show? Surely you should be inspired by the dresses, at least."

I suck in a breath, trying to figure out how to thread this very thorny needle. I don't want to lie to my friends. But I also don't want to tell either of them the truth. I would hate for them to know that I am just playing a part.

Then again, I have been playing a part for so many years now that it's hard for me to tell the difference.

I opt for changing the subject very slightly. "Lars is fine. I just haven't slept much in last month. You know how that is, surely." I raise a frank brow at both of them.

"That we do," Margot agrees.

"So, it's easy dating Lars, then?" Nika asked. "I always imagine that it would be sort of a nightmare. Seeing him settle down with you instead of running around with a new blonde supermodel every week is just sort of… gratifying, yes. But also somewhat mystifying. I genuinely thought he would never get it together."

Margot sits down beside me, shooting Nika a glare. "I'm sure what she means is that we're very glad for both of you. I just want to make sure that you know that you have us to talk to, no matter what."

"Seriously, just knowing that I have you two to vent to does worlds of wonder." Nika says.

"Thank you, girls." Trying to hide my discomfort, I smile and take another sip of my champagne.

Brigid returns with a rolling rack full of dresses, smiling brightly. "Do you want to come look, ladies? Er… Your highnesses, I mean."

Margot and Nika bound to their feet, eager to look at the dresses. I am slower to move as I follow them, wistfully touching the first dress on the rack, an off-shoulder cream number with full skirts. I run my hand down the satin, my mouth twisting sourly. "This dress is lovely. Actually, all the dresses I've seen today have been."

Margot peeks her head out from behind a rack, her eyes bright. "Pippa, tell Brigid your size. Let's start trying on some dresses."

I set my champagne aside and give Brigid a little smile. "Do you have a restroom that I can use?"

She smiles back at me. "Of course! If you go out this door, it's all the way at the end of the hall. Will be waiting for you when you come back."

I press my lips into a smile and rush out the door that she pointed to, my face heating. I'm not a very good liar, not in the average proceeding of things anyway. I rush down the hallway to the ladies room. When I find it, it's quite nice, all granite inside with a large mirror over the sink and a beautiful looking antique chair separate from the stall. Walking over to the mirror, I run a little bit of water and what a paper towel, pressing it against my face. I look in the mirror, my eyes scanning my own expression.

"This is too much," I say to my reflection. "No one ever said that I was going to end up lying to Margot and Nika. What do I do about it?"

I sigh, steeling myself. If I can just get through this little part of my girls day out, I think I will be happier.

I turn and march to the door, opening it.

And I come face-to-face with Ms. Olson, her arms crossed across her chest. She arches a brow.

"I haven't heard from you in some time, Sylvie. Did you forget about me?"

My skin flushes hot. I begin to tremble. "What are you doing here?" I drop my voice to a whisper, peeking out into the hallway where she's standing. "It's almost like you want be caught by the royal family."

Ms. Wilson smirks at me. "I thought it would be better if you were motivated to give me what I want so I can leave."

Shooting her a glare, I reach out and grab her arm, pulling her roughly into the bathroom with me. I close the door, rounding on her. "This has to stop. I don't know anything. I don't want to be your spy. If you don't leave me alone right now, I'll call the authorities. I'm not joking."

She gives me a cool little smile. "Aren't you going to ask me how Stella is doing?"

Her question catches me off guard. I frown. "I... I don't know..." I shake my head. "Just because I'm curious about this girl that you keep talking about doesn't mean anything. You think that you know who I am but you don't."

Ms. Olson clicks her tongue at me. She shakes her head. "I'm not here to listen to your lies, Sylvie." She looks at her watch. "I do have to be running along. But I came here for reason. Your fiancé is going to get some very precious news at work today. And I need you to find out exactly what that news is. It's too sensitive to just talk over the phone, so I will be dropping in on you again, Sylvie."

I ball my fist up. Stepping closer to the middle aged woman, I show her my teeth. "I don't want to see you again. If you leave right now and don't come back, I can forget that all of this ever happened."

Ms. Olson doesn't even blink. "Oh, Sylvie. You need a display of force? Really? Something to show you that I'm not full of hot air?"

She pulls out his cell phone and types of brief message. I give her a look, turning to open the door. This woman is unbalanced and I should have already reported her to the police. There's nothing stopping me from doing that right now.

I yank open the door, sticking my head out. "Nika, Margot? Will someone please call the police? I think I have a stalker…"

Ms. Olson gives a little sniff as she pushes past me, turning right and heading to the exit. Just before she gets there though, she stops and turns around. "I would check my bank accounts if I were you. When you find your money missing, call me. You'll know I am serious and I'll know that you are going to be a good girl."

She whirls and pushes out of the back door just as Margot and Pippa arrive in the hallway, Brigid at their heels.

"What's going on? Who was that?" Margot demand.

I turn to her, my eyes filling with tears. "I don't know," I tell her honestly. "It isn't the first time I have seen her though…"

Margot rushes to my side, hugging me hard. And I hug her back, taking a small matter comfort in her gesture. But I feel a strange pull to check my bank account, even though I'm pretty sure that Ms. Olson is full of crap.

When I finally go home, I do just that. And sure enough, one of my accounts is overdrawn, missing thousands of dollars. I bite my lip, trying to decide what to do.

Should I just tell the bank that my money was stolen?

Maybe I should tell Lars what's going on.

I sit down on my couch, unable to decide. My phone chimes, alerting me to a new text. I check it, finding several photos of me and Lars in bed together. We obviously don't realize we are on camera, because we are smiling and laughing in a few of the photos.

Another text comes in. Are you sure you want to ruin this?

My heartbeat races. I'm not sure. I'm paralyzed.

So I do nothing for now, although this situation clearly needs some kind of resolution… I am just too scared to make the wrong move and put Lars in jeopardy.

27

LARS

The next week is made up of seven days of nonstop royal visits. I drag Pippa along to open factories, speak at schools, see various cultural exhibitions, and just generally just try to represent the royal family as well as we can. Pippa, for her part, seems very distracted. She's right there by my side, holding the giant ribbon cutting scissors for me or tasting the newest wine. Always with a smile plastered on her face.

But she's not really there, not completely.

After a week of touring, I surprise her with a getaway to Monte Carlo, feeling like the only cure for whatever Pippa is experiencing is somewhere out there in the white sand beaches and yacht parties.

"Whoa," Pippa says, staring out the window as we arrive at the palatial beachside mansion I've rented. It's three stories high, beautifully made, and looks like the home of a tech billionaire. She turns her eyes to me, almost disbelieving. "Is this ours?"

I grin at her. "Permanently? No. But for the weekend, it is."

Her phone chirps and she looks down at the screen, frowning. I reach over into her lap and take her phone, turning it off and then pocketing it. She glances up at me, her expression mildly alarmed.

"Hey, I might need that. There are a lot of things still happening in Copenhagen even though we are not there."

I shoot her a coy smile. "It can wait until you get back. Can't it?"

She bites her lip, her frown increasing. But she does nod. "I guess it can."

Our car stops outside the big entrance to the house. We slide out of the car and I slip my arm around her waist, hugging her body against mine. She looks up at me, her expression unreadable. But instead of pulling away as I thought she might do, she leans up, puts her hand on my cheek, and kisses me firmly on the lips.

Her kiss is the kiss of a desperate woman, hungry for my touch, demanding my attentions. I sink into that kiss a little, letting it go on for too long. When the limo driver clears his throat beside us, indicating that he is ready to leave, I finally pull back from her in brace.

I nod towards the house. "Let's go inside. We should technically make it into the house before we start fucking."

Her lips quirk at that. "If we must."

I hustle her inside. I wait until the door closes, then rip off her clothes and have her right then and there, on the cold hardwood floor in the foyer. There's a desperation to our sex, a unspoken worry underlying every moan. I bury myself in her curves, worshiping her, the very act of being inside her feeling like some sort of sacred ritual.

"Faster," she whispers. "Please, Lars. Harder. I need you. I need this."

I thrust into her, my hips moving as fast as I can go, every single thrust like a prayer. The whole time, I restrained myself from saying what I really want to say.

That I love her.

That I need her.

That being with her, being inside her, completes me in a way that nothing else can.

We come together, her breath drawn ragged, our cries rising to the high ceiling. After we catch our breath, I help her up and pull her along to the main bedroom, touching her and kissing her as we both get in the shower.

We're both spent by then. She stands under the water with me, pressed against me. Her eyes are closed as she enjoys the simplicity of my touch and the heat from the shower.

I kiss her, not knowing quite what is going on in her head. When I cup her cheek and raise her face towards me, she opens her eyes a slit.

"This is nice," she murmurs. "I didn't think I would be glad that we came away for the weekend… But I think I really needed it." She pauses. "I think I really need you most of all."

My heart beats faster at her words. I band down and kiss her mouth, taking all of the love I feel but can't say out loud and putting it into my kiss.

We fuck again, exhausted, falling into the tangled sheets. At some point, I lose track of time. The sun goes down as I lie on my side, breathing heavily. Pippa falls asleep on my chest, curled against me.

I do daydream a little bit, letting my mind drift. I get the feeling that I am in a fast moving stream, the water swelling as it reaches a low point before dropping away down a waterfall. That's how I feel about my current relationship with Pippa. I'm worried that if I don't go along with it and ease into the flow, I will miss something. But I already know that the date of our break up is looming up ahead.

In two months, I'm supposed to give her up. And I don't know how I'm going to do it.

I'm not sure what I am supposed to do about it, exactly. All I can think of is that I have to just muster the courage to tell her how I really feel.

I think that she wouldn't dismiss it out of hand. She would at least give me a chance.

But I'm not sure. And my uncertainty about her reaction causes me to feel dread.

The idea of Pippa not being present in my life anymore looms large. If I somehow cause that, I would not know what to do with myself.

Somehow I managed to fall asleep and I wake up a few hours later, finding Pippa beside me still. We seem to wake at the same time, our eyes meeting. She smiles at me.

"So much for seeing the sights in Monte Carlo," she says shyly.

I kiss her lips briefly, savoring her taste. Then I sit up with a sigh. "This is Monte Carlo. Some of the best spots are only to be viewed at night. That is, as long as you're willing to take a little risk."

Her eyebrows raise a little. "Oh? You mean go out right now?"

I cast my gaze down her naked body, pursing my lips. "That is, unless you have other plans…"

She chuckles, rolling her eyes. "Even I have limits on my libido. Give it a couple of hours and I'm sure it will be back in full force."

I grin. "Well, I say we hit the strip, then. Downtown Monte Carlo it's basically a bunch of large hotels and casinos, all spaced out by shops and restaurants. We can get something to eat or grab a drink…"

She brightens. "Does that mean we should dress up?"

I smirk at her. "Monte Carlo demands nothing less of us."

Just like that, she's climbing on the bed, rushing to her suitcases. She unzips a white garment bag, rifling through its contents excitedly. To my delight, she dresses herself in a simple but stunning black gown. It has high slits on each side and the satiny material is soft to the touch. I watch her get dressed, opting for a pair of dark dress pants and a white button up with the sleeves rolled up in the collar undone.

Then we hit the strip on foot. Out to our left is the dazzling sea. Up ahead, the city lights gleam from gorgeous Mediterranean style buildings, the sandstone facades and the red copper roofs flickering against the night sky.

We walk for a ways, Pippa clinging to my arm. We talk about nothing, laugh at everything. I look down at Pippa as we hit the crowded part of Monte Carlo, my heart so full that I can't even speak. She looks at me, grinning, and pulls me into the first crowded bar she sees.

The party is in full swing already, judging by the intensely loud music and the insane crowds once we get in the door. As I make it up the last couple of steps, I can actually feel the floor vibrating.

At the top I stop and stare. The doors are thrown open and the party is so packed that it's spilling out into the hall. Men in tuxes yell into the ears of ladies in ballgowns. There are people lined up for drinks from the bartenders at the bar set up just outside the doors.

The liquor is flowing freely too, from the looks of it. We grab a couple of drinks and then head into the dance floor, shuffling and maneuvering to get past the crowd at the door. Inside, the electronica music is bright and sounds vaguely distorted, but I suppose that's probably on purpose. The lights are lower here by the door and brighter over across the dance floor, centering on a small, tightly packed dance floor.

Everywhere I can see, there are people dancing and chatting and drinking. Pippa dances against me and I try to keep up with her. I finish my drink quite quickly, ready for another. I don't see any waiters, so I guess I'll have to head back to the line outside.

"I'm going to get another drink for both of us," I shout into her ear.

She sways to the music, giving me a thumbs up. I head out to the bar line, standing in it for what seems like forever and being sure that the bartenders make my drinks doubles. The music throbs as I wait.

I'm annoyed by the loud, persistent booming. I want to move on from this bar, to continue down the strip, to go back to laughing and talking like we were doing before.

And that's when I see my fiancée and another guy.

Without question, I know it's Pippa. She is wearing a simple black dress, fitted and full length with thick straps. She pushes a strand of her curly red hair back as she stands by the wall, talking to a man in a tux. Her expression is unreadable, but I can tell by her body language that the man is hitting on her.

I can tell she doesn't like it.

As I start to push my way through the crowd towards her, I see the man grab her arm, lean in, and try to kiss her. She makes a face and turns her head slightly, avoiding direct contact between their mouths.

That's when I start seeing red.

Fuck anyone who touches her against her will.

Fuck any guy that touches her and isn't *me*.

As I start plowing my way through the crowd, I see her protest as the guy tries to pull her closer.

"Stop!" she yelps. "Seriously, you don't even know me—"

"If you would just—"

That's all the guy manages to say before I get close enough to yank him off of her. Pippa's eyes widen when she sees me and takes in my expression.

"Lars, don't—"

"*Foutre le camp!*" the guy says. It's clear to me that he's very drunk, but that doesn't excuse his behavior.

I punch him right in the nose, knocking him down to the floor. The crowd instantly parts, He makes a startled sound and holds his face; bright red blood starts to bloom on his face.

"Lars!" Pippa says, looking tense. She rushes to my side, tugging at my arm.

I glance at her, then back to the guy on the floor, who is just now getting surly.

"Who the fuck are you?" he yells.

I step closer, ignoring Pippa's hand on my arm. "You don't fucking touch her," I tell him. "You don't touch anybody unless they ask you to, you fucking asshole."

"I didn't do anything!" he cries, holding his nose.

"Bullshit," I tell him. "I saw it all. And if you think that I'm the only one who would've stepped in, you're wrong. You can't just step all over a girl nowadays and expect that no one will stop you."

Pippa makes a frustrated noise. "Seriously, Lars—"

"Okay! Okay." I take a step back, gripping Pippa's waist. My gaze meets hers. "I'll go if you go with me."

"Yes," she says, tugging me toward the door of the club. "I'm going with you."

I let her pull me away with one last glare at the man, who is just now getting to his feet. Then he's gone, obscured by the dancers and people talking that stand in between me and the wall. Turning toward the doorway, I step in front of her to make a path.

Soon we are out of the bar. I don't stop there on the landing, though. I grab Pippa by the waist and halfway carry her down the stairs, not stopping until we hit the front door.

There are a few people who drunkenly watch as I carry my fiancée a little ways, finally putting her down in front of a white sandstone building. I grab her and pin her against the wall, my eyes fiery.

"Fuck that guy," I grit out.

She looks up at me, her eyes slitted. "I think you showed him who's in charge," she says.

I roughly kiss her, forcing my lips down on hers. She sinks against me. Burying her hands in my hair, she opens her mouth to me, letting my tongue slide against hers. When she finally breaks away, pulling back, I can see the desire written in her blue eyes.

"Take me home," she asks quietly. "Show me just what went through your mind when you saw him trying to kiss me."

I pull away from the wall, grabbing her hand, and rush toward our rented home.

LARS

In the late morning, I look at Pippa gathering her things.

"Are you thinking of heading up to the beach?" I ask.

"Err… yes." She colors, lifting the tote bag that is on her shoulder. "I brought a book and a towel."

"And sunblock, I hope," I tease her. "I'll come with you."

I feel her gaze slide down my chest. She bites her lip, turns even redder, and then nods. "Okay."

She turns and starts walking away, leaving me to grab my water and catch up. As we walk, I keep an eye trained on her.

Pippa has never said anything even remotely romantic to me. I mean, we've shared our bodies with each other. That's for sure. But nothing about her feelings.

Certainly nothing about wanting to make our relationship real.

Still, gazes like the one she's giving me now speak volumes in their own way.

She thinks I'm hot. She thinks I'm funny. She thinks I'm worth knowing.

I just have to find the right moment to pop the question, as it were.

Will you make our fake relationship real, little witch?

I sigh. She casts an eye over me, squeezing my biceps. "Did you run too hard this morning or something? I saw you get up to work out."

I smirk at her. "I like running. It's just me time. Besides, I have to keep it tight for you." I say the last with a wink.

She shakes her head. "You know, you're lucky you're hot."

I grin. She's not wrong. I am hot. I work my body hard to maintain it.

"So, um…" She ducks her head as we walk, tucking her hair behind her ears. "I've been thinking about what I want you to fund. You know, after we… break up."

My heart speeds up. "*Ja?*"

"Mmhm. I've narrowed it down to three ideas. Tell me what you think." She ticks off the numbers on her fingers as she goes. "One, I think maybe some kind of newspaper for women my age. Good reporting, a mixture of fun stuff and serious stuff."

I nod. "That sounds good."

"I also was thinking about taking a year off, writing a book, and launching myself as a brand."

I cock my head, thoughtful. "What would you write?"

She blushes. "I guess I would have to figure it out."

"What's the third thing?"

"Some sort of publishing house for punk rock and feminist writers. I haven't really defined that idea very well."

Blowing out a long stream of breath, I nod slowly. "Cool. I mean… what if I just gave you the money now? We could still carry on the fake engagement and everything. It's not like you're about to ghost me."

Pippa looks at me, surprised. "If that would make you happy, I guess." She frowns. "You're still happy with our arrangement, right?"

I shrug. "I guess. We do have the four month mark coming up, creeping closer and closer. I feel like we'll have to decide what we want to do then."

Her lips quirk. "What do you mean?"

The back of my neck heats. I clear my throat. "I mean, do we keep fucking? Do we… stay engaged for longer? Do we stop everything all at once?"

Her eyes widen. She looks out at the beach, biting her lower lip. All I get from her is a grudging, "I have no idea," mumbled quickly out of the side of her mouth.

Before us, the road gives way to the sloping beach. It's rocky after we cross the road. The ocean glides gently up toward us and then back again, leaving a sandy beach in its wake.

Pippa picks a spot, laying her tote bag down. "God. It's beautiful out here." She shivers. "It's unexpectedly chilly. I guess there isn't anything to keep the wind off of us."

I toss my shirt down next to her bag. "It's nearly brisk. I like it. But I don't think that I want to get in the water, though. It's not the right time of year for that, I'm afraid."

A smile tugs at her mouth. "I suppose not. Maybe I'll just sit here and read."

She purses her lips and sits down in the pebble-strewn sand, well away from the water. Normally I would just look at the sea for a minute and then head back to the shelter of the house. But since Pippa seems intent on staying, I sit down next to her.

She is pretty quiet, dragging her book out. It's big and thick, not beach reading at all. My knee accidentally brushes hers as I settle in, and my touch leaves traces of crimson in her cheeks. Then she apologizes, as if she had done something bad.

"Oops, sorry!" she says, scooting herself another inch away from me.

As if we didn't start this morning with amazing, steamy shower sex. As if I didn't cup her tits, pull her hair, and fucking come inside her gorgeous body mere hours ago.

My first instinct is to drag her a little closer, put my calloused palms against her smooth skin. Just to see how she would react.

I blow out a breath. "I hate to be one of those people, but what are you reading?"

She wrinkles her nose, showing me the cover. The cover is hot pink and designed to look very 1990s. "It's a look back at how music and feminism shaped millennials."

I look at the sand in front of me, reach out two fingers to trace a figure eight. "I think it's been a while since I've read anything more complicated than a Wired article."

"Oh," she says carefully, gripping her book to her chest with both hands. "I think my brain needs to be fed a steady diet of new and thought provoking material." She wrinkles her nose. "All I ever did as a kid was read." Her cheeks stain again. "Actually, my childhood wasn't that different from my life right now in that regard. I'm still a giant nerd." She crinkles her face up and huffs out a laugh.

I smile a little. I've known her since she was thirteen. And for the most part, she's right. When I picture her, her nose is always stuck in a book. "I wished I was a nerd sometimes. I wished I was basically anything but a prince." My mouth flattens. "I think that sometimes the royal family is sort of trapped. They are set in their ways, always performing the same ceremonies, fragile beings kept under glass."

She straightens her spine and frowns. "I can see why you feel that way." Her mouth twists. "Do you ever dream of escaping this life? Just starting over somewhere that no one will know you?"

I push myself onto my back, laying out against the sand. "*Ja*. Of course. When I was little, I would spend hours studying maps, trying to chart a course for a great ship to take me away. "

Pippa pushes her hair behind her ears, her expression a little sad. She reaches out and touches my arm ever so gently, causing goosebumps to raise all over my body. "I'm glad you didn't sail away. Is that selfish? I'm so glad I met you, especially when I did."

Her words are so earnest, making the back of my neck heat. It's a little weird that she has such complete faith in me when I've never really done anything to earn it.

"Well, me too. I guess I could wish that so many things had turned out differently. But if they did, I might not be here right now," I say, tilting my head. "And I would hate to miss out on this."

Pippa leans over and kisses my lips, a small smile on her face. I feel myself growing sentimental, so I change course. "We should be talking about something more interesting. Like…" I grasp for straws, eager to talk about easier things. What am I good at?

Sex. How do I work that into the conversation?

"Okay…" I say. "Ah! Who was your first crush?"

Her cheeks color. "I don't know…" she hedges.

I'm enjoying her embarrassment too much. "Mine was Star Wright. I don't think you knew her, but when I was a kid, she was a super popular singer. Tall, sexy, and she always wore these bright colors. Oh, and she had really great hair." I wrinkle my nose at Pippa. "I guess you two have that in common."

Pippa looks at the ground. "I had a crush on all of the Beastie Boys," she mumbles. "I liked how they all dressed. They had a lot of style."

"Oh *man*," I say, cracking up. "You liked how they dressed. Of *course* that's your answer." I laugh about that for second, my eye on Pippa. "All right. How about a tougher one?"

She gives me a look that says she couldn't imagine anything she would rather be talking about less. I grin, my shoulders feeling looser.

"How about… are you a boobs girl or a butt girl? Or… what's the female equivalent? Hot arms or strong back muscles?"

She scrunches up her face. "I would rather crawl under a rock than answer that."

I bump her with my shoulder. "Relax. I'm not going to tell anybody. Me, I'm a butt guy, all the way. Boobs are great, but I like an ass. Gives you something to hold onto when you're fucking."

Pippa pinches her eyes closed. "I hate you."

"Just tell me. Which do you fantasize about? Arms or back? Oooh, or abs maybe?"

She grabs her book, holding it in front of her face. "I like the adonis belt, I guess…"

That gives me pause. "The fuck lines, eh? That's pretty raunchy, little witch."

She moves her book to the side and shoots me a glare. "You are seriously the worst. *The. Worst.*"

My grin widens. "What's the hottest sex you've had? Hmm?"

She goes bright red in an instant, glancing away. She drops the book, but she won't look anywhere near me. "Ummm…"

I grin. Reaching out to touch her bare knee, I rib her a little. "Come on, you can tell me."

She looks back at me, her blue eyes full of mortification. "You're going to make fun of me."

"Me? No." I shake my head. "I would never."

Pippa shakes her head. "Would it be too dorky to say the first time we had sex? I feel like I wanted it for a long time before it happened."

My heart thuds in my chest. "Really?"

She pins me with a look. "Yes. Well, it would be a tie. The sex we had on the plane ride here was pretty hot too."

"It really was," I say, my imagination kicking into high gear. I let my gaze slide down her body, biting my lip.

"What was your best sex experience?" she asks, frowning just a little.

I smirk at her, pulling her against my body. Leaning down and cupping her face, I kiss her, deep and with tongue. By the time I pull back, I'm breathless.

I lean my forehead against hers. "How about we work on making some new memories instead of talking about the past?"

Her lips curve up. "I think that sounds like a great plan."

Helping her up, I hustle her toward our lavish rental house, feeling exactly like the desperate man that I am.

29

PIPPA

It's a race to the bedroom, both of us giddy and laughing as we strip off our sandy clothes. Lars looks at me as he takes off his shirt, his eyes glinting.

"Take it all off," he says, pointing at the clothes I've already shed. "I want you naked and ready."

With shaking hands, I unhook my bikini top and let it drop. Then I push my bottoms down my legs, making eye contact with Lars the entire time. He watches me, his eyes slitted, biting his lip.

I'm left bare, no bra or panties. Lars buries his face in the space between my breasts, pushing them both toward his mouth. He takes his time with each one, kissing and licking it, running his tongue over the nipple. He even uses his teeth, setting me on edge and making me ridiculously horny.

All the while, my hands roam over his body, feeling different muscle groups flex. I wrap my legs around him, pressing my pussy against the outline of his cock through his jeans.

He knows just how to make me crazy. He makes this sound deep in his chest, while his mouth is on my breasts. It's a rumble, or a growl maybe. I just can't get enough of it.

He pulls back. "I want you to ride my mouth, Pippa."

I turn red all over. "I don't know, Lars…"

"Yes. Come on, try it. I think you'll like it," he says. I look in his eyes, blue as the sea in the morning, burning with lust.

"I'm embarrassed," I admit.

"Don't be," he says. Your hair tossed back, your breasts thrusting out, a book of pleasure on your face… I can't think of anything hotter."

I pull my lower lip between my teeth, but he's already getting off of me and laying down on the bed. *I guess I'm doing this, then.*

One thing I know is that Lars will never laugh at me or make me feel awkward on purpose. As we spend more and more time together, that becomes readily apparent.

I move up the bed to the wall, kneeling beside his head.

"Ready?" I ask hesitantly.

He nods, caressing my thigh with a smirk. "Extremely ready."

I maneuver myself over his face, straddling him. It's a balancing act and I'm glad that the wall is right there to lean on for a second. I have never felt so awkward in my life, but Lars's hands come up to the tops of my thighs, gently pushing me down.

I spread my knees a little wider, biting my lip. I feel the warmth of his breath just before he kisses the inside of my thighs. I close my eyes, forcing myself to breathe.

I can feel my pussy growing wet as he kisses upward toward my mound. It makes me squeamish, but at the same time, I bite my lip and think of how hot he'll look after I come. Wiping my juices from his face?

Ja, that makes me fucking hot.

He presses the tops of my thighs down further until I fully rest on his face. At the same time he kisses my aching clit, ever so lightly. I moan.

"Oh god," I say as he kisses it again, increasing the pressure a little.

I bite my lip, unsure what to do with my hands. I run my hands over my body, ending up enjoying the sensation of cupping my own breasts. I lean my head to the side, groaning at the stimulation of Lars slowly licking my clit.

I pull on both my nipples at once, and buck against his wicked tongue a couple of times. I keep imagining him after I come all over his face, which makes me crazy.

He shifts for a second, moving his arm. His big hand splays out over one ass cheek, then he coaxes me back down to his mouth. Lars does figure eights with his tongue over my clit, the hand on my ass trailing lower and lower, teasing the cleft of my ass.

He closes his lips over my clit and sucks, which makes me cry out. At the same time, he slips a probing fingertip just to the pucker of my ass. I immediately moan so loud that I embarrass myself. The sensation of him playing with my ass like that just makes me fucking wild. I freeze up, even though Lars sucks harder on my clit. I feel myself blossoming like a flower, a feeling of fullness growing low in my body.

He feels me lock up, and pulls back. "Easy, Pippa. What's going on?"

I go red as a beet. "I like it. I like it too much, if that's possible. But I feel like you should get off, too."

He kisses my inner thigh. "I can, if you want to turn around. You can suck my cock and ride my face at the same time."

How... dirty.

I nod, awkwardly repositioning myself. When I am facing his cock though, I have something to do. My fingers unbutton his jeans, pushing down his boxer briefs to reveal his long, hard, perfect cock.

As Lars closes his lips over my clit again, I take his cock in my fist. He groans, which is eminently satisfying. I strain to wrap my lips around his tip, which is too far away for much else.

I *mmmmm* at the male taste of him, salty and bitter earthy in my mouth.

I try to concentrate on his cock, wetting my lips and covering my teeth with my lips. I try not to worry about what Lars is doing, try not to focus on every single stroke of his tongue.

It's very difficult, though. I run my tongue around his cock and carefully pump my fist up and down his length. I can feel my inner spring winding up, becoming taut. I am aware of his clever finger slipping down to my ass again, penetrating it with just the tip.

Fuck, I think, *it feels good so damn good.* I moan against the tip of his cock. He works his whole finger inside my ass, and I am suddenly aware of the sensation of fullness. The knowledge that I'm going to come soon pops into my mind, and it makes it very difficult to try to pay attention to sucking his cock.

I pause and raise my head, eliciting a groan from him. "I'm close," I whisper.

He moans and doubles down on my clit. I sigh as I sink my mouth down on his cock again, moving my hand in time with my tongue. His taste changes a little, grows saltier as I moan around his cock.

"Oh god," I whisper. What he's doing with his mouth and his naught finger up my ass feels so good. I can't take it anymore. "Oh god, I'm—"

Suddenly I erupt, going over the precipice into a world of pleasure. He starts to come right after me, emptying lash after lash of his salty cum into my mouth, getting a lot of it on my face.

When we finally slow, I slide off his face, pushing myself upright. I finally get that moment I've been waiting for, watching him lick and wipe away the moisture from his mouth and chin.

I lean over and kiss him deeply, loving that I can taste myself on his lips and tongue. He starts chuckling, high on endorphins. I giggle sheepishly, laying down beside him.

He grins and holds me close, his breathing still ragged. No words pass between us, but none are really needed. I've never been achingly aware of the fact that I love someone before, but I would definitely say that's what I'm feeling just now.

We just lie there, basking in each other's afterglow. I curl up on my side, laying my head against his chest, and try my best to breathe through my feelings.

30

PIPPA

The weekend goes too fast. One minute, I am in Monte Carlo, buried in Lars's arms. The next moment I blink and everything is changed. Suddenly I am looking at a sea of people in the royal palace, blinking as Lars steps close to me, sliding his arm around me. I barely remember getting dressed for this event, but here I am, wearing a shimmering pink floor length gown, blinking into a photographer's flashes. Lars is just beside me, wearing his tux. He leans close, whispering in my ear.

"Are you okay?"

I lick my lips, looking up at him. He looks back down at me, his eyes concerned. I want to do nothing but smooth those worry lines from the corners of his eyes. I smile instead, though it feels a little forced.

"I'm fine," I say. "I was just wondering how our weekend away went so fast."

A slow smile spreads over his face. "I can think of a couple of ways how a whole day or two might slip away..."

I give him and knowing look. "I bet you can."

The photographer who is shooting our pictures calls for our attention. "Your highness? If you could just look over here for another minute…"

I look forward, repressing a sigh. We are off to one side of the ballroom that we're in, having our official engagement photos taken. Just outside the thin screens set up by the photographer, the crowd mills around. People laugh, I hear the clinking of glasses together. It's the same as it ever has been, the same as the last five parties that we attended here as an engaged couple.

I glance at Lars, wondering how he doesn't lose his mind with boredom. I thought that I knew exactly what his life entailed, but I had no idea that he was sheltering me from so many boring royal events.

One of the camera flashes catches me off guard and I wrinkle my whole face up. "Can we be done?" I asked the photographer. "Please, you've gotten at least fifty good photos of us together. Surely that's enough."

I feel Lars's fingers tighten on my waist. The photographer looks shocked; Lars quickly steps in, smoothing the situation over.

"We just got off a plane," he said quickly. "Jet lag, you know?"

The photographer seems a little worried but agrees to let us go. Of course, there is no stopping Lars if he doesn't want to have his picture taken anymore… But whether or not that privilege extends to me, I don't know.

Lars steers me out of the little portrait studio, immediately taking a hard right turn toward the ballroom doors. I glance up at him, a little anxious. "Where are we going?"

His expression is unreadable as the moves me out of the room. "We need a break. Or I do, anyway."

Just as we make it to the doors though, a servant stops Lars. "Your highness? The king wishes to speak with you. Do you mind?"

Lars is gaze hardens. He doesn't roll his eyes exactly, but he doesn't look pleased either. He turns to me, apologetic.

"I'm sorry. I'll be right back. I think I saw Nika over by the refreshment table, if it helps."

My lips twist. "Go. You are a prince, after all. If the king summons you, what choice do you have?"

He gives my arm squeeze and then disappears from the ballroom, following the servant that was sent to summon him. I suck in a deep breath and turn around, eyeing the crowd.

I don't want to be here. I am experiencing something like burnout. Worse, I'm doing it publicly.

How do the royals do it this day after day for their whole lives? I've only been doing it officially for two and a half months and I feel so fragile and brittle that I am about to break.

I clear my throat, looking around the room for Nika's small frame. As I am searching for her, Queen Ida spots me from across the way. Petite but elegant, with eyes of steel and sleek silver hair, she zooms in on me. I see her coming, her chic black dress looking as expensive as ever. She arches a brow as she advances.

"There you are, Pippa. I was just wondering if I was going to see you here or not. I have something to show you." She steps forward and takes my arm, towing me along as she makes a beeline for the exit. I don't know what to say so I just clear my throat nervously.

When I let myself be pulled outside the ballroom, I frown. Queen Ida murmurs hello to a passing servant as she toes me along. I finally get up the nerve to speak.

"I don't want Lars to miss me…" I say, glancing back at the rapidly disappearing ballroom behind me. Around me, the soaring white hallways ceilings and majestic red carpeting go on and on seemingly endlessly.

"You'll love this," she says confidently. "I have just had it flown in from being tailored in Milan."

My brows rise a little. "Milan?"

She sneaks me a look. "Yes, dear. That's what I said. Come on, it's in here."

She pulls open a random palace door, ushering me inside. I swallow and step through into a small office. The only thing worth seeing is hanging on a dress hanger in the middle of the room. It's a wedding dress, and an old one at that. It's entirely the wrong size and shape for me, a tall and slender person. This dress is made of crepe and lace, so short and wide that… Well, I would call it serviceable if I were being nice about it. I squint at the dress, as if the garment has answers for me.

"Well, what do you think?" Momse asks.

Careful to keep my face perfectly blank, I turn and face her. "I'm not sure what I am looking at," I admit.

Her eyebrows fly up. "Why, your wedding dress, of course. I thought you would want to get married in the traditional wedding dress that all the second son's wives have shared." She pauses, arching a brow. "Are you not pleased?"

I flush, though I'm not exactly sure why. I lick my lips. "No one said anything to me about already having a dress." I frown. "It's not really my style."

"Nonsense." She moves around me, touching the sleeve of the wedding dress with two fingers. "It's perfectly functional. Just like your engagement ring. I took one look at you and I already knew that I would send for this dress."

I blink rapidly. This has to be some kind of joke. "You have to be testing me or something. Margot didn't wear a proscribed gown. Why would I have to?"

She huffs. "A lot of women would kill for the opportunity that you are turning your nose up at. Lars is my grandson, and he's strong stock. I know that I didn't have much of a choice over this engagement, but I'll be damned if I will be cut out of planning the wedding."

My mouth opens. I don't quite know what to say. "I was under the impression that you were planning the wedding entirely, and I was only expected to pick out what I'm wearing. I didn't even get a say on what day my wedding date will be."

I can feel my face growing hot, feel something like rage creeping up in my tone. Queen Ida looks at me, gives another little half smirk, and looks back at the gown. "You'll wear the dress. And while we're on the topic of things you need to do, I think that you and I should sit down and talk about how it is appropriate to comport one's self when you're representing the royal family. Because I for one don't want to be embarrassed any further."

My hands curl into this. I narrow my eyes at Queen Ida, feeling myself start to shake. "Does Lars even know that you are talking to me right now?"

"Should he?" she shoots back.

It takes everything in me to keep from lashing out. Instead, I press my fingernails into the palm of each hand, speaking slowly and clearly. "I'm not sure what kind of game you're playing. I'm not even sure if you are playing on the same field as I am. But this need for control that you have, this bizarre compulsion that you feel, it won't go on. Not with me. I won't have it."

My voice rises until I'm almost but not quite yelling by the end of the sentence. An elegant little smirk appears on her face. "I think you will do just exactly what I ask you to do."

I turn, elbowing my way past her and heading for the door. "This is outrageous. I'm just going to pretend like this little tete-a-tete never happened. You would be wise to do the same."

Momse clears her throat. "Where are you going?"

I don't even look back at her. "I'm going to find my fiancé and tell him that I'm not feeling well." I fling the door open, taking a step outside.

That's when she drops the bomb.

"I wouldn't do that if I were you, Sylvie."

I freeze mid-step. Turning around slowly, my brow hunches I squint at her. "What?"

She gives me a smirk. "You heard me. What, did you think that I didn't know who you really are?" She laughs. "Like I would just let *anybody* be friends with one of my grandsons. Fat chance."

My face is so hot, I'm sure that I must be flushed all over. I take a step back towards her, dropping my voice. "I don't know what you think you know, but I'm sure that you are mistaken."

She rolls her eyes. Please. "Maybe you haven't been listening for all these months. Apparently my envoy wasn't clear enough for you."

I give her a puzzled look. "What?"

She folds her arms across her chest. "Ms. Olson said that you had the nerve to kick her out of a wedding dress shop last week. And I am here to tell you personally, that won't do. You are going to smile and play along and marry my grandson. You're going to have his kids and go on vacations and do all the royal handwaving that I ask of you. And you do it without being asked. Because I know your dirty little secret, *Sylvie*."

She looks a little proud of herself as she says it. "I also know all about Stella."

At this point, I'm so dumbstruck that I don't even know what I could possibly say. Anything that floats to the top of my mind seems like a bad idea because I would have to acknowledge that I am in fact Sylvie Martin. And something tells me that I definitely don't want to show this woman my belly.

"Pippa?" I turn my head to see Lars zooming over to me, concern for me weighing his brow. Are you okay?

I turn away from Queen Ida, automatically pulled toward the one person I feel the safest with in the world. I tried to force a smile on my lips but I know I have failed by looking at his puzzled expression.

"I'm not feeling well," I tell him. "Will you take me home?"

He looks surprised, striding up to me and taking one of my hands. It's only then that I realized my fists is still balled up. He looks down at my hand and then catches sight of his grandmother in the office. She inclines her head but otherwise says nothing.

Lars slides his gaze back to me, trying to figure it out. But I don't give him that kind of time.

"Can we go please?" I ask him softly. "Please, Lars."

He gives his grandmother one last glance and then puts his arm around me, pushing me toward the exit. "Of course," he says.

I've never been so glad to leave the royal palace as I am at that moment.

3 1

LARS

I SIT IN MY KITCHEN, BROODING AS I STARE OUT AT THE EARLY morning light falling onto the city of Copenhagen. The city is quiet right now, in my view is breathtaking. But I'm in no mood for the dazzling panoramic views. I sip my coffee, sighing silently.

Behind me, I hear Pippa's bare feet padding into the kitchen. I turn, casting and eye over her form. She has bed head and wears nothing but one of my overlarge t-shirts. She nods to me quietly and then goes to pour herself a cup of coffee.

"Are you feeling any better today?" I ask.

She turns to me, a steaming cup of coffee in her hand. "Yes," she says quietly. She looks down at the floor as she answers, making me wonder if I'm getting the entire truth. I hate that feeling, sloshing around in my stomach like acid. Still, I try to make conversation. "Do you want to talk about what happened with between you and my grandmother?"

She sips her coffee, shaking her head a little. "I'd rather not. It was just a petty disagreement about my wedding dress. Nothing to be worried about."

I walk over to the kitchen counter, setting my coffee down. I straighten my tie, trying to read the expression on her face. She glances at me, her blue eyes pinning me in place for a moment.

Something electric shivers through the air, bouncing back and forth between us. I don't understand exactly why she is so morose and withdrawn, but I'm willing to bet that it has something to do with Momse.

"If there is something wrong, you would tell me, wouldn't you?"

She ducked her head and drops her gaze again, nodding. "Sure."

"Pippa," I say. "Look at me."

She looks up, her eyes flashing with emotion. If I didn't know better, I would think that she was feeling guilty about something. But what could she possibly be guilty for?

She sets her mug down too hard on the counter, sloshing coffee over the edge. She mumbles a curse and turns around to get a wad of paper towels, mopping up the mess. I watch as she moves around the kitchen, that strange acid washing around in my stomach again.

The feeling that she's not being truthful. I hate that.

I clear my throat. "I have to go and meet one of my commanders for coffee this morning. Will you be okay here by yourself?"

She nods, swallowing. "I'm fine. I'll be fine. I just need some self-care, I guess." She frowns. "When you get back, we should talk about your royal schedule. I think… I think it's just too demanding for me." She looks up at me, tugging the hem of her oversized T-shirt down.

My eyebrows rise. "That's what you're upset about? Jesus, Pippa. You had me worried. Of course we can talk about paring my schedule back."

She blows out of breath, nodding. "That would be great."

I walk over to where she's standing, reaching out and sliding an arm around her waist. She comes easily to my side and I place a kiss on the crown of her head, my nose probing her coppery curls. "I have to go," I say. "Be good."

She looks up at me, a small smile appearing on her sweetly shaped face. "Should I plan for you to be back by lunch?"

I can't help but smile when I looking at her. "I think you should," I say.

She wrinkles her nose. "Okay. I'll miss you."

I pull her in for a final kiss, loving the way she fills all my senses. Her scent tickles my nose, she feels so good under my hands, she tastes even better than she smells. I open my eyes, gaze deep into hers, and then it just pops out of my mouth.

"I love you."

The second I say it, my eyes widen. Pippa gives me a shocked expression, as though she couldn't possibly imagine why I would say such a thing to someone like her. My neck heats.

"Lars I…" She bites her lip.

I can't stand here and have her tell me that she doesn't love me back. My heart thunders in my chest. I released her from my hold suddenly, clumsily, and straighten my neck tie. I look in any direction that isn't right at her face. "I uh, I have to go. I… I'll be back."

"Lars, wait…" she says in a pleading tone.

I look back at her, biting my lower lip. She blushes, dropping her gaze to the floor. "I love you too. You know that, don't you?"

On the last word, she looks up and pins me with that blue gaze. I'm a little dumbfounded. She loves me?

Like really loves me?

The thought breaks over me like the sea over a boat's stern. I stand there for a few seconds, staring at her almost blankly. She gets that weird guilty look on her face again, dropping her gaze. "I know you have to go," she says. "I know that. But when you get back, we should really talk. There are things that you don't know about me, things that you probably have every right to know…"

I stop her in her tracks, putting my hand on her upper arm and pulling her towards me. I still don't have the words to communicate what I feel exactly. But when my lips seek hers, my kiss hungry and searching, I pour all those feelings into the kiss. She responds immediately, raising up on her tiptoes and curling her hands into my lapel. She makes a soft sound of want against my lips. I slide my hands around her and take her up, needing her to feel how much I love her.

A moment later, she gently breaks off the kiss, looking me deep in my eyes. "You have to go. You don't want to be late."

I groan a little, not wanting to put her down. "I don't want to though."

She gives me a small sad smile. Running her hand through my hair, she kisses my lips ever so briefly. "I'll still be here when you get back. I'm not going anywhere. I promise."

I kiss her one final time before I put her down, checking the time on my watch. Fuck. If I don't hurry, I'm going to be late. And there is nothing that I want less then to show up late to a meeting with my commanding officer when I'm trying to prove that I'm an outstanding member of the Royal Air Force.

Letting my eyes travel down her body, I step back. "Do me a favor. Don't change clothes. I want you to be in this exact outfit when I get home. I want to tear it off your body." I arched a brow. "Okay?"

She blushes, smiling a little bit. "Okay, okay. Now go. You're going to be late."

Luckily as I hurry out the door and into the waiting car, I only have to go a couple of miles. The second the car pulls to a stop outside the coffee shop, I burst out the door and run into the shop. I'm looking at my watch as I hurry through to the door. I am exactly 1 minute late.

My commanding officer, Gen. Ted, is sitting at a corner booth, drumming his fingers on the table. I push my hand through my hair as I stride over to the table, saluting the general.

"Sir. Sorry I'm late, sir. It will not happen again."

"Capt. Løve," the general greets me with a nod. "Please, sit down."

I slide into the booth, my eyes scanning the general's face for any signs. I don't know why I was called here exactly, but I have a feeling that it's either very good news or very bad news. I sit up straight and try not to appear nervous.

The general frowns at the cup of coffee sitting before him. His expression is unreadable. "I called you here today because you applied for a promotion to our space force." He glances up at me. "I'm sorry to say that you have not been chosen. Not because of any shortcomings about you as a person, soldier. But because of your royal rank."

My heart freezes in my chest. I stare at the general's lips, willing him to not tell me what he came here to tell me. But he just continues anyway.

"Are you listening, soldier?"

I look up, but you my bottom lip. "Sir. Yes, sir."

He puts his elbows on the table, steepling his fingers. "After talking to Royal Air Force high command, it was decided that you were simply more valuable down here on earth then you would be as a potential astronaut. This is a reflection of your value as a royal prince. It's not a reflection of your performance or any inability on your part. You understand that?"

I feel numb as I nod. "Sir. Yes, sir."

He clears his throat. "I believe that if you are still interested in moving up the ladder, there is a position available for you. That is, if you decide to continue with the Royal Air Force. I knew a lot of men in your position that probably would not."

I glance at him, meeting his gaze had on. "Because I am a prince?"

He just inclines his head.

I shake my head, trying to pretend like he didn't just smash all my dreams. "I'm not so spoiled and materialistic as to want to leave the Royal Air Force, sir."

He smiles coolly. "No, I suppose you are not." He checks his watch, clearing his throat. "I have to be on my way now. I suppose I will see you on the base later?"

I slide of the booth, my body immediately stiffening into a salute. "Sir. Yes, sir. Thank you, sir."

He slowly climbs out of the booth and slaps my back, walking away. I turn and watch him walk out the doors, my heart pounding in my chest.

After a moment of staring, I walked to the door, heading out to the street. It's not so busy here, it's far from downtown and the middle of the work day. I don't know what I'm supposed to do or feel, so I just stare blankly down the street, trying to wrap my head around the fact that I will not be an astronaut.

I clench my fist. I've been lying to myself for a long time. I thought that if I was smart enough, if I was fit enough, if I devoted my life to being the best that I could be, I would escape my family somehow. That I would be chosen to train as an astronaut because I had made myself worthy, not because of some stupid title from of a made up hierarchy. But no, now I see all too clearly.

I am still worth more as the spare to Stellan's heir then I am as me, just a person trying to rise through the ranks. It stings like hell, that thought stated plainly.

Looking down, I start walking back to my apartment, ambling slowly while I turn my thoughts over in my head.

32

PIPPA

After Lars leaves, I sit at the kitchen counter, looking listlessly out at the Copenhagen skyline. I'm going to have to come clean to him when he gets back. I know it.

After fifteen years of lies, I'm finally about to tell him that I was born someone else. That thought makes me shiver.

As I finish my cup of coffee, I head to the sink to put the mug down. I hear a bell chime and I cock my head. That's certainly a new sound that I haven't heard before.

I wander into the hallway, where it the chime sounds again, louder this time. I think somehow it's a doorbell, though I don't know exactly where or how to address it.

I run into the bedroom and grab one of Lars's robes, pulling it around myself before I head down to the very end of the hallway near the elevator. A panel of lights is illuminated there, where normally it would blend in with the beige colored walls. I reach out a hand and touch it as the bell chimes again, revealing a screen.

Ms. Olson stares up into the camera lens, her mouth set in a grim line. My whole body runs cold. What is she doing here?

I look around for a second, wondering if I can just claim that I wasn't at home. Then again, now that I know that Ms. Olson works for Queen Ida, it probably goes along that Ms. Olson will know exactly where I am. Exhaling a long breath, I press the button at the bottom of the screen labeled *admit*.

Ms. Olson quickly appears as the elevator doors open, a little smirk on her face. "Hello, Sylvie."

She doesn't ask, she just barges in, her shoulder bumping mine.

"Excuse me," I say. "This is the prince's house. You can't just come in whenever you feel like it."

She throws a smirk over her shoulder, heading toward the kitchen. "I can do whatever I please, Sylvie. The sooner that you hear my demands, the sooner I will be out of your hair. So let's hurry it up."

I trail after her, my eyes widening. "Are you serious right now?" I ask as I walk into the kitchen. "Did they have to pick someone who was such a bitch to deal with me? Because I am not inclined to work with you. Actually, scratch that. I'm not inclined to work with anyone. I wish that you spies would all talk to each other and get your stories straight."

She checks her silver watch, looking bored. "We have your sister, Sylvie."

I look up at her, my expression puzzled. "What do you mean you have her?"

Ms. Olson pulls a phone from her pocket, showing me this screen. A video starts playing of a younger version of myself, standing in front of the Royal Palace. The cameraman says something inaudible to Stella. Stella smiles right into the camera and says, "Bonjour! My name is Stella and I am here in Copenhagen, on the first leg of my European tour…"

Ms. Olson turns the phone off, looking at me pointedly. "We have her here. She doesn't know that you even exist. She thinks that she has won a songwriting contest and is now on the tour to represent France."

My heart beats loudly. I stare at the phone though the screen is powered off, not quite able to put it all together. "And what are you going to do with my sister, exactly?"

"That's up to you. If you do what you are supposed to do, Stella will continue on her European tour and nothing will happen to her. But if you don't, the man that filmed this video will hurt her. You understand that? Stella's life is in danger."

I stare at her face, trying to weed her expression. But she is solemn and there is nothing more to read there.

I lick my lips. "And what is it that you want from me?"

She smirks a little. "We want you to behave yourself. That means that you'll accede to any and every demand that is put to you by the royal family. You will wear the wedding dress that has been picked out for you, dance to the song that has been selected for you, and generally be a perfect princess all through the wedding. And then, the real work starts. You will keep track of Lars's movements and report everything back to me. Oh, and you will absolutely have Lars is children. That's not in question."

My heart dies. My first inclination is just to laugh in her face. But my gaze is drawn down to the phone again. I don't know that the video that she showed me is even really Stella, although they did find a young woman that looked remarkably like the photo I saw on the internet. If she's an actress, she's a good one.

I must take too long think to think about it because Ms. Olson claps her hands at me, startling me. "You are taking too long to respond. I'm not here to offer you a plethora of decisions. I'm here to tell you exactly what is going to happen from here on out."

I squint at her. "How do I even know that this the woman that you have on video is really my sister?" I give my head a tiny shake. "I mean, for all you know, that may not be the way to control me. I may be heartless. I may not care."

Her lips twist into a cool smile. "I think we've already established the fact that you do care for Stella."

I narrow my gaze at her. "You're threatening me with the harm of someone that I am not even sure is actually my sister. I'm trying to tell you now that I could very easily just tell you to shove off."

Her eyebrows rise. "Is that so?" She reaches down to the phone, turning it on and dialing a number. She puts the phone on speaker.

A man answers. "Hello?"

"Kill the girl," Ms. Olson says. "Make sure you capture her death on film."

"Are you sure?" the man asks.

Ms. Lowe's and looks at me, raising a brow. "I don't know. Am I sure, Pippa?"

I stare her down for a good five seconds before slowly shaking my head. "No," I mutter.

She smiles at me and tells the man on the other end of the line not to worry about it.

As she hangs up, I swallow nervously. There's no way of knowing whether she's serious or not about killing the girl. There's no honest way of telling whether or not Stella is in fact my sister. But one thing is very clear to me: it's obvious that I am bringing danger and pain into Lars's world by continuing to pretend to be his fiancée.

So, Ms. Olson says, folding her arms across her chest. "Do we have an understanding then?"

I nod. I would've said just about anything to get her to call off her dogs. And knowing that, I realize what must be done.

I have to break up with Lars. I can't risk being an enemy to him while I was supposed to be engages to him. I would never put him in any peril. And I fear that by remaining his fiancée, I'm putting him in danger.

So I have to break off the engagement. And the sooner it's done, the better.

That realization makes my eyes well up with tears. My heart breaks, thinking about the conversation that I'm going to have to have with Lars.

He is my heart, love of my life, but in the grand scheme of things I would rather know that he is safe then to risk putting him in danger over and over again just him with my presence.

Ms. Olson looks pleased with herself. "Well then, "she says. "I've already made an appointment for you with the royal tailor. He will fit the royal wedding dress on you. And don't feel the need to respond to any wedding planning invitations, because everything has already been dealt with. There will be no detail left unattended."

I nod a bit glumly. Ms. Olson looks satisfied with herself and picks up the phone, putting it in her pocket. Under normal circumstances, I would ask her more questions about where my sister was and what she intended to do with her. But today, I don't.

If she finds the lack of questions unusual, she doesn't say anything about it. In the back of my mind, I am trying to figure out what the best plan to save Stella would be.

"Sylvie?" I look up, wiping at my eyes.

She starts walking towards his door, smiling her particular little smile. "I think you will see that you made the right choice. I think you will be satisfied. After all, isn't it every little girl's fantasy to marry a real life prince?"

I don't say a word. I just cross my arms across my chest and look at her blankly. She smiles at me, gives me a head to toe glance, and then shrugs. "I'm sure we'll see each other soon," she tosses over her shoulder as she heads out of the room.

After she's gone, I sit and stare off into space. I don't know how I will find the strength to do this. But I'm going to have to break up with him, no matter how much it tears my heart into pieces. Worse than that, I know that my secret, the one held closest to my heart for so many years, is going to get out one way or the other. I have a choice I suppose.

I can take my story to a newspaper and hope that they don't sensationalize who I am and what my father did. Or I can wait until someone else slips the paper this information.

God, if I could do everything all over again, I would tell Lars the whole and unvarnished truth on the day that we met. It might've changed the course of our friendship... But I wouldn't be staring down the barrel of this terrible decision right now.

It occurs to me that maybe Lars won't care about who I used to be. It's possible. But if I tell him, layout the whole tragic truth, there is always the possibility that he won't understand.

In any event, I will have to break off our engagement. No way will the royal palace let him marry someone who has lied about who she was for so many years. The daughter of an anti-monarchist terrorist?

Ja, I'm definitely not going to be welcome at any kind of family event.

I hear Lars in the hall and I suck in a breath. Do I have to do it right now?

On the other hand, can I stand to wait?

When Lars finally comes around the corner from the hallway, I can see the sadness written all over his face and in his slumped shoulders. My heart wrenches.

"What happened?" I ask him softly.

He looks up at me, shaking his head. "I didn't get into the space program," he says. "My commander said it is because they need a prince more than they need me as an astronaut. The palace probably shot down the idea."

He walks over to me, ripping off his tie. His eyes are so full of pain that I don't quite know where to start.

I open my arms to him and he steps into them, hugging me hard. He lays his head on my shoulder.

I close my eyes and suck in a deep lungful of his unique scent, thinking only that I can't possibly break up with him right now. Not when he's just gotten such terrible news.

When he straightens and cups my jaw, I lift my face to his and let my eyes flutter closed. His mouth finds mine, his tongue teasing my own. And I think that just for now, just for today at least, this is enough.

33

PIPPA

I SHIVER AND INVITE HIM TO COME CLOSER. HIS LIPS FIND A pulse point at my neck, his big body coming down on top of mine. My breath stops when he grinds his cock against my pubic bone.

Ohh. Yes, I had almost forgotten how delicious every single touch could be. Addictive, almost.

Lars's lips touch my collarbone, trailing down to my breast. I gasp and arch into his kisses, making him chuckle.

"You missed me," he says, pulling back. His expression is amused, but his bright blue eyes are hungry.

"Maybe," I tease.

He kisses me, making me lose my breath as his tongue slides against mine. Then he pulls away again, standing up fully.

"I want you naked and in my bed before I'm out of the shower. I hope you don't have anything planned because I'm going to fuck you so hard that you won't be able to walk straight tomorrow."

My cheeks turn scarlet as my eyes widen. With that, he turns and bounds up the stairs. I can hear him as he goes, taking the stairs two at a time.

It feels more naughty than usual, being left to prepare myself for him. For the specific purpose of readying myself for his needs. I climb the stairs slowly, heading into his bedroom and stripping down to nothing.

I lie on his bed, arranging and rearranging myself, trying to figure out which way to present myself to him.

When Lars steps out of his bathroom, drying himself with a towel, he is the only thing I can concentrate on. My eyes travel down his form, taking in his muscled, toned body. He ambles over to me, his eyes still ravenous, and he drops the towel on the floor.

I look at him, six and a half feet of perfect olive skin and well-toned muscle. He's all arms and abs, pecs and muscular thighs. And his face, with those angular cheekbones, icy blue eyes, and his dark eyebrows.

Not to mention, he has the nicest cock. I don't have much to compare it to, but when he fills me up with his cock, I almost implode every single time.

All in all, the perfect package. He comes over to the bed, grabbing me by the ankle and pulling me to the edge of the bed. But that doesn't shut me up. As he nuzzles my neck, the question bubbles up to my lips.

Lars's big hand slides around the front of my throat, squeezing. My hands come up to pull his hand away, but he growls so loudly I can feel it where our bodies touch. The sound vibrates over my naked skin, sending out goosebumps.

"Oh, little witch." He leans close, inhaling the sudden scent of my fear. Knotting his fingers in my hair, he seems almost amused. "I'm going to fucking ruin you tonight."

Yes. God, yes.

His fingers tighten in my hair, making me moan. He smashes his mouth to mine, as much kissing me as showing his dominance. He pulls on my hair again, making me gasp, and then uses that moment to invade my mouth. He licks and rolls his tongue around the entirety of my mouth, biting my lower lip until I groan.

When he pulls his mouth away, I gasp for breath. He doesn't let up on his grip on my hair. Instead, he sits down on the bed, forcing my head down to his lap. I can barely open my mouth before he's shoving his cock in it, pushing my head down onto his long, thick dick.

Lars moans a little. He keeps his thrusts shallow, his cock coming just to the point of making me gag, then pulling back.

"Christ," he mutters, keeping my head moving steadily. "Pippa, holy fuck. I love watching you. Fuck, I love knowing I'm giving you exactly what you need."

The whole time, he just bobs my head up and down on his massive cock. He groans and leans back a little, watching my mouth traveling up and down his cock intently. There is so much saliva that it starts to drip down to the base of his dick.

For some reason, that is the thing that flips a switch for me, turning me on. I close my eyes, loving the feel of his slick flesh in my mouth. But before I can really do anything crazy, he stops me.

"Enough," he grates, pulling me off of his cock. My mouth makes a satisfying *pop* sound as he pushes me off.

I can't go far though, because he moves to flip me over onto my knees. He leans down and spreads my legs, pushing my head down. As he strokes my clit from behind, I can feel myself grow wet.

Fuck, with Lars teasing me just like this, I can't help but give in. He's dominating me, giving me pleasure while exerting control. And I love it.

I can feel his clever fingers skating over my pussy. I shiver.

He surprises me by pushing his face against my pussy forcefully. He presses his hand on my lower back and puts his mouth to my pussy, his tongue finding my clit without fail.

He circles my swollen clit a few times, then traces his tongue to my aching entrance. He delves inside. I let out a moan, pushing back against his face.

Then he moves again, pushing me down on the bed. I feel him settle against the back of my legs, his big cock nudges my entrance. I moan.

"Yes," I whisper, closing my eyes.

He thrusts into my pussy without a second's hesitation, filling me to the hilt, stretching my pussy out in the best way possible. We both make a sound as he drives his cock all the way home.

Lars grips my hips, slamming himself into me, heedless of me. His touch is brutal, the swing of his hips frenzied. I can just barely hang on, riding the waves of pleasure building inside me.

When I come, it's sudden and unexpected and bright, a burst of magnificent color and melodious sound. Lars is right behind me, groaning his release.

34

LARS

When I wake in the morning, Pippa is still asleep beside me. She faces away from me, scrunched into a ball. Her amazing curls look like nothing so much as a bright fire. I sweep them off her neck, placing a kiss at the place where her collarbone and her neck meet.

She awakens sleepily, yawning and stretching as she rolls over. Then she sees me and her whole face falls. I frown, reaching my hand up and touching her hip.

"What is that about? Don't make that face at me."

She bites her lip and swallows. "I have to tell you something." Her eyes fill with tears. "It's serious."

Propping myself up on my hands, I look at her with mock seriousness. "Okay. I'm ready."

She wipes away her own tears, shaking her head a little. "Don't joke right now. Please."

She pins me with that blue gaze of hers. A little wrinkle of worry appears in her forehead, right between her brows.

I push my cheek out with my tongue, exhaling along breath. "You can tell me anything, Pippa." I catch her hands, squeezing her fingers together. "Don't you know that by now?"

A shudder runs through her. She squeezes my fingers, releasing them. She looks so damn guilty that I don't even know what to say about that.

"A story is going to come out about me in the press. A really bad story."

I squint at her. "A story about what? Not that it matters. You know I don't care about what's in the press."

She looks at me, her gaze scanning my face. "I'm afraid to tell you what I have to tell you because I don't want you to stop looking at me the way that you do. I don't want you to stop loving me."

I frown, reaching out for her. I pull her close, shaking my head. "Just tell me. It can't be that bad, whatever it is."

A fresh round of tears fills her eyes and she wipes at her face, not stopping them in the least. "You may not care… At least I hope you don't. But I think it will keep me from ever being able to marry you."

My eyebrows shoot up. "Tell me. What could possibly be that bad?"

She looks down for a beat, her eyelids fluttering closed. Then she looks back at me, her eyes filled with pain. "I'm not Pippa Welch. Pippa Welch is a complete fabrication."

I blink a few times. "What?"

She licks her lips, her hand finding mine. She clenches my fingers. "I'm not Pippa Welch. I was born under a different name. I've been lying for most of my life."

I know that she is looking at me and saying these words, but I shake my head in disbelief. "No, that's not right. I mean, you were Pippa Welch when I met you. We have known each other for ages."

She grips my fingers so hard that it's almost painful. "I'm telling you the truth, Lars. I was brought to St. Matthews after being smuggled out of France. My father was Ansel Martin, the terrorist who bombed French Parliament. He *killed* people."

I squint, trying to make sense of her story. "So what? So your father was a terrorist? I don't understand why that qualifies you to change your name and move to another country…"

She swallows heavily. "I was just a little girl. I was only twelve when it happened. A family friend took my sister and I in for a while. She thought that eventually we would stop being harassed by everyone that we met… But after a year, she made the decision to split us up and change my identity." She shakes her head. "I agreed to it. I agreed to be separated from my sister and to go live a new life under a new name. None of this would ever have come out except…" She bites her lip, her eyes steady on mine. "Except for you are a prince."

She falls silent then, tears overwhelming her once more. I sit up, shaking my hand a little. She lets go of it and I make a fist to regain blood flow. "So you're… you're not Pippa Welch." I look at her, frowning. "Are you even from England?"

Her cheeks burn red. "My mother was. She died a few years before my father… killed all those people." She dropped my gaze, looking down at the sheets.

"What's your real name?" I ask.

"Sylvie. Sylvie Martin," she whispers.

I crack my knuckles, shaking my head a little. "I guess I am in shock of some kind. Why didn't you just tell me? Literally you could've told me anytime in the past fifteen years. You could've told me before we got engaged, for Christ's sake. I think it would be nice to know that you are not really who you say you are."

She sits up, pulling up the sheet with her, and touches my arm imploringly. "That name… that girl is dead. She died on the way to St. Matthews. I am Pippa. I've only ever been Pippa since I met you."

I blow out a long breath. "Why are you telling me this now?"

She looks down again. "Because your grandmother found out somehow. And she's been blackmailing me for months." Pippa glances up at me, tucking her hair behind her ear. "It's a long story, but essentially she has known since before we were engaged. And she's been… trying to get information on you, I guess."

I stare at her, feeling like for the second time in as many minutes she's speaking a language other than my own. "What? We…" I shake my head angrily. "My grandmother has been blackmailing you?"

Pippa's face grows anguished. "Yes," she answers simply. "I didn't know at first that she was behind the person black-mailing me. But it turns out that she expected me to play along with her and her schemes. Your grandmother had a woman name Ms. Olson come visit me. She wanted to know everything that you said to me." She bites her lip. "She had pictures of my little sister. She had photographs of you and I in a compromising position. And she threatened me that if I didn't obey her rules, she would hurt you or my sister."

I squint at her. "Momse threatened you? Seriously?"

Her cheeks turn bright red. She nods. "Ms. Olson threatened me first but when I didn't comply with her, your grandmother quite openly said that she would deal with me and I wouldn't like it."

"And what does the press have to do with this little story of yours exactly?" I ask.

Pippa dashes away her tears. "The story is out there now. If Ms. Olson knows, chances are that other people know. And while you may not care about who I am, the royal press office is going to have a lot to say about me and how I can't be trusted. The story will get out one way or another. It would be better if I were the one to tell it to a friendly journalist."

I stand up, feeling like the world is shifting beneath my feet. "Maybe you can't be trusted. I mean, for all I know, you're not Pippa or Sylvie or… whoever."

She looks down on her the hands in her lap. "I'm sorry, Lars. Really I am. The only reason I didn't tell you before because it just seems… easier to forget who I used to be, I guess."

Reminding myself to breathe, I walk to the huge glass window, looking out at the dark and city skyline. I have a million questions, I feel like. I try to go through them methodically, to sort out what I absolutely need to know right now. One thing that sticks out in my mind though.

I turn to her, a frown on my face. "You said my grandmother asked you about what I said and did?"

She swallows. "Well, mostly Ms. Olson asked me. But yes, she asked me for reports on you. I refused, but she wouldn't let me go that easily. I told her as little as I felt I could."

"Did you tell my grandmother about me trying to be an astronaut?"

Look of surprise on her face is complete. "Well, *ja*. I did. I thought that was kind of an open secret."

"And did you tell her about any of my other job details? Any of my confidential conversations that I had with Royal Air Force personnel?"

Her cheeks flush. "I… I don't know. I don't I don't think so but… I could have. Is that important?"

My lips twist. "I don't know Pippa. I don't know about that. I just…" I shake my head. I need to think. I need to… run or something."

Heading to my closet, I grab a t-shirt, a pair of running pants, and a light windbreaker. I change quickly, my mind racing. When I leave my closet and return to my room, Pippa is sitting on my bed, tears in her eyes. She looks so sorrowful that I desperately want to wrap my arms around her.

But I don't. I can't yet. I'm going on a run.

I just walk right by her, stalking out of the apartment, needing to clear my mind and digest all the information that I have just received. I head onto the darkened Copenhagen streets and push myself, running as fast and as far as I can handle for almost two hours. By the time I am jogging back into my apartment lobby, the sun has risen.

I'm fucking exhausted. I'm still not sure what I'm going to say to Pippa, but I am a lot more centered than I was two hours ago.

But when I get into my apartment, it's still and silent.

"Pippa," I call. No response. "Pippa?"

But she is nowhere to be found. I grab my phone and try to call her but there is no answer there either.

Pippa Welch or Sylvie Martin or whoever she is… She's definitely not in this apartment anymore.

Fuck.

3 5

PIPPA

I'M STANDING OUTSIDE IN THE FREEZING COLD, LOOKING OUT over the frosty majesty of landscape. I don't know what exactly drew me to this skiing cabin again. When I left Lars's house, tears streaming from my face, I had no place to go. I suppose that I came here because I only have good memories associated with this cabin.

But those good memories have driven me out onto the balcony, away from the memories of everything that happened in that bedroom, on the couch, on the dining room table…

I sniffle and blot at my eyes with my mittens, feeling like I've lost everything that I ever held dear. I turned off my phone the second that I left Lars's place. The thing is that I know him pretty well and I think that he would have forgiven me eventually.

But I can't be a part of his life.

Not if my part in it is to be a marionette, my strings being pulled by his grandmother. Not in exchange for my sister being tied up in all of this.

I'm not even sure what I'm going to do now. Maybe I will go back to France. Or England, I guess.

There's no way that I can stay in Copenhagen and not see Lars every single place that we've ever been, or at least the memory of him.

I shiver and pull the edges of my coat closer around me. I have no job. I have no boyfriend or fiancé. My best friends are both entangled with the royal family.

There's nothing left here for me.

Inhaling a shaky breath, I blow it out in a long stream. It clouds in the air, hanging for a moment. I hear the crunch of gravel.

Whirling, I watched as a huge black SUV comes climbing up the snowy driveway. My heart starts racing. Could it be that Lars has tracked me down?

I push down the hope that rises in my chest. Even if he does get out of the car, even if I do see his face, even if I want him so badly I don't know what to do with myself…

That doesn't fix or solve anything at all. It would only prolong our mutual sadness.

The car comes to a stop. I head across the porch to watch as the back doors open on both sides of the car. And then I see Margot's face.

The Queen of Denmark is here to see me. My eyes fill with tears. I cover my mouth with my hands, almost missing that little blonde Nika follows Margot up the last few feet of the driveway. They both look chilled to the bone despite wearing layers and layers of clothing.

Margot locks eyes with me and sees that I am crying. She burst into a run, trotting up the steps to where I am standing. She doesn't ask questions, she doesn't say anything. She just barrels into me, wrapping her arms around me.

A ragged sob leaves my lips, unable to be controlled the longer. I've been so miserable these past four days and seeing her is bittersweet. After all, she essentially is the royal palace personified.

But mostly, I look at her and see the same girl that I met when I was a freshman in college, figuring out my roommate situation. She looks almost the same as she did then, only now she pulls back, brushes back my hair, and looks at me sternly.

"Where have you been?" she lectures. "Do you know that I had to pull all kinds of strings and track your credit card to find you? I'm not even sure what I did was technically legal."

Nika comes to stand next to me, throwing an arm around me. She smiles brightly at me. "You got her all riled up. You should've heard her talking about you in the car. She was pissed."

I wipe my eyes, apologetic. "I'm so sorry, Margot. Both of you. I just… I don't have a good reason. I'm just pathetic right now."

Nika shivers. "Let's go inside. We can talk about how wrong you are until we're blue in the face but I personally do not want to be out here for a second longer."

I huff out a watery laugh. "Of course." I lead the way into the house, holding the door open for Margot and Nika. I feel like a fool as I usher them in, taking their coats and telling them to make themselves welcome. I rush to take off my coat and I am a little bit self-conscious because my normally carefully chosen outfits are still in Lars's closet. I'm wearing what I could pick up from the ski lodge's store: a long sleeve T-shirt and a pair of ski pants. I see Nika look at my outfit was some surprise but luckily she is a good friend that she doesn't say anything.

I flush as I hurry into the kitchen. "Do you want tea?" I call. "You guys like tea, right?"

Nika settles in on the couch, her expression disapproving. "We want answers. That's what we want." Margot turns to her and gives her a look. She stands up, putting her hand over her belly. I realize that she has actually started to show.

For some reason, that actually makes me cry all over again. I have a mini breakdown over the sink, crying as I fill the kettle. Margot comes up behind me and hugs me, slipping her arms around my rib cage. She rests her cheek against my back.

I can't help but love her. It seems so unfair that among all the things that I am about to miss, I'm going to miss out on Margot and Stellan's first child. I may get a picture now and then, but I won't really know him or her. It won't be the same.

"Do you want to tell us what happened?" Margot murmurs. "Lars just said that you got into an argument with his grand-mother. Which let me say, I have been there personally."

Nika calls out. "Margot's too nice to say that she's a bitch, but my grandmother is definitely a bitch."

I wrinkle my nose. "I hate that word. Let's just say that she is… a monster."

I wipe my eyes and sniff a little. Margot steps back and I turn around, drawing in a shaky breath.

"What else did Lars tell you?" I ask, my eyes going from Margot to Nika.

"He said something about how you said you weren't who you claim to be or something? Honestly, it was pretty hard to follow. At the time that he was telling me, he was technically on a run and he was pretty out of breath."

"*Ja*, it's been hard to get him on the phone even." Margot wrinkles her nose. "He's been very distraught since you disappeared from his apartment. So?"

"*Ja*, spill the beans. Tell us everything."

Margot takes the tea kettle from my hand, setting it aside and guiding me back to the living room. I sit down on the couch and suck in a breath. "I don't even know where to start. It's all so confusing and sort of fucked up and…"

Nika leans forward, putting her hand on my knee. "I'm gonna need you to stop talking like that. I feel like you are editorializing a lot and making yourself look as bad as possible when I just want the facts. Okay?"

My cheeks turn pink. "Sorry."

Margot sits down on the other side of me and sighs. "I'm also going to need you to stop apologizing. Weren't you the one that told me that when I first met you? You told me that I apologize too much. I want you to take some advice from yourself."

I run a hand over my face. *Ja. Ja*, okay. It just… It involves some deception. Of Lars, but of you guys too. So be prepared for that, I guess."

I tell the story of the fake engagement, of Ms. Olson and her demands, and of Lars's grandmother in as few words as possible. I try not to editorialize, as Nika called my derogatory view of things.

When I'm done, I look at Nika and Margot, trying to read their expressions. Nika just looks vaguely confused. Margot on the other hand looks furious. I don't really know how to deal with furious Margot, so I steel myself.

"Are you telling me that Stellan's grandmother knew who you were the entire time? That she threatened you, Lars, and your sister because of some… some *gossip?*"

I pause, not sure how to answer that for a second. I wasn't really expecting her to be angry with anyone but me in this scenario. "Um? *Ja*, I guess I am telling you that."

Nika up pipes up. "That is so fucked up. I can't believe that Momse would do that." She scrunches her face up. "Well, I can believe it, I just don't want to. That makes me *so* mad."

Margot shakes her head. "My question is, where does Lars fit into this picture? Because I don't think that he is so upset with you that he is never going to speak to you again. I think that he would really like to know where you are and to be allowed to come here."

I sit back on the couch, shaking my head. "I know. He's way too forgiving for his own good."

"Lars?" Nika asks. "I don't think that forgiving is among the top fifty adjectives that you would use to describe my brother. I do however think that he is more understanding than you give him credit for. You didn't even really talk about it. You just like told him what happened and then he was super confused and he went for a run and…" She makes a gesture. "You were gone."

Margot touches Nika's arm, letting her know that she's said enough about that.

Margot looks at me. "Why did you run away?"

I swallow against the lump in my throat. "Because I know that the royal family can't forgive what I did. They can't forgive me not telling them the truth about my identity. They can't forgive my father or what he did."

Margot squints at me. "I think it would be a mistake to equate everyone's personal feelings with the amount of forgiveness that you receive from the royal family. Also, I think that you overestimate Stellan's grandmother's power. Whether she likes it or not, Stellan and I have been making decisions mostly on our own. She's losing a lot of her steam these days."

I bite my lip, glancing between Nika and Margot. "If you are here to talk me into going back, you are mistaken. Lars is better off without me. He's better off finding a girl that he can settle down with that will not create as much political drama as I will. As soon as that story comes out…"

Nika cuts me off. "It's been out for three days."

I don't quite know what to say to that. I flush and cover my eyes with my hand, shaking my head. "Of course it has. Because the royal press office has absolutely zero chill."

"I just talked to Stellan this morning about how I was going to try to find you and make you come back with me. He didn't seem opposed to it. I think that you spent fifteen years waiting for the other shoe to drop, thinking that you did something terribly wrong. And you didn't. I mean… Maybe it wasn't on the up and up, but it really wasn't that bad." Margot scrunches her face up.

"And you were a child," Nika adds. "You didn't have that much of a say in whether or not you started a new life or not."

Margot nods. "*Ja*. Everybody is on your side. Everybody that is not Stellan's grandmother, of course."

"Who sucks, by the way," Nika says.

I give my head a tiny shake. "I'm so glad that you guys came up here. I am glad that Lars is okay. But I'm not going back. I can't."

Margot and Annika look at each other, Margot sighing. She cast an eye over my outfit, looking me up and down. "Do you have any more comfy clothes?"

"Well, I have the ski shop right down the street," I hedge.

Margot looks at me, dead serious. "I will need to go hit that store up. Because I'm not coming back without you. So if I have to get comfortable, that's what I'll do."

Nika pulls out her cell phone and starts scrolling through this screen. "I'm ordering new clothes for all of us as we speak. One of my assistants is going to drive them here. No arguments."

I cross my arms, frowning at both of them, and get ready to make my case.

LARS

I AM GLOWERING AS I STARE DOWN THE LENGTH OF THE polished dining room table, pushing my cheek out with my tongue. At the other end of the table is Momse, looking quite tense. I make a gesture, ready for her to start explaining herself.

"So? The papers have got Pippa's story. I believe that you have been working behind the scenes and pulling the strings, whatever you need to do to make Pippa look bad. How can you defend yourself?"

She looks affronted. "Lars, I think if you just put aside your attachment to Pippa, you'll see that she was never the right girl for you anyway…"

I slam my hand down on the table, my eye twitching. Momse looks at me, her eyes widening just a little bit. "There's no call for that, is there?"

I ignore that. "So you essentially have no justification for your actions. Blackmailing my fiancée, bullying her, driving her out of Copenhagen… This is all part of your plan?" I shake my head, disgusted. "The only reason I even agreed to this meeting today was to give you one last chance to explain yourself."

My grandmother stands up from her chair, walking over to the window. "I know that it seems like I'm intruding. But really, I have to make sure that my grandchildren have the best chances for continuing the royal bloodline. I went wrong with Stellan. Annika got away from me too. So you are my third attempt at trying for the best outcome."

She shrugged, turning and looking at me innocently. "You can't blame me for wanting to make sure that everything goes right. And I knew the second that you said that you were engaged to Pippa that she couldn't make you happy. Not really, not in the long run."

I raise for my chair, sighing. "Well, it doesn't matter now."

A little smile crosses her mouth. "No, I suppose it doesn't. With Pippa gone, we can focus on finding you a more suitable girl."

I shake my head. "No, you misunderstand me. It doesn't matter anymore because you are kicked out of the royal family. I'm not sure exactly how I'm going to do it or by what means, but you have meddled with not just one, not just two, but three serious relationships. Luckily your grandchildren are stronger than you think and we all see what you done… But you have caused so much chaos and turmoil between the Løve siblings and those that we are partnered with. It's time that you retire from royal life and go live out your remaining years in solitude. Somewhere far away from Copenhagen."

She lifts her chin and scoffs. "You don't have the authority to do anything like that."

I give her a cool little smile. "Enjoy the last days of your royal reign. Because I have Stellan on my side and now it's just a matter of figuring out how to strip you of your title and remove you from our ranks."

She narrows her eyes at me. "You wouldn't."

I make my way toward the door, my hands still punched into fists. "I've already done it. This is just a courtesy, letting you know that it's already been done. So with that, I feel like we have nothing left to say to each other. Goodbye, Momse."

I pull the door open, stepping outside. I hear Momse's plaintive voice, trying to pull me back in.

"Lars… Lars! You can't do this…"

I march down the palace halls, heading for Stellan's office. I knock on his door.

"Come in," he calls.

I enter his little study, finding him and Erik sitting on the long couches that bracket the fireplace. Stellan raises a brow at me.

"Was it good? Do you feel remotely better now that you finally told Momse to fuck off?"

I walk to the same couch as Stellan, collapsing on it with a sigh. "I think it would've felt good if I didn't have so much else to worry about. Is there any word about Pippa's location?"

Erik squints toward the window. "I think if you really wanted to find her, you probably could. There are ways. But the question is, does she want to be found?"

"And what are you going to do with her once you find her?" Stellan chimes in.

I blow out of breath. "That's a good question. All the papers have pictures of Pippa plastered across the covers, with headlines that call her a liar and a fallen princess. I think that she was at least partially right in the fact that she shouldn't hold her breath, waiting for the royal family to forgive her for her sins."

"Can I make a suggestion? Retire from public life." His gaze slides to Stellan. "I know that you like having Pippa around to do some handwaving, but I think if you allow him to retire from public life, he can still get married eventually."

Stellan grunts. "I think he is right. As much as it pains me to say it, I don't think that we can have you being married to Pippa and still be a member of the royal family. You'll still receive your inheritance, I think. But you would not represent us anymore."

He shrugs. Erik nods his head.

I take a deep breath, sighing loudly. "I hate that I have to be worried about what I feel is something too advanced for our relationship. Like, I think that in the normal course of things, we wouldn't even mention marriage. But I got the ball rolling by fake proposing to her…"

"I'm still mad at you about that, as an aside." Stellan jabs his finger at me.

"Get in line. There's nothing that you can say that I probably haven't thought myself."

"What are you going to do to win her back?" Erik asks again. "You need to figure out the grand gesture. Something that will make her realize how much she needs you in her life.

Because I guarantee you right now, she is doing the math and sorting out whether you are worth it."

I shoot him a glare. "I hadn't really thought about it. I'm just focused on finding her.

Stellan fishes his phone out of his pocket, frowning at the screen. "Well, it looks like the girls found Pippa. I don't know how, but I'm glad that Pippa is safe and sound."

I blow out a breath. "She's all right? Where is she?"

Stellan looks up at me. "Margot says that the three of them are talking things through. So if I tell you, I need you to promise that you are not going to just immediately rush over there. I know it's been a few days, but Pippa needs some reinforcement from her lady friends."

I give him a droll look. "I promise."

"She's up at a ski cabin about an hour north of here. Margot said that you would know which one."

My eyebrows rise with surprise. "That's where she went?"

"Maybe she felt like getting her exercise in every day," Erik jokes.

I shoot him a cool look. "That's the place we were staying when we first hooked up."

Stellan quirks a brow. "Wait, was that not just a couple of months ago?"

My neck heats. "*Ja*, we might've lied about some stuff. We didn't start fucking until we were already fake engaged."

Stellan shakes his head. "You really are a bastard, do you know that?"

"Wait, wait," Erik cuts in. "That doesn't really answer the question of what you're going to do to prove to Pippa that you are the only choice for her."

Eager to get away from talking about my past deceptions, I latch onto that question.

"I should propose again. I mean, for real this time."

Erik shakes his head at me. "That's obvious enough. But how should you do it?"

"Yeah, what does she like?" Stellan adds.

"Hmm", I say thoughtfully. "A lot of things, obviously."

"Duh," Erik says. "Name some stuff, Get the juices flowing. There are no bad ideas."

I purse my lips. "She likes dressing up and being elegant. She loves parties. She loves people. She likes…" I chuckle. "Pippa loves getting me to dance."

Stellan lifts a brow. "It sounds like you need to throw a huge party, with everyone she knows in attendance."

A light bulb goes off for me. "Actually…" I glance at both of them with a sly expression on my face, biting my lip. "I think I have the perfect idea. I will just need a shit ton of help…"

PIPPA

It takes the better part of two whole days for Margot and Nika to convince me to return to Copenhagen. When we are about to leave, Margot pulls me aside and shows me a garment bag. My eyebrows lift a little as I unzip the bag.

Inside is the most gorgeous dress I have probably ever seen. It is made of sheer lace with light pink and purple splashes all over it and an elegant train that trails behind it.

I look up at Margot, arching my brow. "What is this?"

She gives me a secretive smile. "Just put it on. I'll see you out in the car."

I change into the dress and pin my hair up, wondering what exactly Margot has planned. I don't know and that fact gives me a lot of anxiety.

The ride to Copenhagen is practically silent. Margot and Nika are on their phones, probably checking in on all the things that they have willingly missed in order to talk some sense into me. I bite my lip and look out the window, thinking about how I will show up at Lars's house, apologetic that I ran away.

Will that be enough for him to take me back? That's the real question.

When we get into downtown Copenhagen, we don't go to either the palace or Lars's apartment. Instead, we pull up beside a row of shops on a busy street in downtown Copenhagen, not far from the palace. I arch my brow at Margot. She's quick to reassure me.

"I thought that you could do you with a little bit of shopping before your big reunion with Lars. You know, let off some steam, get your ducks in a row."

I squint at her. "Are you sure I shouldn't just go straight to wherever Lars is?"

Nika opens the car door, ready to get out. "This sounds fine. Let's do it. We can go back to the mission at hand once we are through."

"Yeah, it will be half an hour or an hour at most. Besides, this bakery over here has these éclairs that I am currently fetishizing." Margot pulls a face. "Do it for my poor, pregnant self."

My lips quirk but I give in fairly easily. "All right. I mean, I do love to shop…"

We slide out of the back of the SUV, shielding our faces against the bright morning light. I see the pastry shop that Margot mentioned. Looking across the street, I start heading there.

As I cross the street, there is a young woman dressed as a ballet dancer, dancing for the public. My gaze snags on her, on her delicate light pink dress and elegant form. Suddenly music starts playing. The strains of The Cure's "Friday I'm In Love" start to rise into the air. I look around but don't see where the music is coming from. It's loud enough that it's obviously part of the dancer's performance, as she doesn't bat an eyelash at the loud sound.

She waves her hand at the audience and five people emerge from the crowd, all lining up equally distant from the ballerina. They are all wearing full-face white masks, making me frown as I study them.

They all start to dance, their moves smooth and organized, sort of a hip-hop style. Instantly there are plenty of crowd members, curious about the music and what other people are looking at. The ballerina joins the line of dancers, dancing along with the same moves.

I can't help but smile. Nika and Margot come stand by me, urging me forward a few steps to get closer to the performers. I study their faces, but I can't see much other than their blank white masks.

Margot leans in with a whisper. "They're quite good, aren't they?"

I don't take my eyes off the dancers, but I whisper back to her. "They are good. I don't know about the bloke at the end, he seems like he might not be a professional dancer like the rest of them. But they're all pretty decent."

The ballerina gestures to the crowd again and six more people join them, white masks and street clothes on. My eye keeps wandering down to the guy at the end, who is honestly trying to do all the moves but seems to be partially failing.

Nika grasps my elbow, smiling at the dancers. "Doesn't this just lift your spirits?"

I give her a rueful smile. "It does, actually. Do you think that these dancers work on an hourly basis? And I just hire them to come and cheer me up whenever I'm feeling blue?"

Margot shushes me unexpectedly, nodding toward the ballerina. The ballerina heads toward us, a beatific smile on her face. Margot squeezes my forearm, earning a look from me. She has tears in her eyes and I wonder if being pregnant has made her a little bit more prone to cry or if she knows something that I don't.

The ballerina dances up to us, bowing elegantly and looking me straight in the eyes. She doesn't say anything, but she does hold out a hand. My cheeks burn bright red as I accept the invitation to dance. She pulls me toward the center of the wide circle of people.

The music rises, reaching a crescendo. The dancers all move into a triangle position and I dance along beside them despite not knowing the steps at all. All the dancers but one suddenly kneel.

One of the dancers is left standing, the awkward dancer. That one person walks over to me, reaching out and taking my hand.

Then he takes a knee, pushing his white mask up. My eyes widen as I realize that Lars is kneeling before me, looking more nervous than I think I've ever seen him. He pulls out a ring box.

"Oh god," I gasp. "Lars, you planned all of this?"

My hands fly to my mouth, my heart beats so loud that I almost can't hear anything else. He cracks the box open and takes my hand.

Lars has to almost shout over the sound of the music, but he makes himself known. "Pippa, I did this for you because it's something that you like. I hate dancing but for you I will go anywhere, do anything. I did it because I love you, more than I can possibly say."

I try to interject. "But what about my history and the royal family…"

Lars shakes his head. "What about it? I would rather be with you than to be part of any institution that wouldn't welcome you with open arms. I talked to Stellan and I think that we can work something out."

My chin wobbles, my eyes brim with tears. I just nod, too overwhelmed for a long speech. "I love you too," I say.

Lars doubles down on his proposition, as it were. "I know you've been my fake fiancé for too long, but I'm hoping that you will make it real. Would you do me the honor of being my wife?"

My eyes fill with tears as I nod. "Yes. Yes, Lars."

He frees the ring from its box, sliding it onto my finger beside my old engagement ring. I recognize it; it is the ring that I looked at for so long when we were at the jeweler's, a large princess cut diamond with sapphires around it.

He stands up and embraces me, his demeanor quite emotional. I press up onto my tiptoes, seeking his mouth. His lips brush mine and I can't help my tears as I kiss him.

The music ends, the dancers fade away back into the audience. But Lars and I stay in that spot, holding each other and kissing for what feels like a lifetime. When at last he steps back, beaming down at me, I am almost too emotional to speak.

Erik and Stellan appear suddenly, clapping Lars on the back. Margot and Nika grin and congratulate me. The audience seems to get the biggest kick out of their royal family acting out their lives where the public can see.

No one says anything to me about who my father was or anything else; they are just seem to focus on the fact that I am a princess and I am here, within their reach.

To my delight, the music starts again, playing something slower this time. Lars grins and takes my hand, pulling me into a slow dance against his body. I look up at him, feeling so overwhelmed.

He looks down at me, wrinkling his face. "What?"

"I just… when I think about you and me and how we finally got together, it makes me smile. But I also know that there will be critics." I pull a face. "Your grandmother is a prime example."

Lars cocks his head, smiling. "My grandmother is no longer a part of the royal family. She has had it coming for a while now, but this was the nail in her coffin."

I blink up at him, unsure that I heard him right. "What?"

He shrugs. "I told Stellan about how horribly Momse treated you, how she blackmailed and threatened you. And he agreed that we don't want to give her a chance to get her hooks into our children. So she's not banished from Denmark, but she is forbidden from all of the palaces and all the family events."

His lips quirk. "To tell you the truth, I really never cared for her much anyway. Momse was one misstep away from me just deciding not to talk to her anymore. And you were a hell of a misstep, Pippa."

Tears threaten to overtake me again. "Thank you, Lars."

He shakes his head. "Don't thank me. I'm the reason that such a poisonous person was ever in your life. I don't think we will miss her one single bit. Do you?"

I lean my face against the firm wall of his chest, shaking my head. "I don't think so."

For half a minute, we just dance like that, totally wrapped up in each other. Eventually he dips me, kisses me, and makes me laugh again.

"God, I fucking love you," I say, breathless from laughter.

"And I love you, little witch," he says, squeezing my body tightly against his. "I've loved you since the first second I laid eyes on you back in school. And if I am lucky, I will love you for the rest of my long, long life."

I wipe my eyes and feel incredibly lucky. My friends surround me, Lars holds me close, and though I know that there will be some more things to figure out, I am just so glad that my best friend has become my fiancé for real this time.

LARS

I MARRY MY BEST FRIEND TWO MONTHS LATER ON A COOL early spring day. After much discussion, it's decided that we should just keep it private, only invite people that we actually want there.

So now I am standing in the nave of a church, anxiety pumping through my veins, as my family and friends look on. I'm wearing a dark pair of dress pants and a white button up; Pippa didn't want anything too fancy or fussy. And I am willing to give her whatever she wants.

Stellan and Margot, Nika and Erik, and my parents stare up at me from the pews. That's the entire group that will see us get married today. That's it.

The door opens at the other end of the markedly somber church, revealing my bride. She enters in a rose-colored lace gown, simple and elegant. I grin at her as she glides down the aisle toward me.

This is the moment that I have been slowly building to for fifteen years. Of course, I didn't know that this exact thing was what I wanted, but I think if you'd have told me that I would end up marrying beautiful redheaded Pippa, I would have been okay with it.

And standing here today, as Pippa climbs the steps and takes my hand, I feel like all my dreams are coming true. I lift the delicate veil off her face, pushing it back a little. Pippa looks up at me, tears shining in her eyes, and she just looks so fucking beautiful. It takes my breath away.

The minister keeps our ceremony short and simple. We hold hands and recite our vows to each other. The minister pronounces us husband and wife and suggests that I kiss my bride.

I grab Pippa's waist, pulling her in and dipping her back for a dramatic kiss. I can feel her smile.

It matches my own, I am certain.

I offer Pippa my arm, cocking a brow. "Are you ready, Ms. Løve?"

Her cheeks go pink but she beams up at me, ridiculously happy. "Yes, your highness."

I grin at that. "You know, you are now the Duchess of Marion. And your children will be titled too," I remind her.

She looks me dead in the eyes and utters the words I most need to hear. "I couldn't really care less about the title, Lars. You're the only one I care about."

I kiss her on the lips, jubilant. She takes my arm and I lead her down the steps, the following a procession made of my family.

Afterward, we toast our vows at an upscale brunch. Pippa insisted on picking a restaurant for the reception, such as it is. So soon I am pushing in her chair at a white linen table set for eight, looking around the brightly lit space. Pippa beams at me as I take my seat beside her, incredibly excited about everything.

"So? What do you think?"

Finding her hand under the table, I give it a squeeze. "You have to be more specific, love."

She wrinkles her nose at me. "I know that you didn't want this small of a ceremony…"

I chuckle. "No, I didn't have any feelings about even having a ceremony. Honestly, I thought that I would never get married. Obviously, I was wrong."

She wiggles her eyebrows at me. "You were. I forgive you, though."

All the family that we invited finds their seats around us, chatting amongst each other for a moment. Everyone gets a flute full of champagne or sparkling cider. The food has already been ordered so we all just sit back and relax.

Stellan stands up, bringing a knife to the rim of his glass, calling for a toast. He raises his champagne flute. "To the bride and groom! May you live a long and happy life together."

"Hear, hear!" everyone agrees.

Margot pushes up out of her chair, cupping her pregnant belly. She also raises her glass, looking at Pippa and I. Tears shimmer in her eyes as she smiles broadly at us. "It was a long time coming. But that doesn't make it any less special. I'm glad that you two found your happily ever after. I wish you all the best."

Pippa wipes at her eyes, blowing Margot a kiss. I glance at the faces around the table, faces of the people that I hold dearest, and I feel like the luckiest man on earth.

39

———

PIPPA

I REACH BEHIND MY BODY AS I STEP OUT OF THE AIRPORT'S cargo terminal, needing reassurance. Luckily Lars is right there, grabbing my hand and giving it a kiss. He is always right beside me when I need him, a solid presence. Today of all days, I cling to him.

"I know you're anxious, little witch," he says. "But you've got no reason to be nervous. The doctor said that you being stressed is bad for the baby. So just breathe."

I wrinkle my nose. "I know. I'm just not sure I'm ready for this, you know?"

Lars pulls me close, kissing the top of my head. "It will be okay. You'll see."

Holding my hand, he leads me over to the waiting SUV, putting me in the back seat. As we pull out of the airport, I look at the city of Paris looming in the distance. Against a steel gray sky, it is a dark shape, taking up more and more of the horizon as we approach it.

This was where my little sister Stella finally agreed to meet me. I press my palm against the window, frowning at the darkening sky. It starts to rain a little, giant fat drops from above. I do my best to breathe instead of tensing up my entire body, but I know that my blood pressure is higher than the doctor would like.

As we make our way into the city, turning down dark gray streets, I reach across the seat and take Lars's hand again. He doesn't say anything, but he does wrap my small hand in his big one, squeezing and reassuring me. We get out of the car at the address that Stella gave me.

It's in a nondescript part of the outskirts of Paris, on a block where there are a few little shops on the side. Lars points to the shop that obviously has a giant coffee cup on the window. I think that's the spot we're looking for.

I stand in the street, staring at the coffee shop for a few seconds. Someone on a Vespa honks their horn at me, startling me into motion. Lars leads the way across the street and into the shop.

From outside, I can see Stella perched by the window. Her halo of red curls is on full display as we walk in the door. The coffee shop she's chosen is very small and she's essentially the only customer. She is sitting with a cup of coffee, nervously jiggling her crossed legs. She looks up and our gazes connect.

The fact that I ever doubted that she might be my sister is immediately erased from my mind. She has the same blue eyes that she did when we were kids, the same earnest stare. She stands up, nervously running her hands over her light blue sweater and tucking her hair behind her ear.

Lars steps forward, stretching his hand out to Stella. "Bonjour," he says. "I'm Lars."

He uses a hand on the small of my back to propel me forward, so I stick my hand out too, still nervous that my little sister might judge me poorly. She grips my hand and blushes, obviously fairly nervous herself.

When she lets go, she motions to the service counter. "Would you like something to drink?"

The fact that she just offered to buy two of Europe's richest people coffee is not missed by me. I blush and turn to Lars, that he is already waving me down. "I'll get it. You just sit down."

Stella takes her seat back, leaving three padded chairs facing her in a loose semi-circle to choose from.

I take the closest one, feeling like I have so many questions and so many apologies to make that I don't even know where to begin. Stella pulls out a pair of wire-rimmed glasses and perches them on her nose, wrinkling her face daintily.

"So…" I start, clearing my throat.

She surprises me by leaning over, touching my hand, and looking at me very directly. "You don't have to be nervous. You don't have to explain anything or apologize for anything. I just want to know what's going on in your life, that's all. I hope that's okay."

I'm instantly overwhelmed, my eyes filling with tears. I glance at her as I wipe away tears from my face, trying to find the words for exactly what I need to say to her.

"I know you said that you don't need me to apologize. But I am sorry. I'm sorry that I ever let you go."

She smiles a little bit, but her eyes are emotional. "I wish that we had never been separated. I wish that our father hadn't done what he did. But that's not really important, is it? All we can do is try to be better moving forward."

She glances down at my hand, raising a brow. "Are you married now?"

I nod a little. "Lars and I got married two months ago in a private ceremony. Just friends and family, you know. I wish… I wish that you had been there. But I understand why you said no to my invitation."

Her cheeks go pink. "It was just bad timing. I have my big move from Nantes to Paris and I was literally in the middle of that. And let's be honest, I was nervous, too. I'm sorry about it, for what it's worth."

I clench her fingers, smiling. "I'm glad to see you in person. There's so much I want to get off my chest and clear my head before the baby comes."

Her brows shoot up. "You're expecting?"

I nod. "Yes. I'm due in about five months. It's going to be a girl."

She bites her lower lip. "Can I… Would it be okay if I were a part of you and the baby's life?"

Tears brim in my eyes again. I'm hoarse as I answer. "Of course. I would love that."

She bites her lower lip. "I want to hug you."

I nod vigorously and throw my arms open wide. She comes in and hugs me, her body feeling so strange and yet so familiar all at once.

"We have so much catching up to do," I whisper into her hair.

She pulls back, wiping her eyes, and nods. "I'm going to go get another cup of coffee and then we can really drill down on everything that we've missed. Okay?"

"Okay," I answer. "I can't wait."

As she leaves, Lars steps into the circle, holding two steaming cups. He glances backward over his shoulder at Stella. "Is everything okay?"

After he sets the steaming cups down, I grab his shirt and pull him in for a kiss. He goes along with that, clearly not about to resist me. When he pulls away, he cocks a single brow.

"What was that for?"

"Just a way of saying thank you. Thank you for pushing me to do this. I'm so happy to see my sister and I know that without you, I would've been too afraid."

He crouches down next to me, cupping my jaw in his hand. "You are very welcome, little witch. And remember…" He looks at me, his eyes scanning my face. "I love you."

I grin, kissing him, knowing that I always have him at my back and on my side. No matter what, forever.

THE END

ABOUT VIVIAN WOOD

Vivian likes to write about troubled, deeply flawed alpha males and the fiery, kick-ass women who bring them to their knees.

Vivian's lasting motto in romance is a quote from a favorite song: "Soulmates never die."

Be sure to follow Vivian through her Instagram or join her email list to keep up with all the awesome giveaways, author videos, ARC opportunities, and more!

VIVIAN'S WORKS

RUINED CASTLE SERIES
Forbidden Billionaire Romance
THE SINNER
THE BEAST

THE NANNY
THE CARESS

BROKEN SLIPPER SERIES
Forbidden Billionaire Romance
THE PATRON
THE DANCER
THE EMBRACE
POSSESSIVE

RAVAGED DREAM SERIES - COMING 2023
Forbidden Billionaire Romance
THE ROGUE
THE INTERN
THE SECRET

MARRIED AT MIDNIGHT SERIES - COMING 2023
FORBIDDEN BILLIONAIRE ROMANCE
DEAL WITH THE DEVIL
LIE LIKE THE DEVIL
FOREVER WITH THE DEVIL

DIRTY ROYALS
Forbidden Royal Romance
THE ROYAL REBEL
THE WICKED PRINCE
HIS FORBIDDEN PRINCESS
ROYAL FAKE FIANCÉ

LYON DYNASTY WORLD
Dark Billionaire Romance
KING'S CAPTURE
QUEEN'S SACRIFICE